Nyifie Brothers Publishing

PLAGUE OF DEMONS

THE ZEN ELEMENT CHRONICLES
BOOK THREE

JOHNNY B. TRUANT

SEAN PLATT

For my most constant readers.
I love you guys!

PLAGUE OF DEMONS

I

SIX MONTHS AGO

"Swipe with this end, stab with this one," he said.

Laurel looked up and found herself lost in Ray Porter's big blue eyes. He'd handed her a collapsible Rollard, but for a dumb-headed second Laurel would have believed anyone who told her it was a bouquet of roses.

They were in the middle of a sulfur storm, the air and soundscape chaotic, all three of their hair blown back by the exhale of the rift, and yet here she was drifting. If Ray and Adrian were right, Matt Baker had just gone through the rift in front of them now, which meant he at least thought it survivable — and given he seemed to be working with the fiends, it probably was.

Still, there was no denying that the Porter boys — one Laurel's love and the other her ex — were about to enter Hell. She might never see them again.

While Ray waited for Laurel to acknowledge the Rollard and his instructions, his hand lingered a moment too long. The way he'd handed her the weapon was tender. She found herself thinking of how they'd been close before she was with Adrian. *Close,* but definitely no cigar.

She nodded, touched. Ray still held the prototype multi-weapon, but a Legion's Rollard was his right hand. The fact that he was about to enter battle without it because he hoped it'd keep her safe was disarming: a spark of beauty amid the horror.

The brothers put on their rebreathers and pulled on Stitcher's hoods. Asbestos coats and pants would hopefully keep them from burning before they reached whatever passed for this rift's other side.

They waited for her to turn away. Laurel wanted to watch them enter the rift — to see if, once past the barrier, they simply burst into flame — but she was the unequipped and barely-armed one cursed to linger on the Earthly plane as the apocalypse dawned. If watching her walk out of sight made them feel better, as if she'd survive, she supposed she could do them that favor.

She kissed Adrian. Hard.

And then she walked away, back through the valley cut into the earth the way they'd come. She gave in and looked back after ten paces, but the valley was empty, and the Porters were gone.

You're NOT GOING, Adrian had said. He'd sounded surprised and wary.

Laurel had shaken her head. *I don't have a heat suit. Besides, someone has to monitor things out here where the equipment still works. I'll see your signature when you come out. If the cavalry comes, I'll tell them where to find you.*

At first, she'd been able to keep her word. Despite the EMP-like nature of the rift's initial opening, the most-shielded of the brigade's gadgets still worked. She'd made her way to a cellular tower, then hooked into the emergency services box at its base — a GEN project she knew about but hadn't worked on.

The box didn't need a key — that might be like requiring a key for an emergency exit in a fire — and she was able to hook the handheld monitor into its universal port. From there, she'd had to improvise. The system was meant for broadcast, but Laurel wanted its receive functionality instead.

Her work was imperfect, but good enough. She could see rift energetics across most of Fortune, stopping hard at the Rampart wall's interference ore. The city was in chaos. The many small rifts Baker's sabotage had opened and the brigades had closed were open again, forced asunder as pressure built from the other side. She didn't have the equipment necessary to measure planar cohesion, but it would have to be incredibly low.

They'd been right: One big punch in the field's-side center of this pockmarked mess would drop the bottom from the world like tearing perforated paper.

Her first usable visualization was compiled and ready just in time. She saw a rift swell and disgorge something out at the site of the old GEN warehouses — a place she'd taken Adrian to see when they started dating. There was enough bioelectricity in the disgorgement for two humans: Adrian and Ray emerging, presumably safe, through the rift's other side.

She exhaled, then looked at the time display on her device. How much time had passed since they'd entered? How long had they endured the heat, pressure, and lack of oxygen in the fiends' plane before finally exiting at the GEN facility?

Gods. Almost seven minutes. And to to think: Before now, the longest incursions had been from Stitchers briefly entering to close the rifts. Fifteen, thirty seconds at most.

Laurel watched the display, knowing Ray and Adrian would be searching for their exit now, looking for Matt Baker. He would have a planar bomb, no doubt — enough Zen Element and Thulemite in proper ratio to turn Fortune into New Hell.

Laurel heard something behind her and spun. Nothing was there. But from her high-up place, near Baker's place in the mountains, she could see the Rampart. It wasn't just a wall. The Gore Point was inside Fortune, and until last week everyone thought rifts could only open in the Gore Point.

The Rampart, made largely of anti-entropic ore pulled from the other side and permanently polarized, acted like a demon repeller. The way two same-pole magnets will push away from one another, that's the way the polarized Zen in the Rampart acted with the Zen fiend bodies.

Maybe it would hold. Maybe it wouldn't.

Laurel waited, returning her attention to the screen. She'd promised to monitor, and if she saw a chance, she'd do whatever she could to help. For now, there was nothing.

Maybe she had signed up to watch the Porter boys die.

On her screen, Laurel watched something new open out at the GEN warehouses: a rift like she'd never seen before. It was ...

What was it, other than different?

It wasn't really *larger* than other rifts, but *more potent*, perhaps. Its energy packed a lot more punch per cubic centimeter than other rifts, and there was very little "noise energy" in it: not a lot of rift-made heat, or light, or other kinds of waste radiation. *Precise* might have been a good word for it.

If most rifts were shotgun blasts, this had a sniper's precision.

Untold amounts of Zen emerged from the new rift. Laurel

watched with a hand over her mouth, knowing how overrun Adrian and Ray must be.

What was happening there? If she'd expected anything dire, it was for Baker's Zen bomb to blow. If that happened, the boundary would shatter and the planes would mingle. Our plane, in this place, was the more fragile one. She wouldn't have to wonder, if the bomb went off. She'd find herself in an airless broiler.

But this was something else. If Laurel had to guess, it was untold tons of fiends — including one that had to be building-sized — entering the human plane but not yet cutting it open. Why?

The fiend signatures swarmed toward the human signatures. There was no chance for Ray and Adrian. They were being devoured.

She heard something behind her.

Laurel spun as she had before, but instinct told her to hold the handle latch and let the Rollard swing into extended position this time.

Creepers. Six of them, coming right at her from the direction of Baker's occupied cabin.

No time to think. Ray had given her simple instructions on using the Rollard, but her mind couldn't see even that much now. She lashed out, swiping in big arcs. Creepers were slow and stupid things. She practically decapitated two of them in the first go.

The remaining creepers kept coming. Laurel stutter-stepped backward quickly, ducking behind a tree. The lead fiend lunged and unhinged its jaw at the first junction, exposing its first flight of teeth.

As Laurel dove for cover, the creeper dove as well. It struck the tree like an errant arrow, actually sinking its teeth in the wood.

Laurel pivoted, rotated the Rollard, and stabbed.

She was sloppy; her too-deep lunge had embedded the weapon's tines in the tree like a fiend embedding its fangs. It took her two hard pulls to wrench free, but the weaponless delay cost her.

There were three creepers left, and two got hold of her: one at the arm, one at the same-side leg. The pain was exquisite. With their teeth in her, they pulled back and clamped down like a dog ripping jerky.

With a desperate heave, Laurel wrenched the Rollard free. The momentum of the tug dropped her to the dirt. When one of the fiends let go of her leg and made for her throat instead, she rolled back and kicked its abdomen.

It was her chomped leg, bitten nearly through. There was enough *oomf* in the blow to knock the creeper away, but also a bit too much. Her splintered tibia gave way, cracking in half like kindling over the knee.

She screamed. The world swam; she was going to lose consciousness. She bit her lip stupidly, hoping the agony would bring her around. But what was she thinking? She had pain for ages.

The creeper she'd kicked away came back at her. She turned the freed Rollard around, held it against her body, and let the thing's momentum do the work. It impaled itself on the tines, then stopped moving.

That was all she had in her. Laurel's mind was almost lost to blood loss and shock by now. She couldn't bring herself to look at her leg, but could tell by its weight that the lower part was now held on only by sinew. The pain was glassy and hot, but growing foggier by the second. Soon she'd lose consciousness, and then, even if the fiends didn't eat her, she'd bleed out and die.

She laid back, breathing hard and now actively hoping to pass out and get it over with, and waited.

But the remaining creepers didn't come.

Long minutes later, kept conscious more by curiosity than biology, Laurel lifted her head as far as she could stand. She could see one of the creepers in the distance, walking away. They'd both stopped attacking.

Get out of here, girl. Before they come back.

But that was a laugh. Laurel could barely think. She wasn't going anywhere.

The tablet had landed beside her. Its screen, though made tough, had cracked in one long vertical line. It was still zeroed in on the GEN warehouse, but to her surprise, the human signatures there were still breathing. Ray and Adrian, despite facing possible thousands of fiends minutes ago, hadn't died after all.

Things there were quiet now. Civilized. As if the Porters were now done with battle, now in discussion mode with their adversaries.

Her head fell back. She was too weak. The pain was too much. Her arm was no better than the leg; she couldn't feel her hand and the mid-forearm area on that side was a storm of pain. Again, she refused to look over. She got only one quick peek, and saw nothing but gore and blood.

Just go to sleep. Forget slitting your wrists. They slit everything for you.

Surrendering, her mind began to swim.

She saw colors and shapes whenever her eyelids drifted closed. A sense of strange peace came over her. She didn't have to fight anymore. She didn't have to worry anymore, or hold up her end of the good fight. All that was left was to retire from the biggest game.

She'd done what she could, and she'd broken Adrian's promise for him.

Come back to me, she'd commanded. He'd said he would. But now who'd let whom down? He'd asked Laurel to make no such promise.

Her eyes opened. Now the light patterns she'd seen earlier were here, too. All around her, in the woods. She was surrounded by aurora — curtains of multicolored light. There was warmth. Perhaps heat. She was floating into death, then falling.

"Adrian," she said aloud to nobody, delirious now. "Baby. Come back to—"

"—ME."

Laurel closed her lips, wondering why they'd come open in the first place. Wondering why she'd spoken aloud in her sleep. Had she been having a dream? The word she'd heard herself say had come all by itself, but she had no idea which thought it belonged to. What *about* "me"?

She opened her eyes. She wasn't actually in her bed. Or her bedroom.

No, she was in a hotel.

She frowned. There was confusion, but something deep inside her understood everything perfectly — down at the bottom of her awareness where she couldn't reach it. Waking in a hotel she didn't really remember checking into was strange and sensible in unison. Saying the single word "me," as if to complete a thought, was bizarre while also being perfectly normal.

A woman had to finish her thoughts, didn't she? Why would *any* of this be strange?

Because it's strange. Really fucking strange.

Just like the hotel room was strange, though again strange in a way that some deep-down part of Laurel understood. She was a doppelgänger of herself: two Laurels sharing the same body and brain.

One Laurel had been on a journey to get here, but the other was just waking up. She needed to merge them. She needed to reach that other Laurel inside her and get to the point where she at least *got* this situation — where her scientist and engineer's mind could determine what came next.

Go to the window, then.

The voice inside was hers: that knowing self giving her confused self a helping hand.

She rose, noting the bed's strange construction. The mattress was soft enough and so were the sheets, but they clearly weren't made of the usual materials. The sheets felt almost like silk, but made by covering something tough with something slippery. The bed's base wasn't metal, but rock instead. *Red* rock. There was no lamp or lighting fixtures of any kind. No bedside drawer in which Gideons might place a Bible. No intolerable art hung above a headboard that wasn't even there. The decor, now that her twin selves were melding and noticing all the strangeness that half of her somehow found sensible, was quite unusual.

Was this some sort of well-appointed cave?

Her bare feet touched the ground, which was also red rock. She heard sizzling, as if she'd stepped into a frying pan, but there was no pain. And that was weird, because she'd swear the leg she'd stepped down with (and this was crazy, but whatever) had been mostly severed. Same for one of her arms, but they were both more or less normal now that she looked. The curious limbs both had patches on them, thick with a blue-colored ointment. She flexed her fingers and toes. No problem there.

Her skin looked kind of funny, though. She seriously needed some hand cream. Industrial-grade Aquaphor. Because goddamn, she basically had dragon skin. Rough and hard, like leather. Warmer than usual. Thicker, too, as if made of flesh-colored scales.

Sense was returning slowly, again accompanied by an equal sense of almost-understanding. She knew now that this wasn't a hotel, but a room somewhere she shouldn't be. Her body was different now: whole, but modified. What was going on here? She almost knew. It was right on the tip of her tongue.

Go to the window.

The voice was impatient for this ignorant version of Laurel to understand, so her whole self could move on.

She went to the window without a curtain and looked out at the landscape of endless, red, superheated horizon of what most humans called Hell.

And she remembered.

COLLAR AROUND HER NECK. Line running from it to a second, thicker, line that'd been stretched ahead. Both lines approximated metal, though Laurel knew by now that neither probably was. They didn't mine the same ores here as people did on the human plane. The material held heat like Earth metals, though, and if they hadn't changed her body to allow survival in this place, the collar would fry her like a steak.

A halfskull was passing by. After her leg and arm had finished healing, they'd moved her to this place that was more like a jail cell and less like a hospital or hotel room. She supposed the halfskulls were prison guards, but they just sort of milled around. She knew by now how they communicated: something her work had suggested long ago. Lower castes here were usually, but not always, part of a hive mind.

This one walking by was probably more like a passing a drone.

"Hey," she said to it.

The halfskull turned. It didn't have a face. Somehow, even in this heat, the visible parts of the inside of halfskulls' heads stayed (or at least appeared) moist. She'd stopped them before, and whenever you had what passed for their attention, their slow breathing elicited squishing sounds from that wet, cut-brain mass. It sounded like squeezing a bag full of shit, over and over again.

"I have an idea." She presumed her spoken words were being translated into concepts the fiends understood. Laurel kept trying to learn to think like they did so she could communicate more directly, but for now this was facile enough. When she asked them for food, they gave her something that approximated food.

She waited. This was the first time she'd tried to say anything to one of her guards that wasn't a direct request. They wouldn't let her go or allow Laurel to leave the cell, but they brought her things if she spoke in nouns. *Idea* was a noun, but not one that could be delivered on a tray. She gave even odds that, after trying to process what she'd said, the halfskull would simply walk away.

Instead, she felt an intrusive sensation. It was like being under many layers of covers, then feeling someone push their way through those covers to reach you.

A strong, fully-English voice came into her mind. She could feel its caution: how much effort it expelled to use real words she could understand. They probably spoke normally in concepts and intentions. She really needed to figure that out if she wanted to escape this place.

You are ready to work?

Laurel waved her arm toward the workbench installed in

her jail cell. It was — and from her first day here had been — fully stocked with approximations of the same lab equipment she used in her work with GEN. After a day of screaming for release, she'd considered what was there, understanding from a lot of gist-catching and dot-connecting that they'd brought her here to teach the refinement of Zen: something that could currently only be done on Earth's plane.

She'd given her assigned task a lone day of effort, then announced at the end of her third full day in Hell that there was nothing she could do with what they'd given her. Even if she had the right reagents (she didn't; her usual reagents were water-based and would boil away here), the atmosphere in which they expected her to use them was entirely wrong. Try doing chemistry experiments inside a furnace full of sulfur ash and no oxygen. Reactions don't work the same there as in a normal lab.

"The entire concept of what you want me to do is wrong," she told the halfskull, fairly confident she was talking *through* it, to their leader. "I told you that days ago. I'm willing to help. Honestly I am."

She'd thought a lot about it and decided her kidnapping had been offset by two less-sinister things that made the issue less clear-cut, and refusal less automatic. First, they'd kept her from dying using Zen Element medicine. If they hadn't brought her here, she'd be dead. Second, she'd learned the fiends were suffering an energy crisis brought about by Zen leaking to the other plane. As usually happened when naive cultures ran across first-world humans, things had gone only in the first-world's direction. Laurel was liberal-minded; she didn't like the idea that even *demons* were being resource-raped to deprivation.

"But I think maybe we need to throw out this way of doing things and try something completely different. I think I *can* teach you to refine your own element ... but not using this equipment. Not in this way."

The halfskull watched her, using a sense other than sight because it had no eyes. She could feel the leader (king?) watching her through it. The king was thinking. Trying to decide if Laurel was telling the truth.

She grabbed the line leading from her collar to the line strung overhead and shook it. "I'm in a cage. You don't need to tie me up like a dog."

You protest.

Laurel nodded. "I protest. You want me to show you how to refine Zen, but you don't trust me. I'm telling you it can't be done the way we do it on our plane. I have an idea of how we *could* actually do it ..." She shook her leash again. "But if you want me to show you how to do something you could turn around and use as a weapon against us — if I'm going to trust you enough to show you that — then you have to trust *me*, too."

Trust. The voice sounded like it was working to understand the concept.

It wasn't an easy thing to explain with words. Figuring what-the-hell, Laurel closed her eyes and focused, hoping the halfskull could read her mind. She thought about relationships in which she'd had trust. People she'd trusted. She thought of deals kept and promises honored. *Trust.*

She tried to project the notion to the king, broadcasting her bond to Adrian.

The sons of Eldon Porter, said the voice.

Laurel's brow furrowed. How did it know Adrian, and who his father had been? Why did Adrian's name, in the tone of this alien non-tongue, sound almost revered — special in a way the king seemed almost willing to (wait for it) ... *trust?*

"No," Laurel said, aloud again now. "I'm not trying to show

you *Adrian*. I'm showing you how *I believe what Adrian tells me.* I'm showing you the *bond*. I'm showing you *trust*."

You and the sons of Porter. Trust.

Well. One of them, anyway. Ray, despite his handing-over of the Rollard, still had some work to do.

The halfskull pressed its hand into the lock on her door, and the door came open.

Trust, said the voice. *Now show us.*

Soon, the king said weeks after her new work began.

Laurel wasn't sure if it was a statement or a question. After working for the underworld, she'd grown used to having grotesque creatures as lab assistants and a five-story-tall boss with massive red horns, but she still wasn't fully used to their style of communication. Language, Laurel was learning, had unlimited nuance. Lifting your voice to indicate a question was one of them, and that seemed harder when the voices weren't really *voices* at all.

Was this a question? Was the king asking her if her work would be done *soon?*

"It depends on how you define 'finished.'" Laurel had mostly stopped trying to communicate using her mind.

She'd had to dumb the science down so far in order to create mental concepts that it'd grown impossible to get anything meaningful across. They spoke now in a hybrid. She used words, then the others reached into her head to grab the meaning *beneath* those words. They didn't understand the word "titration" or Laurel's attempt to mentalize it, for instance, but if she just spoke it aloud, a deeper part of herself seemed to translate in a way they could understand.

"The Zen we're refining is over ninety percent pure at this point. Energetically, it's ... what? ... I think our last batch measured as three hundred and fourteen percent more energetic than the raw material. With the same amount of actual Zen, we're getting three times the punch. Effectively, your plane now has triple the amount of energy available if it was all refined. That's plenty for your base needs, at the current rate of leakage."

Technically, it was plenty at the *old* rate of leakage. From what she'd seen, Earth had hopped-to on the riftfare front, going overboard to close every rift and pre-rift in existence. Now, when new rifts started to form, They didn't wait for the rifts to open wide, patching them in advance. There was no way to patch the planes forever. But if humans kept keeping new rifts from forming and the fiends didn't try to break through, they'd be fine for millennia.

There is a new rift, the king told her.

"I've seen no new rifts."

You must provide closing for the new rift as well.

"First, I'm not a Stitcher," Laurel snapped, having lost her fear of what was technically the Devil a while ago. These days he was just one more lab boss who demanded the impossible of his undergrads and post-docs. "Second, like I said, I've seen no new rifts."

Then look, and see.

What happened next, the king had only done to her once before. He sucked her mind into his, but the feeling was like arms reaching out, grabbing her bodily, and shoving Laurel down some monstrous throat. Her senses, useless in this mindspace, created their own fantasy: She imagined being squeezed through the great being's intestines, coming to an uneasy rest somewhere in a sultry internal theater.

But once there, she saw.

A vast red plain, somewhere unknown. Armies of halfskulls and other soldier castes, most already dosed with the new Zen armament cocktail and glowing blue, stood in loose ranks as if waiting for a show to begin. At first, her visiting mind did not see what they were watching, but then she realized the spectacle was too big. She had to take in the entire forward horizon to see it, sending her internal gaze from stem to sky.

The hot air warbled with the pre-energetics of the most massive rift she'd ever seen, far off the usual top end of the Minghai scale and forming right in front of her.

Then the vision was gone, and Laurel was herself again.

They prepare, said the king, meaning the humans beyond the forming rift.

Laurel didn't ask her next question aloud. Through the pre-aurora of the rift, she'd seen glimpses of a familiar place: the warehouse Adrian and Ray had appeared in after crossing their last rift. The place the king had gone before the sundering almost happened — a place now full of humans in military uniforms, stuffed with Zen-fueled equipment, about to open the largest controlled rift the world had ever seen.

The question she didn't ask was, *What are they preparing for?*

She saw the fingerprints of GEN's military wing all over the scene ... and thought she knew *exactly* what they were preparing for.

An invasion. A sundering of their own.

"Soon," she told the king.

THEY'D MOVED her lab to a small cave off of a plateau so the king, whose head brushed every ceiling, could speak to her from out in the open. More and more he desired privacy — to speak to Laurel, whom he seemed to trust much more now — alone.

The king was just another being. They all were. Evil was a

point of view, and from her current point of view, Earth had birthed the bad guys.

The queen seeks to overthrow me, he told Laurel.

She looked over. She'd been working. It was clear now that her ecological work was being militarized, but Laurel found she didn't care. The big rift had begun to open, and immediately the humans built a small train able to cross it. They kept sending expeditions, killing and harvesting a dozen or so hive-mind caste demons at a time. She'd been in Hell for two months — long enough to see her fiend militarization as self-defense.

The others with separate minds fear the opening, the king explained. *It is foolhardy to act, but the queen tells them she WOULD act, if it was her decision.*

Laurel kept waiting, wary that this was building up to something ugly. She wasn't as charitable in her attitude toward the king as he'd become toward her. He didn't threaten her personally, but he was still more than a menace to her home race. Once he'd realized Laurel's intelligent mind was able to keep up with his (none of the fiends' minds could), he'd begun dumping more and more on her.

It was too much. She knew his views now; she knew he'd only called off the sundering because he was planning something much larger. He still wanted to end the worlds. He still wanted Earth to burn if it meant saving his plane.

You know it was always inevitable.

Laurel didn't need context for the king's quick change of topic — away from mutiny and toward this. Their mental bond gave her all the context she needed, provided without faux-words. He was talking about the sundering now — a belief he had that the universe maintaining two separate planes was an affront to physics.

Worse, after reviewing all the data, Laurel agreed with him.

All things tended toward chaos. It wasn't a question of *if* Hell and Earth would collapse into one another. It was a question of *when*.

"We have time. The refining of Zen has bought time."

Not if they finish opening their rift. Not since Eldon Porter.

The second thing was primary. The massive rift was a threat in terms of invasion and Zen loss, but the chaos of it all had become a ticking clock the minute a human mind touched the interplanar border. On a cosmic scale, the planes were always going to collapse eventually … but thanks to Eldon, it wouldn't take billions of years. Now it might only take thousands, and the king would easily live that long.

Armageddon within one's lifetime. Laurel couldn't imagine the existential horror. No wonder they were scared. No wonder the queen was gaining support, and the king was losing his patience.

We must act. The slow bleed brings suffering.

A strange thing for the king of this place to say. In horror movies, Hell *liked* suffering. But the collapse of the planes (Earth falling into Hell or the other way around) was starting to seem like ripping off a Band-Aid. Maybe it really was best to get it over with, like the king kept hinting.

"You're talking about the destruction of my world."

You are the takers. You are the murderers.

"*You've* done murder, too."

The king waved his enormous hand as if to dismiss the thought as semantics. The hand created so much turbulence, Laurel almost fell over. A human gesture, learned from months spent sharing her mind.

The queen refuses to understand. She will send soldiers. She will arm more and more of us.

"Arming" meant more of the Zen infusion. The enhanced, refined mutagen that Laurel herself had helped make stronger.

She'd begun this by talking about trust — if she was to work with the king, she needed to trust that he wouldn't turn her energy-saving work into a weapon.

Now it was one. Oh, how things spun so quickly out of control.

She'd seen them train. Demon soldiers injected with Zen resin were nearly impossible to kill. They resisted most attacks and could launch new assaults of their own. On the far side of the big rift — increasingly the only one in existence, and this rift hidden from public eyes — the humans were building bigger and better weapons. Strategy here was different. Hell's soldiers were *becoming* weapons.

Laurel wasn't stupid. It'd become quite clear, what the queen's rogue support was doing. The king hadn't sanctioned the armies preparing, from this side, to invade. Soon, she'd take over and he wouldn't have to sanction anything. He'd just be ... gone.

Was that better, or worse? Laurel was starting to feel like a woman who'd tied a noose, then realized one day she herself had stepped right into it. The queen's plan would lead to war like nothing the planes had seen before. The king's plan, though, might end everything for everyone.

Unless ...

Her thought was interrupted when the king spoke again. He hadn't seen what she'd been thinking. Concepts had to be intended as communication to be seen.

We must hasten it. Because it will happen anyway, we must make it happen now.

"No," Laurel said.

Yes. The queen cannot be stopped. The mind-clusters are all infected. Every one of them is afraid. We are not always all interconnected. I sense more and more being hidden from me. Plotting against my wishes. She has the majority. I cannot wait for the plan I intended.

Was that a good thing? Despite knowing scientifically that the planes would inevitably collapse, Laurel still had moral problems with his plan. It was still genocide, ending a way of life for humanity that would otherwise continue for many generations. It was your classic philosopher's dilemma. Do you kill one man with the runaway trolley to save ten?

By the numbers, the answer was clearly yes. The only hitch was that murder still felt like murder.

A plan of her own began to form in her mind. The king wanted to act now? Maybe she had a way to give him exactly that ... and at the same time, give Earth a lifeline it wouldn't otherwise have.

A lifeline with the last name Porter.

"You think that if the queen tries to overthrow you, she will win."

Yes, said the king.

"Then let her."

LAUREL GRABBED the only non-blue halfskull in her lab by the arm as he passed. It was the guard from when they brought her as a prisoner and tied her to a cable like a dog on a zipline.

Now the king was on the other side, having allowed himself to be captured as part of Laurel's plan. The queen was in charge, thinking she'd pulled a coup and building her Zen-enhanced armies. Now the guard — who she called "Prime," because he'd been her first test subject — was the closest thing Laurel had to a friend.

Yes?

Before speaking, Laurel pulled Prime into a corner of the

lab. Nobody else was here, and she'd been moved to a facility with a door that was currently closed. She needed to know, in advance, if anyone was coming to overhear them. They'd talked this way before — in defiance of Hell's groupthink, technically speaking — but Laurel was about to take things to a whole other level.

"Is it safe to talk?"

Prime went still, seemed to think with that squishy, wet, cut-in-half brain of his. Then he nodded because nodding was how his human companion usually expressed the affirmative.

"So it's safe."

None are listening.

"And your separation from the hive?"

Separation. She wasn't sure how Prime felt about that, if he was capable of emotion. She hadn't meant to cut him off almost completely from the halfskull hive mind in this sector. It'd been a side effect, not the intent.

The king had volunteered all the soldiers Laurel needed for experimentation as she worked to refine Zen Element, but to Laurel, experimenting on what remained sentient beings — hive mind or no hive mind — felt a bit too much like what the Nazis did for comfort. Needing test subjects, she'd compromised.

They were all able to push the hive mind back a little, becoming semi-independent. She'd asked Prime to do just that, then requested his permission. She'd given him the first serum once he agreed, but it had done nothing to the Element in his blood, instead making his pushing-back of the hive permanent. He'd become mostly an individual and probably always would be, for better or worse.

My separation remains intact.

Laurel still didn't speak. Prime waited patiently, giving her a halfskull's version of an expectant look. She'd grown used to staring into his ventricles as if they were eyes in the three and a half months she'd been here, and Prime had gotten used to her. They were in sync. They spoke fluidly, without confusion.

Prime had begun to express his own opinions thanks to his cutting-off ... and the doubt she heard in those opinions — his questions about both king and queen — was what gave her the strength to speak now.

She watched him a few seconds longer, wishing he had a real face she could read — that he was a human whose facial expressions meant something. Her ex-boyfriend used to slaughter beings like Prime by the thousands when they spilled from rifts, and her current boyfriend sealed breaches against them.

Was it really so smart that Laurel, now, was about to trust Prime with her life?

She'd know in thirty seconds. He would either hear her treasonous ideas and agree to help her ... or run to the closest guard and turn her in.

"You know what the queen is planning."

Again Prime nodded. *The invasion. Through their very own rift.*

"It will fail."

Prime seemed to consider her.

"I worked for the company that makes our weapons. I know what was being developed when I left. I know how our military complex responds to big, public threats like what almost happened with the sundering. Those weapons, if they're not already ready for use, will be soon. And they are a *lot* more powerful. When the king showed me the rift — almost two months ago now — I saw humans massing a war machine on the other side. The queen's about to launch a one-point attack, thinking her Zen soldiers can seize their machines. But she's wrong. It's a bottleneck. She might cause some damage, but it won't extend beyond the building. And then ..."

Laurel took just two seconds to catch her breath. "And then they will respond, Prime. Do you understand? My race? They will *respond.*"

Laurel waited. Prime knew enough about human institutions from chats with Laurel to know what "respond" meant in this context. It meant *over*-response. A human attempt at annihilation more than war.

Go on.

She swallowed. "The king allowed himself to be captured by the humans. He did it on purpose. It was my suggestion."

Go on.

"He didn't stop the sundering because he wanted peace, Prime. He stopped it because he wanted things to escalate. The buildup to the sundering showed your cards to my side. Humans saw what *might* have happened. The response that's happened already — making all those bigger and better weapons I mentioned? That's what the king wanted. And our response — creating the Zen serum, making your plane's soldiers stronger? He wanted that, too. He made a feint, Prime. That's all the almost-sundering was: a *feint.* He didn't want to break the worlds that day because it wasn't big enough yet. Humans didn't have powerful enough weapons — and your side didn't have powerful enough weapons — for the conflict to go worldwide. Now, though, there's been so much escalation, it *can* go worldwide. Four months ago, what he did wouldn't have ended it all. Now, though, it just might."

Laurel stopped, desperate to know what Prime would think after she'd vomited forth all she knew, believed, and feared. There was treachery implied by what she'd said, even without spelling it out. She wouldn't have told Prime so much if her only intention was to whine.

You think you know a way to stop it. That's why you told the king to let himself be captured.

"It's a plan within a plan. The king doesn't want *anything* stopped. He let himself be captured because he thinks it will *hasten* the end, not stop it. I'm clinging to an ace in the hole."

She paused again. Now her neck was fully exposed: a clear traitor to her adopted home in Hell.

"I need your help, Prime. The plan I gave the king, if things go the way I told him, will collapse both planes. Nothing will survive intact; anyone who knows it's coming can bunker in and come out the other side, but when it's over both sides will have to start from scratch. I think there might still be a way to survive, chaos and inevitability be damned. But I couldn't tell the king. His mind is poisoned. He *wants* this, if only to get rid of the queen. I had to give him a plan that, if we do it right, *will* work." She took both of Prime's clawed hands in hers, immune by now to the alien feel of his skin. "But we can't let it work. Do you hear me? *We can't let the king's plan work.*"

Tell me.

"Where they're holding the king is close to a man named Adrian Porter. He's—"

I know who Adrian Porter is.

"I can use the king's influence to give Adrian dreams. Of me. I can call out. There's another man, J. Dixon. He used to be in charge of a lot of this, and Adrian still talks to him about rift-fare, though I think by now Dixon's keeping secrets. If the king puts me inside Adrian's head enough, I think he'll go to Dixon. He knows about energetics and resonance; he'll see the sense in sending Adrian into the rift. I know your kind can read intentions, and by now people like Dixon must know, too. He's an ass, but tries to do the right thing. He'll want recon before any invasion. I'll just have to hope when he talks to whatever grunts are in charge of that big rift, they'll hear him out."

And send Adrian Porter into the rift. To find you. Here.

Laurel nodded. "It's a kind of a pincer. Adrian comes here, the king stays there. It'll allow them to build a bridge — to open a rift into the queen's inner sanctum. It'll put him inside her defenses, not outside where she's kept him."

He'll take over, Prime said.

"Yes."

Kill the queen. Commandeer her armies.

Laurel nodded again. "With the queen dead, he'll be this plane's only capable leader. There won't be any resistance to him this time, with no queen to support instead. Not when he puts those armies to work, completing the work the queen's already begun."

And launches the invasion.

"Not right away. The queen wants to rush in with weapons blazing. That's why she'll lose. The king is more strategic. Before his invasion, he'll stack the deck in his favor. Like the game I taught you. Chess. The king is a chess player, Prime. Instead of a frontal assault, he'll carefully plan his attack. He'll put the right pieces in the right places *before* the incursion begins. That's why he, unlike the queen, will succeed."

They both went silent. That was it. That was almost everything. Laurel was now laid bare, all her traitor's cards on the table. She'd betrayed her own world by helping arm the fiends, and was now betraying the fiends.

She watched Prime, wondering which way he'd fall. He thought for himself now, but that didn't mean he was willing to hop with her aboard the saboteur's bandwagon.

What can I do? he asked.

"Go to the queen," Laurel answered gratefully. "Volunteer.

She knows who you are and what my experiment did to you. Tell her your new nature lets you understand humans better than anyone else. Ask her to send you to the front. Then ..."

Then?

"Find a way through. Somehow. I don't know how, just find a way. Cross the rift. Then find Dixon. Special Agent J. Dixon, with the department of Spread and Containment in the city of Fortune. Tell Dixon what I told you. We'll just have to hope he's willing to listen. Like I said, he and Adrian are already in touch and he might already be thinking of sending Adrian in. If he isn't, tell him to. With luck, he'll send both of you in. But *don't* tell Adrian about any of this, okay? If he knows it's a ruse, it'll fog his intention. He'll suddenly be on a mission of conquest, not a lover's quest to reach me. If that happens, the queen will see him coming. He'll never make the gate, let alone get inside to build the king a bridge."

Prime digested all of this, then said, *But when the king returns, it still starts the war.*

"Not if we can help it." And then she told Prime the rest of her plan, and why.

"Will you do it?" She had to pray for yes; without Prime as liaison, her subversion of the king's big plan would fail right now.

I will do it.

"Tell the queen to send you to the rift. Cross it. Find Dixon."

Find Adrian Porter. Make friends.

That made Laurel smile — something she hadn't realized she desperately needed. Her fiend partner had turned friend. Amazing what the addition of one small R could do.

"I should warn you about something, if you're going to be friends with Adrian. Seeing as you can't tell him yet that you know me, and that I call you 'Prime' ..."

You're saying I need a new name.

"I'm saying you should let him name you, so he has a subconscious reason to trust you. But this is Adrian we're talking about ... and that means the name he chooses will be something ridiculous."

2
NOW

NOW

"Anything from Carl?" Adrian found himself hoping the answer was yes. It'd been weeks, and he missed his gross little halfskull buddy.

Special Agent J. Dixon had acted almost human for the six months between near-sundering-day and the day Adrian caused something much worse. Now that Adrian was back on the human plane, though, Dixon had become a cartoon again. He always sounded like a hard-charging, old-school newspaper boss, talking in a too-loud voice full of clipped ends that made everyone think they were in trouble ... or possibly that the *Times* was going to get the scoop and he needed his ace reporter on the story, *pronto*.

"Carl? No." Dixon held up a long, slim FedEx box he must have retrieved from the lobby since he was getting up anyway. "Your fans? Yes."

He tossed the box into Adrian's lap. The address on the airbill stuck to the front was hard to see through the heavy strokes of a triple-thick marker: some street-level critic's addition to the label, presumably written while the box sat on the stoop. It read, *TRAITOR.*

Adrian sighed and made to hand the box to Dixon.

Dixon pushed it back. "Don't give me that. It's got shit in it."

Adrian's attention was lost to the addressee on the airbill. "This is for me. Why am I getting mail at your office?"

"Because it's got shit in it."

Adrian ripped off the pull strip and peered inside, wincing as he tossed the box aside. Inside were turds, neatly packed in sandwich-sized bags like snacks for later.

"Jesus."

"Why did you open that?" Dixon said, annoyed and waving away stink. "Asshole. I *told* you it had shit in it."

"How did you know?"

"Because you get them all the time. Do you want me to start passing them on?"

Adrian stood, using the sleeve of his left hand to cover his nose while his right hand pinched the open flap of the box, held at maximal length. He headed for the door.

"Where the fuck do you think you're going?"

"Dumpster?"

"Through the front door? Without a gun? Idiot. It's not a hundred percent chaos out there yet. When it's a hundred percent chaos and everyone is eating everyone else alive, maybe you won't be special anymore and you can take shit to dumpsters as often as you want. For now, though, it's going to be really inconvenient for me if someone sees you. More inconvenient if they kill you. Although ..." He seemed to think. "At least the shit-boxes would stop that way."

When Adrian froze (he wasn't sure which protocol was required here; Dixon usually only said what *wasn't* okay), Dixon rolled his eyes and went to one of the windows that faced the alley. They were on the second floor above a bakery that had gone out of business when people learned who had an office upstairs.

"Dumpster," Dixon said, raising the sash.

"The dumpster's all the way down at the end."

"Come on, come on," Dixon said, making impatient circles with his arm. "The alley's one big toilet. You really think you're going to make it worse?"

When Adrian was halfway to the window, Dixon impatiently came forward, took the box, tossed it out, then closed the window. The entire sequence seemed to ask why Adrian was alive and why that was Dixon's problem. He sat back at his desk and resumed working on something amid annoyed mutterings.

"So nothing from Carl," Adrian said, deciding the best way to move past whatever the hell had just happened was to ignore it.

"You're welcome to look."

"I don't really think that's necessary. Not if you just did."

"Great. Big fucking help. Thanks, Porter. I'm glad you're here."

"Did I do something wrong?" Adrian asked.

Dixon stared back.

"Recently?" Adrian clarified.

"Not since you rang the dinner bell for Satan, no! Not since you undid everything Patel's unit was doing out at the base."

"You act like it wasn't part of Laurel's plan."

"I act like a lot of things."

The room was silent for a while. Adrian had figured Dixon out after he'd returned and they'd become reluctant partners.

Dixon's problem was that he had the emotional maturity of a third-grader. When something displeased him, he shouted about it to whoever happened to be nearby whether that person was in any way responsible or not. They both knew Dixon had been part of this whole bad idea from sundering day onward — arguably, a much bigger part of it than Adrian himself.

Yes, Adrian had opened the rift, but Dixon had known from the start that he'd do it and had taken great pains to make sure he did. It's why he'd sent Adrian into the other plane, trusting that Laurel Gantry and her halfskull accomplice, who Adrian named Carl, knew what they were doing. The GEN team, Dixon later explained, had even reached some of the same conclusions as Laurel had from the other side, pre-disposing Dixon to agree when Carl came to him and made contact. Word from Laurel, when she'd still been Hell's prisoner-slash-accomplice, had merely confirmed what Dixon was already prepared to do. If there was fault here, it was Dixon's as much as Adrian's.

Blaming Adrian was just his way of processing the anger he had at himself, the situation, and the world. *Nobody* liked what had happened last month, whether they understood why (like Adrian, Dixon, Laurel, and of course Carl) or whether they just thought Adrian Porter was a traitorous fucker who'd sold humanity out to Hell so he could get his girlfriend back (like literally everyone else, including Adrian's brother Ray).

Adrian could fight Dixon's weird psychology or he could just let it ride. The latter was easier and probably the least contentious. It's not like Adrian was brimming with supporters these days.

"Nothing from Carl." Repeating Adrian's question in a non-accusatory voice was as close as Dixon got to an apology.

Adrian went to the window — the front window, this time. He always did so slowly now, checking the street view from a distance before committing himself to stepping all the way into it. He'd never been shot at, when someone saw him up here, but rocks had been thrown. Eggs, too. It seemed Dixon wasn't the only one around who had a childish way of dealing with anger.

The streets were clear. Almost normal. That was the thing about the new armageddon: Everyone felt it coming, but nobody could point to evidence it was happening. Adrian didn't understand that part, and the lack of comprehension bothered him. Only three humans and one demon knew the whole of what was supposed to happen next ... and trust Laurel though he did, Adrian couldn't shake a feeling that she and maybe Carl still knew more than him and Dixon.

If she wasn't letting Adrian in on a hidden corner of her plan, he supposed she had her reasons, but it was still cruel. She'd asked Adrian to end the world for her, and he had. Now he was paying the price, yet felt like he was still somehow in the dark.

He watched two people stroll down the sidewalk, walking a dog. They seemed to be chatting to each other amid small, affectionate smiles. A carefree sort of conversation, not one full of angst and anger. There was still a lot of that out there. With most people.

The official story was that prominent GEN scientist Laurel Gantry, believed dead, had been found after six months missing by ex-Stitcher Adrian Porter. A lot fell neatly between the lines of those simple facts: Laurel had been abducted and pulled through a rift when the sundering nearly happened, undergone a mutation that allowed her to live in the other plane (the internet was rife with rumors of GEN's work to facilitate such mutations), and Adrian had crossed over to get her. That, too, was accepted as official story.

Between *those* lines, though, were rumors ranging from

outrageous to no-way-it's-not-true. If Laurel had been abducted but was free now, was it really possible that Adrian had battled through to save her?

No. Of course not. The reality TV show *Brigade* had shown anyone interested exactly how impossible a rescue in Hell would be, leaving just one option: Instead of being *rescued*, Laurel had been *released* — let go voluntarily. Why?

Well, nobody knew the answer, but it was *also* true that on the same day Adrian and Laurel re-emerged through a rift that opened right in the middle of a public park's yoga class, the so-called "dreadnought" had mysteriously vanished. The giant demon — which some were now calling "Hell's King" — hadn't broken through his bindings or the walls of his prison, meaning he too had escaped through a rift.

Was it coincidence, or had Adrian made a deal — the king for Laurel?

Because Adrian never made a statement (brigade orders, though for PR reasons maybe he should have been allowed), the public decided a king-for-Laurel deal was *exactly* what had happened. The research-and-development think tank GEN, which had openly begun liaising with military after sundering day, had shaken up around that time, making the story worse. Malcontents who used to work there began dropping all sorts of knowledge bombs on the press.

GEN was divided on riftfare strategy, half trying to repair the planes and half helping the government profit from their fracturing. It painted the bleakest of pictures. The worst thing that could ever have happened — from an end-of-the-world standpoint — would be for King Dreadnought to retake his throne and command the fiends again. Now that had happened, and GEN informants theorized that it was only a matter of time before all Hell broke loose ... literally this time.

Laurel and Adrian's return was now a month in the past.

Nothing had happened, except for Adrian becoming a pariah and Ray becoming a bit of one too, just to be safe. A lot of the population was shit-scared, stockpiling gasoline, guns, and water as if those things would protect them from planar collapse: keep them breathing when the air was gone, keeping them cool when the rivers started to boil.

But a lot of the population — like this pair of happy, chatting dog-walkers — was exactly the opposite. For them, no news was good news. Maybe it was all a mistake. Maybe the fiend king had just wanted to go back home. Now that he was, he'd probably go away and never bother humanity again.

Deep down, nobody believed that. Everything simmered with foreboding anticipation. Everything waited for disaster that felt inevitable.

But how? When? From where, and in what way? Adrian and Ray had met the king. They'd watched when he'd stopped the sundering, though Laurel had told him from outside his fiend-plane jail cell that "stopping the sundering" was part of the ruse. The king, Laurel said, had brought the planes to the brink of collapse that day because he'd wanted the human government and military scared. They had been ... and the fact that the sundering *didn't* happen meant they could now stockpile weapons, stockpile dangerous refined Zen Element, and develop newer, deadlier ways of waging war so no sundering could ever happen again.

The king knew that the queen, who he'd allowed to overthrow his rule after permitting himself to be captured by humans, would prepare and stockpile on her own. The sundering, in other words, had amped the human/fiend arms race to eleven. After both species were armed to the teeth, there was enough force and fury — a big enough "mutually assured destruction" — to *truly* collapse the planes.

The original sundering would have been a skirmish. This was nuclear war.

Laurel and Dixon *supported* this plan? They'd talked *Adrian* into supporting this? After a month of reflection, Adrian wondered what he'd been thinking. He'd freed the king just like everyone secretly knew he had because in the moment, Laurel's argument had made sense. She said the planes had been weakened long ago and were going to eventually collapse no matter what anyone tried to do to prevent it. Getting that inevitable collapse over with now would, through some twisted form of logic, save lives versus the slow and steady decay that would happen otherwise.

But now back on Earth in this shitty little office with Dixon, both of them disgraced and Adrian seen as the world's biggest traitor — Adrian wondered what would have been so bad about slow and steady. So rifts might open. He'd already been fighting rifts his entire life, and was used to it.

He watched the two people and their dog vanish around a corner, wondering if those who Laurel felt were in denial might actually be right. It'd been a month. Dixon's comment about Adrian "undoing all Colonel Patel had done" wasn't entirely true but close enough: the enormous, magnitude 35 rift had been closed to doorway-sized, and the expeditions to abduct and render fiends for the Zen in their blood had stopped.

As far as anyone was admitting, that single rift — which the public didn't even know existed — was the only one left unless you counted Dixon and Adrian's private little portal. Even the tiny, flash-in-the-pan popcorn rifts that had sucked fiend prisoners back into the other plane hadn't recurred. Everything had gone cold. If not for Carl's updates, it might be possible to believe that no other plane — or its demonic residents, or its threat — had ever existed.

Maybe everything really was okay. Maybe Adrian wasn't a traitor, but a hero instead. Maybe he was the Henry Kissinger of the modern age, negotiating the peaceful exchange of prisoners. Maybe that's all they'd wanted — to have their old leader back. Maybe that leader, once home, had decided to call off all hostilities. Maybe the world was fine now — or at least *would be* fine for the lifespan of everyone Adrian would ever meet.

Good enough for now. The future was the future's problem.

Adrian returned to his desk. He sighed, then looked at his charts, his files, his computer — at the whole of the futile, wheel-spinning "research" he and Dixon did here while they pretended to still have both dignity and authority.

He stopped when an alien thought entered his brain.

Come here.

He looked at the broom closet, with the false back wall, hiding the portal.

It seemed there was word from Carl after all.

3
THE VIRUS

Adrian called it a portal. Dixon, who had no sense of humor and meant the term derisively, called it the Magic Mirror.

"Mirror mirror on the wall," Dixon recited with fairy tale cadence as Adrian stood and made for the closet, "go fuck yourself."

"That's not how it goes."

"The hell it isn't."

Adrian opened the closet and stepped inside, closing the innocuous-looking door behind him. He didn't like the claustrophobia and usually used the portal with the door open, but with Dixon in a mood he wanted some privacy away from Dixon's verbal jabs throughout the conversation.

There was a catch on the closet's back: a coathook that pushed up to release a latch. He pushed it, thinking of Scooby Doo-style secret passages like always. With a tight squeeze, he sucked his stomach in so he could accordion-fold the false wall out of the way.

The window-sized rift behind it was already swimming

with aurora. It didn't always, but they'd still sealed the door to conceal it like a darkroom so no light could escape and give them away. The hot thing was always exhaling sulfur. Before the lightproofing, which doubled as scentproofing, Dixon complained it made the office smell like farts.

Carl was already on the portal's other side, waiting for Adrian to settle in. In the time since the king returned, Hell's soldiers had started wearing rank and authority insignia. Carl's — equivalent to the pull of a human senator — was visible as an armband just below his shoulder. Because fiends had never worn anything at all before, some at GEN who knew about the insigna theorized it was humanity's influence, leaking through, that prompted the change. Carl had picked up some of Adrian's mannerisms and "speech" patterns, and Laurel said even the king had adopted some of hers, so that made sense: More interactions with humans made them a tiny bit human.

Adrian tried to think of that as a good thing. Knowing humans, though, it probably wasn't.

For a while, he had tried to learn Carl's way of speaking: telepathic, not using out-loud words. He'd eventually given up. Mentality was mentality, and his mind had learned how to translate Fiend as well as Carl's mind had learned how to translate English. The communicators he'd used when first crossing over weren't even necessary anymore.

Greetings.

"Greetings," Adrian echoed. It was a formal way of saying Hello, but it's how Carl always began.

Are you well?

"Not particularly, but who is? You?"

Carl's mouth was all teeth and he couldn't smile, but the tone of his thoughts conveyed a tiny bit of ironic levity. *About the same as you.*

"I was starting to think you'd abandoned us." *Or been killed,* he silently amended, careful to hide the thought from Carl. Thanks to Laurel's work, Carl was the only soldier-caste fiend who thought entirely on his own, mostly divorced from any of the lower castes' hive minds. In one sense, individuality and his ability to understand humans made Carl invaluable to the king, who was also an individual but tied into every hive on his plane. But in another way, individuality made Carl dangerous. Free-thinkers had a history of causing problems for tyrants.

There has been little chance to get away. Mental bonds are being rearranged and strengthened. I am often asked to open my mind. It's important that I am able to hold back what others must not see.

"'Rearranged and strengthened'?"

Carl nodded — one of the many human affects he'd picked up. *It's being done for the incursion.*

Adrian's blood went cold. Oh, the apocalyptic incursion he'd just tried to convince himself was never going to happen? *That's* the "incursion" Carl meant?

"When will it happen?"

It's already begun.

"What? Where?"

Spreading out from the Gore Point.

"'Spreading'? I don't understand."

It is difficult to explain to a being who's never known a hive mind.

Adrian made a wondering face. There was something here he wasn't getting. Incursions from the other plane came through rifts, and as far as Adrian knew, there'd *been* no new rifts. There were barely even brigades anymore — just Brigade One's skeleton crew left for show, with the real defensive work now being done by the military, no longer trying to hide its involvement.

People knew the end was nigh. Seeing soldiers carrying

multi-weapons and Zen grenades that would surely accomplish nothing in the face of an invasion helped frightened citizens sleep better at night.

Not like that. It's not an incursion like your mind shows me now.

Adrian reminded himself to be more careful. He didn't care if Carl saw his thoughts because Carl was an ally. Carl, in fact, had put his newly-individual neck on the line when he'd returned to the king and pretended his allegiance had never wavered — something the king seemed to believe because Carl, through Laurel, was only reason he'd been able to escape, overthrow the queen again, and take Hell back over as its leader.

In truth, Carl was loyal to a cause he thought was right: Laurel's cause, Adrian's cause, Dixon's cause. It wasn't the same cause as the king's anymore. Carl's contining to live depended on Carl (whose singular mind was still very new to duplicity) walking a very fine line. He could admit to working with Laurel's crew because she had helped the king ... but he could only admit it so far, because although Laurel had revealed nothing new, Adrian felt sure she wasn't really on the king's side anymore if she ever had been.

The smallest slip could be the last thing Carl ever did.

Adrian said nothing, allowing his mind to open because Carl was the only fiend nearby. He had indeed been picturing the "incursion" Carl spoke of as an armed invasion: ranks upon ranks of Zen-stuffed fiends marching across a rift and into the human world, taking up stations and doing battle.

Not like that, Carl repeated as if maybe Adrian's thoughtfulness meant he hadn't heard.

"Like what, then?"

Has Laurel told you that she thinks of the king as a master of your game chess?

"A little," Adrian replied, though he'd thought it was just a comparison of the king's way versus the smash-and-grab military tactics the queen had been planning.

It's true. He knows that if he tried to enter your world in force, he would be quickly defeated. Your side does not want to invade our side anymore. Your people seem to know that even with Zen mutations, there is no way to win on our plane.

It was more than that, but Adrian didn't say so. The military complex seemed to have given up on raping the other plane for Zen Element, too — maybe because they already had enough or maybe because it just wasn't worth the risk anymore.

The king wants war. Your side is content to simply prevent *war. The king wants to win, and winning means collapsing the planes — but humans don't care about conquest right now and are happy just to* keep *the planes from collapsing. Do you see the problem he has?*

"You're saying we have home-court advantage. The king has a bigger, harder job to do if he wants to reach his goals than we have to do to reach ours."

Correct. Brute force will not accomplish what he wants. Rifts and bombs only worked for the sundering because the sundering was never meant to succeed. From the king's perspective, the sundering was all for show. To succeed now, he cannot try to open rifts and plant bombs. It is very difficult for us to open rifts and bombs will only be met with your bombs. You remember what it took to open all those rifts last time?

Adrian felt a shiver, suddenly understanding. The other plane hadn't actually done the work leading up to the false sundering. It couldn't. Except within very limited ways in very limited conditions, fiends couldn't open controlled rifts. That had always been mankind's work, starting with Adrian's father. Seven months ago now, the hole that nearly punched the worlds open hadn't been Hell's doing, but Matt Baker and Erika Dale's instead.

"You're saying his troops won't do the job. He needs collaborators on our side."

Carl nodded again. *Helpers among the humans. But he has a problem. Your people know what is at stake this time. They know what we can do and they are very afraid — not just for themselves, but for the end of everything. There are some among you with minds that can be twisted, or already are twisted.*

"Minds like Erika and Matt."

There are only so many minds like that, especially now that worlds hang in the balance. Our king needs more human helpers than are available. He also needs them in specific places, doing very specific and specialized things. The key is your city — Fortune. As goes Fortune, so goes the war. The first phase, within Fortune, must be very precise. It's not enough to hope human allies will appear in exactly the right places at exactly the right times, able and willing to do exactly what needs doing, without failure or conscience. To secure Fortune requires strategy. You do not attack right away in chess, correct? First you must arrange your pieces. Only then can the attack, once begun, have a chance of succeeding.

Adrian felt doom climbing his spine like a ladder. He didn't know where this was going, but he didn't like it.

"So what did you mean before? About how the incursion was spreading out from the Gore Point?"

The old Gore Point, in your dead forest, was the original point of breach.

Adrian didn't need to be told that. He hadn't been around for the first opening from the human side, but he'd been around when his father was ripped to pieces by a hellbringer in almost the exact same place.

As such, the Gore Point is the thinnest place between the planes, like the worn patch of carpet in Dixon's hallway, trod too long by too many feet.

Adrian tried to smile, to distract himself. Watching Carl traipse through Dixon's apartment had been amusing. Dixon had complained about that, too, because just as with the smelly rift, Carl's clawed feet had ground sulfur into the rug.

It was easy enough to punch a small rift there — one that didn't need to be precise or controlled. It could be more like the tiny rifts our side opened in the prisons holding our soldiers. Just big enough to let the virus through.

Panic came. Adrian hadn't heard about any virus before now, and a lifetime of living in the modern age had taught him fear of viruses. They could be benign, or world-enders. Even without Hollywood's apocalyptic viruses, ranging from Ebola to the kind that made zombies, there were real-world phenomena that at times felt unrelenting.

"He's made a virus?"

He is *a virus.*

"What?"

The king is *a virus. Or at least he can be. Not in the way you think of viruses. Using your words, "contagion" is more accurate.*

"I think you'd better explain, Carl."

There was anger in Adrian's voice that he hadn't consciously put there — the kind that came with impotence against terror. When something was coming and you felt you couldn't fight it, instinct sometimes suggested that fury was the solution: as if rage was the same as power, as if enough anger might cause the world to decide it was being unfair and take the bad thing away.

Your kind believes it has no hive mind. Our scholars say that's untrue. You cannot communicate and share thoughts directly in the way we do, but that doesn't mean your minds aren't linked. We are linked in a usable network. You, by contrast, are linked by prefer-

ence, protection, and favor that exists below the conscious level, but above the level you'd call telepathy.

"What the hell does that mean?"

It means that when everyone starts buying the newest gadget, you need to buy one, too. It means that when your neighbor disapproves of something you're doing, you feel the need to change even if you don't have to — or to dig in and make him disapprove even more just to make the point that nobody can tell you what to do. But don't you see? That's just a different kind of control. Your neighbor asks you to turn down your music, but whether you do what he asks or defy what he asks, his request is still controlling you.

Humans are still a herd, governed by a herd instinct. You don't want to be alone, whether that means being actually separate or just believing or doing things that others don't believe or do. Deep down, you all want to belong to your tribe. We have studied your behavior extensively since the first opening. It's clear to us that all humans control one another whether you want to believe it or not.

"Influence?" Adrian asked.

Deeper than influence. You prefer what others prefer ... unless you notice it and make a choice to prefer something different just so you can be different ... which, like with the music and your neighbor, is just an upside-down kind of preference of its own. You want favor from others so you can share their resources and be part of the tribe, so you do what your society does and become what society says you should be. It's not something you can easily fight. It's instinct, done for protection. One human is vulnerable, but in groups, you are safe.

"Conformity, then. You're talking about conformity."

Call it whatever you'd like. The king's incursion begins with a contagion of mind, not an invasion of soldiers. It plays on your instincts. It has been specifically crafted to manipulate human psychology. It will spread like a rumor. Like opinions that alter society's mind. The way books and movies and phenomena on your internet become popular out of the blue, that is how his virus will spread.

It all made sense. There was an expression to describe exactly what Carl was talking about when it happened in the usual human world. Ironically, that expression was "going viral." The New Hot Thing always seemed to come out of nowhere. One day, nobody had heard of it. The next, everyone everywhere would be talking about it, consuming it, passing it on to everyone they came into contact with.

Spreading it. Like a virus.

"It won't be that easy. We don't control — or even know — what will catch on next. It's not something you can engineer."

He already has.

"Since Laurel and I came back?"

Since humankind felt the first hint of inspiration beyond what they could see. Since the first time a human heard a dark voice whispering in their ear.

Adrian felt his head shaking on its own. This was all so familiar. From his childhood. From church. From Father James, who Matt Baker said long ago had told him Eldon Porter was going to Hell.

Haven't you ever heard the expression, "The Devil made me do it?"

4

KNOCK DOWN DRAG OUT

"Ray! Ray! We—!"

Adrian's shout was interrupted when his brother wrenched open the front door and hit Adrian in the face.

Adrian fell back, his ass striking the hallway's opposite wall and sliding down to an awkward crouch.

"You've got some nerve," Ray said.

Adrian touched two fingers to his lip. They came away wet with blood. He looked up at Ray, more annoyed than angry.

"Seriously?"

"Get up. Get up and get out."

"We need to talk."

"*You* need to go. That's what *you* need to do."

"So this is what it's come to?"

"This is what it's come to."

Maybe the best strategy here was to press on. Ray had always been impulsive. Sometimes that gave him memory like a goldfish. "Listen. Carl just told me—"

"Carl," Ray interrupted.

"Yes. Carl."

"The same Carl who led us into the belly of the beast. Into an ambush."

"He didn't know we'd be ambushed."

"But you did. Didn't you?"

"I ... *What?* No, of course not!"

"Piss off, Adrian."

"I'm your brother!"

"No. You're not." Ray stepped back into his apartment. Before he could slam the door, Adrian lunged forward and stuck his foot between door and jamb.

He'd never done it before. No real person had. Sticking a foot in the door was either an expression without grounds or something that only happened on TV. That much was clear when Ray, oblivious of or uncaring about the foot, didn't temper his slam at all. Wood attempted to crush wood and crushed the flesh between instead. Adrian's ankle caught some of the rebound, resonating a funny bone down there he didn't know he had.

Ray, unsympathetic, kicked at Adrian's throbbing foot. When that didn't clear his threshold, he slammed the foot in the door again instead.

"Goddammit, get your fucking foot—!"

Ignoring tremendous bolts of pain, Adrian somehow managed to pogo-jump back toward standing, bearing most of his weight on the good foot. His balance was forward of vertical, more or less by design. The resulting trajectory was like a torpid missile that technically failed its launch but hit a valid target anyway. In Adrian's case, the rocket was the pocket between his head and right shoulder, and the target was Ray's middle.

He hit Ray in a tackle. Not at all expecting it, Ray wasn't so much as braced. His top half folded down and his back half fell like bricks.

When Ray's butt hit the floor, his head whipsawed back so hard, Adrian thought later that impact with the floor could have killed him. Ray was a slob, though — something Adrian knew from living in this very apartment on and off. He had never repaired the coffee table they'd annihilated the last time they'd done this, and he certainly never bothered to put his clothes anywhere sensible. As a result, his skull was pillowed by a pile of boxer shorts. Hopefully they were clean.

The hit dazed Ray. All breath, totally unprepared for a blow to the abdomen, had been forced out of him. He heaved like a man choking, sucking at oxygen that wasn't there.

"Ray. *Ray?* Are you okay? I'm sorry. I didn't mean—"

He'd climbed atop Ray to assess the damage. As he reached forward to slap his brother's cheek back to awareness, a heavy fist struck Adrian in the kidney. Then Ray was over him, on knees and then feet. He still hadn't caught his breath. He swayed in dukes-up stance like a boxer low on fuel as Adrian, backing out of striking range and gripping his side, rose to match him.

"I don't want to fight you."

"Too." *Wheeze.* "Bad."

"What happened that day isn't what you think."

"Con—" *Wheeze.* "—venient."

Adrian considered his brother. They didn't usually have one-sided fights, and for the first time in a very long time, Adrian suspected he might be winning. It was uncharted territory for the famous — now infamous — Porter boys.

Ray looked like he might fall over. His ability to breathe was returning, but not yet keeping up with the oxygen demands of all this exertion. He was burning more than he was getting, his eyes foggy and his limbs shaking like a man with palsy.

"Do you want me to give you a minute?" Adrian asked.

"Fuck off."

"Not bad. You got out an entire sentence that time."

Ray threw a lamp. It missed.

"Dumbshit. That's *your* lamp you just broke."

"It's your *dick.*"

Adrian took a second. Then he said, "Good one."

"I told you to leave."

"Yeah, Ray, you did. But here's the thing: I'm not going to. You're not stupid, even if you did let your fans think of you as the handsome, brave moron."

"Fuck you."

"Come on. Tell me something original. At least have some dignity to your insults."

Ray rushed forward. Except it wasn't a rush, in his weakened state, so much as a controlled fall. Adrian had never taken judo, but his brother's languid maneuver was so slow, he was able to improvise based on clichés. You were supposed to use your opponent's own momentum against him, right? That meant the correct counter to Ray's attack was to step slightly aside and push him as he passed.

Ray struck the front room mirror, shattering it.

Adrian squatted beside him after he hit the floor again, careful to stay out of fist and leg radius. "It's like I said. You're not stupid."

Ray didn't answer this time. Maybe because he didn't have any new vocabulary and didn't want to chance more witty rejoinders from Adrian.

"You know we're just going to keep pummeling each other until we can't move, then end up talking anyway."

Ray was breathing like a man just trying to keep up. Adrian, watching him, felt strangely sad. Ray was always on top of these encounters, *always.* The fact that Adrian was winning this fight — and handily so — wasn't triumphant. It was pathetic.

No matter how much they fought as both boys and adults, which was constantly, Adrian had always looked up to his older brother as something unshakable. Ray had never really been an opponent to Adrian. He'd been more like the Rampart itself. You could fight a wall if you wanted, but it was unbreakable. A wall would unfailingly kick your ass ... but when all the fight was out of you, that wall would reliably still be there: support and protection when you needed it most.

Ray now was that wall in ruin. That wall toppled, as if humbled by age. Adrian felt a strange impulse to look away as Ray just sat there, as Ray accepted his impossible defeat. It was seeing the beautiful without beauty, the strong without strength. Even though Ray was the one at mercy, it was Adrian, watching it happen, who felt frail and mortal.

"Are we done?" Adrian asked.

"I hate you."

"I know. But are we done?"

After ten or so seconds, Adrian decided Ray's agonizing non-response was as good as a yes. He stood from his crouch and offered his brother a hand.

Ray half-rose, cringing as he did. He slapped Adrian's hand away and finished standing on his own.

5

REALITY

They talked. And talked. And talked.

It became clear to Adrian after a while that the biggest obstacle to getting on the same page was the fact that Ray had already committed to his version of what happened when their other-plane adventure ended. It'd happened a month ago, and they hadn't spoken since. Without Adrian there to nudge back against Ray's perception of events, he had only dug in deeper. Ray had asked himself questions about the mission, the intention of the mission, and what Adrian may or may not have known all along ... then answered them himself. Suppositions created suppositions. Theories became fact. Now Adrian's simple request to discuss the matter had become less like shaping clay and more like drilling into concrete.

Ray had needed to keep on living with himself over the past month. He'd needed to be able to look into the mirror and see his face every day. He'd needed a way to understand what felt like (and, in some ways, *was*) a whole new world, and he'd done all of it in isolation. Most of Adrian's work, through their multi-hour, often-contentious conversation, was reminding Ray that much of what he'd taken to be true were actually guesses he'd made himself.

"Stripped of all the bullshit," Adrian said, "what are you *actually* mad at me about?"

Ray grunted. He wasn't going to answer questions that direct and Adrian should know better than to ask. After Eldon died and their mother got cancer, Adrian went to therapy and Ray doubled his shifts at the brigadehouse. They both battled demons during that time, but Adrian's were internal while Ray's were literal. He didn't like confronting his feelings. The idea of explaining to Adrian why he was angry felt repugnant. He'd rather just be mad.

"Okay," he said, changing tacks away from emotion and toward facts, "what do you think happened?"

"When? In what?"

"In the mission as a whole."

So Ray, beaten into line at that point by Adrian's superior verbal skills, told Adrian the story.

Adrian reminded him: *Don't guess. Pretend you're writing a report, and tell me exactly what happened as if I didn't already know.*

Ray did exactly that. He didn't invent things and by then he'd realized it was futile to sneak in a few jabs about what an asshole Adrian was. Still, sticking to facts with which Adrian actually agreed, it was fascinating to see the tilt Ray had given those truths. He wasn't telling Adrian the *story* of their quest to infiltrate the fiend city, make contact with the queen, and hopefully free Laurel along the way. He told Adrian his *reality* ... and it was different from Adrian's:

After the near-sundering, a few rifts opened and there were a handful of skirmishes, but slowly the fiends had been repelled and all rifts were closed. During this final push, the human side had scored a massive win.

They'd captured the fiend king and held him prisoner. The military had then opened a single massive rift in the warehouse complex and begun mining fiend bodies for Zen.

Meanwhile Adrian had started talking to Laurel in his dreams. She called him to her, to save her. At around the same time, Dixon had word from a halfskull double-agent and learned that the queen, who'd replaced the king, was plotting an invasion. Her troops had assembled — troops the Roughnecks later saw in person — outside the rift. War was about to break out.

When the Roughnecks entered the alien city, having lost two of their best friends along the way, they were captured and held prisoner because Laurel and the queen had made a deal. It was all a scam: the Roughnecks lured under false promises.

Then Adrian, instead of standing up for his squad (and for humanity), had helped the dreadnought escape in exchange for letting Laurel go. The Roughnecks had been released first, allowed to re-enter the human plane through an adjunct rift. Laurel and Adrian were released later, presumably so they could welcome the returning king.

"'Presumably,'" said Adrian.

"What?"

"You *presumed* that's why we were released later. It's another guess you made. It's not fact."

"Well, then, *fuck*, Adrian," Ray said, collapsing his risen arms and shaking his head: a full-body gesture of surrender. "I guess I don't know what facts are, so why doesn't your enlightened ass tell me. You already admitted you opened the door for that motherfucker. You set him free."

"Yes, but—"

"And you were there when he arrived. And you talked to him. You admitted *that*, too."

"Well yeah, but 'welcoming the king' makes it sound like we were happy about it."

"Jesus Christ."

"What?"

"So now 'reality' depends on your feelings. You said to be objective. So, okay, you weren't happy when the king came back to Hell. You were sad. Or mad. Or you thought it was hilarious."

"We were—"

"It's not the point. Who the fuck cares? You wanted me to tell you what happened. That's what I saw happen with my own eyes, or what I heard happened and you confirmed for me like a half hour ago. I don't know what else you expect me to say."

"What you have is right," Adrian told him. "But you don't have everything."

So Adrian told him. He didn't know why he'd thought he could keep secrets from Ray. He couldn't — not in the long term. They should have had this talk right away. Laurel told him that Ray was too volatile to know the truth: his tendency toward rash action would end up giving them away. But Laurel, despite having dated both brothers, didn't understand why "Ray plus Adrian" did not equal "Ray and Adrian." Their bond was more than the sum of its parts.

Ray *was* rash. Ray *could* give them away. But he wouldn't, if the two of them worked together.

"Goddamn, Ray, I'm sorry. I really am."

"I told you to go fuck yourself with your sorries."

"Yeah. You did." Neither man's comment had any teeth. They'd always be brothers, and that meant that once the fight was behind them, their worst insults were basically *hello*. "I still am."

Ray looked away. "Well, yeah."

"I *did* open that rift — or, really, co-opened it. The king did return through it. So yes. He's out of his prison because of me."

Ray made a *Well, there you go* gesture with his arms.

"But I didn't tell you why."

"You said you did it because the queen was worse."

"By a lot of people's standards, she actually *wasn't* worse. Whatever she did would have been messy, but there was always a solution."

"But the king — against what he's up to, or what Laurel told you he'd be up to, there isn't a solution."

"Right."

"How's that the right choice, Adrian?"

So Adrian explained. Ray tried to understand — really he did — but Adrian himself barely understood Laurel's science. Part of Ray's incomplete comprehension, when it was over, was surely Adrian's fault.

"It still sounds like the end of the world," Ray said.

"It is."

"And yet here you are, telling me you knew that in advance and did it anyway."

"Right."

Ray thought, then settled on saying again, "Goddammit, Ade."

"You have to trust me."

"How can I trust you, with what you said?"

"I'm not telling it right. *Laurel.* Do you trust her?"

That was a hard question to ask. Laurel was an ex, and "trusting Laurel" meant validating her judgment — the same judgment that once upon a time had kicked him to the curb.

"On this, yeah. I guess I trust her," Ray finally said. "But it's fucked. I don't like it."

"Nobody likes it. But it had to be done."

Ray made a discontented noise but said nothing more. They'd reached a strange impasse. Both men agreed that the king was bad news and was about to ruin the world. Ray was — barely — willing to accept Adrian's word that *despite* being bad, the situation was ... *somehow?* ... the best option — this despite Adrian being unable to clarify why. But it was worse than that: Explaining his actions, hearing his own words as he spoke them to Ray, was starting to make *Adrian* doubt, too. He was attempting to defend himself while not believing himself especially defensible.

Their trust — their willingness to move past this worst of all possible choices — was wafer-thin. Breathing too hard would snap it, sending them both down a hopeless spiral in which everything was over and Adrian was the arch villain.

But fortunately neither of them breathed much beyond that. They didn't utter another word. The issue swelled with protest, then thanks to the silence abated like a strained hose finally breaking through a clog.

The pressure of the moment drained away. Then they were two very tired, very battered men in a shitty apartment, wondering what to do next.

Five minutes passed. Ten. Each started to think the other had fallen asleep.

"So it turns out Dee Scott is gay," Ray said.

"I know that. Everyone knows that. We've all known for ages."

Another ten seconds. They'd devolved to neighborhood news. That's how dumb this fight had gotten.

Ray spoke into the silence: "Goddammit, Adrian."

6
LOCK-IN

Once upon a time, they'd been heroes: brave Ray, the Legion, and insightful and intelligent Adrian, the Stitcher. The reality TV show following their compatriots as they fought creatures from the other side (everyone knew Ray and Adrian were the stars) had been the most popular program in the world. They'd had sponsorships, personally and as part of the brigade. Ray was the chiseled jaw representing razor blades. Adrian, the brain, represented tech gadgets. Their brigade uniforms had been covered with sponsor patches and their faces were always on the covers of magazines. They'd both been stopped constantly back then in the streets of Fortune: celebrities a little less reluctant than modesty should have allowed. Everyone loved the Porter brothers the same as everyone had loved their famous father.

Not anymore, though. The public had turned on the Porter family like the crack of a whip after the dreadnought vanished and the rumors began. Adrian was an obvious target: People believed — correctly — that Adrian had been the cause of it all. But Ray's reputation was dragged through the mud right behind his brother: the rumor mill working doubly hard to add him to the list of pariahs.

Dixon, for one, was delighted to see them together again. His comment when Ray followed Adrian into the office was, "Oh, fuck my mother."

"Don't," Adrian told Dixon.

"Laurel specifically told you not to tell him." Dixon meant Ray.

"He's my brother."

"He's a hothead. The people who hate me and you at least think *we* believe the shitty things they think we did. *He*, on the other hand—"

"You know, *he* is right here," Ray interjected, looking around.

Dixon ignored him and continued yelling at Adrian. "—is just a bumbling fucking pretty boy. He'll believe whatever people tell him. He'll do whatever you say. So what's this look like, Adrian? I'll tell you what it looks like, if anyone saw you bring him in here. It looks like we recruited muscle. We brought in your big, stupid brother because *clearly* we're up to something; *clearly* we aren't laying low now that everyone's pissing themselves, sure the world's about to end."

"Hey, where's your Satan bobblehead? I thought you said—"

"Dixon ..." Adrian started, ignoring his brother as he realized he didn't even know the man's first name. A first name was called for here, but what was he supposed to say? "J"?

"Out," Dixon said, pointing at the door as his attention finally turned to Ray. "There's a reason we didn't bring you in before now."

"I'm here to help."

"We're good. Fuck off."

Ray stepped forward. What Dixon didn't seem to realize

was that Ray wasn't much for verbal sparring. You could push most people with words until their bluff got called, but Ray wasn't bluffing. Dixon was barely half his weight. In about two seconds, Ray would tie him up like a pretzel.

Adrian stepped between them, then spoke to Dixon. "We need allies."

Dixon rolled his eyes. "Oh, so *this* is my lot now? You, your idiot brother, and your girlfriend who always knows better than me? You know what? Great. Great. I love it. Let's start a band, the four of us. I've even got a name: Dixon and the Three Treasures."

"I told you what Carl said."

"About the king peeking some psychic part of himself through the rift and taking over people's minds one by one? Yeah. You told me. *One*: Whatever. *Two*: Even if that's really a thing, I don't see how Rambo here is going to do anything to stop it."

Ray stepped forward again. Before he could push through his brother to punch Special Agent J. Dixon in the throat, the entire building shook with the force of a nuclear blast. Ray staggered, nearly falling on the desk. Glass fell from the cabinets in the kitchen. Frames, hung on the wall, detonated on the floor.

Seconds later, something boomed in the distance. It sounded almost like artillery. Then came a chorus of screaming.

They looked at each other, their near-fight paused for the moment. Then all three men went to the window.

In the hills, maybe three miles distant in the direction of the highway, a plume of orange fire bloomed into the ash-gray sky.

• • •

THERE WAS no time to be subtle. Hated or not, Adrian had never surrendered his tie to the brigade. He was still technically a Stitcher, though there was nothing left to stitch. They'd driven Ray's squad car to Dixon's not-entirely-incognito office, so both brothers piled back into it. Heads turned as Adrian arrived. He saw loathing in the onlookers' eyes, but this wasn't the time to look away. Adrian stared right back, darting between his haters and the fire in the distance — a mushroom cloud now haloed in black smoke.

My brother and I are going to go and deal with that, he tried to project. *Unless you hate and distrust me so much, you'd rather I didn't?*

The haters looked away. Nobody rushed forward now to stop them — to call Adrian a traitor and Ray his accomplice, demanding they resign and die. Seeing the way they set aside their insults so the brothers could deal with the thing that scared them, resentment bubbled inside him.

Adrian could see resentment bubbling inside his brother, too.

Cowards. Turncoats. Spineless, back-seat-brigade assholes, Adrian thought, staring right back at the deer-in-headlights fools that Fortune's angriest people had become. *I guess you're not too good to want our help.*

They slammed the doors too hard, then sped off with the siren screaming.

It was hard to see exactly where the trouble lay from a map's point of view, so Ray simply kept his eyes on the orange-and-black cloud and did his best to drive in its general direction. It didn't look far as the crow flies, but getting there took over ten minutes. There'd clearly been other incidents that were less showy than the fireball in the hills, and a good amount of the population was starting to lose their minds. Fortune was now a thin veneer over a layer of fear and chaos that had permeated recent weeks.

They had to steer around two car wrecks. Ray nearly ran down no fewer than a dozen people, all milling aimlessly in the streets. A woman with her hair in curlers ran at the squad car, leapt onto its windshield, and hung on by the wipers until Ray, unsure what else to do, simply turned them on to dislodge her.

They were hearing more and more bad news in the distance now: crumpling sounds, crashes, gunshots, shouts. It was audible even through closed windows.

"Maybe Carl was wrong." Ray's tone and the washed-out, gobsmacked look of his face told Adrian that the argument between them was completely over now; there were bigger fish to fry than fighting brother-to-brother. "This is how it was for the sundering."

That wasn't really true. The sundering, when it almost happened, had been much, much worse. That had felt like the literal end of the world, the air itself hot and poisoned. They'd had to don rebreathers and full suits to leave the brigadehouse safely, because particulate Zen had been spilling from scores of rifts to be circulated by the wind. The people on the streets then had done nothing but run from one place to another, out of their minds. This was subtler, but everyone in Fortune had severe PTSD from last time.

This felt like mild disorder compared to the sundering ... but with an added edge, because everyone they saw seemed to be waiting for the other shoe to drop.

Adrian didn't answer. He didn't know what to say. His gut and his faith in Laurel's analysis from the start (confirmed today by Carl, who'd added the part about this new offensive being both coy and slow, under the radar instead of flames and spectacle) told him that what they were seeing now was something less than the end. What it was, though, he had no idea.

So he kept his lips pressed together and his eyes ahead. He could see Ray looking at his profile for a long time, waiting for Adrian to respond. Then their vehicle rolled jarringly over something in the road — something Adrian thought at first was a human being, but turned out to be a knocked-off car bumper — and Ray's attention jerked back to the windshield. He weaved through the debris of a two-car smash, then around a downed and sparking power line. After that, he couldn't spare more looks at his brother.

The streets cleared out somewhat closer to their destination, though at the very end they had to honk at a group of rubberneckers around it to get them to move out of the way. Then Ray threaded the squad car through the gap, aware instantly of the problem's nature ... and why, instead of driving closer, he'd do best to keep the car a fair distance away.

The fireball was coming from a gas station. Something big had ruptured — probably one of the underground gasoline tanks. The heat of the petrol blaze was immense, rivaling even the heat of the fiend plane through an open rift. They'd come from an office, not the muster room at the station, and were therefore in street clothes. After Adrian lost face, he'd kept far from the brigadehouse lest he be mobbed to death. He didn't even know where he'd find heat-resistant clothing and equipment if he needed them, and he needed them now.

"Tell me you have a coat and gear in the trunk," Adrian said to his brother.

"This is Captain Kaur's car. So no."

"Shit."

"Shit," Ray agreed.

But the fire wasn't even the biggest *shit* on the scene. Adrian and Ray had both noticed something much more troubling — something the rubberneckers seemed more wary of than even the blaze. Fire from a gas station, while terrifying, was at least something a person could understand.

The other thing wasn't.

The fire wasn't burning in the open. In an impossible-to-fathom way, it wasn't even a whole fire. It looked a little like a fire set right up against a wall, but even a fire against a wall would be a complete fire. This, by contrast, looked like a fire that had started to burn before getting cut in half by something. Gasoline fueling the blaze was directly below the fire itself, with only the front part of it visible from where the brothers stood.

Bisecting the fire was a smooth gray field that stretched endlessly upward.

"Adrian, what the hell is—?"

Adrian saw. Adrian needed the exact same answers as his brother, but right now the fire was the bigger problem. They had to extinguish it somehow first … and *then* deal with the reality-bending thing before them.

There were sirens approaching from all around: firefighters coming with the exact same goal. Somehow Adrian and Ray had gotten here first — maybe because the fire engines were larger than their sedan, and would have more trouble navigating the obstructions to get here. They could see the flashers of the nearest one now, trying to make its way forward. It would still have to arrive, unload, and hook up to a hydrant. It would be minutes before that happened.

"Let's see if we can find the cutoff," Ray said.

Adrian was already changing his mind about coming here. He'd been amped up, like everyone of late. They weren't firefighters; they were riftfare. They understood heat, and they'd been conditioned to run toward trouble while other people ran away. Those impulses — plus the unknown of Carl's warning, suggesting terrible things in waiting — had made them come here. Now that they were on-site, it struck Adrian how inappropriate it was that they get involved.

Yeah, said a voice inside Adrian's head, *but what about the big, weird, impossibly tall gray thing that probably caused the fire in the first place? That's not a firefighter thing, is it?*

"Adrian. The cutoff?"

Adrian closed his eyes for a half second, then took a quick breath. The air, even this far from the blaze, was nearly hot enough to blister paint. It scraped at his lungs. They should have gear, but neither Ray nor Adrian had thought of it.

Rifts required gear. This, to the animal parts of their brains, was more-generalized danger.

Adrian forced himself to push a few steps forward, around the blaze to one side, trying to see the station. The emergency pump cutoff was always prominent on the front of any gas station. He tried to ignore the fact that this was a *tank* fire instead of a *pump* fire, and that triggering the cutoff would be a little like turning off a hose so a nearby river would stop overflowing.

Even where the black smoke was thin, heat haze made it nearly impossible to see past the fire. They hadn't brought goggles, so their eyes weren't cooperating: The fire's heat dried them like grapes becoming raisins and the petroleum fumes made them ache and water.

Adrian squinted his lids. He was more used to heat than most, as was Ray. He forced himself to move closer, until he saw a new problem: There was no cutoff, because there was no station. The big gray thing, which looked like a wall made of shimmering and shifting matte-gray stone, seemed to have smashed into the ground (and the underground tank) from above somehow, between the road and the station itself.

The station was on its other side.

Ray had realized it too. Brother looked at brother, lost with no idea what to do.

Impatient, authoritative shouts came from behind. Something charged past Adrian, nearly knocking him over. Then another thing of about the same size rushed by his other side, this one actively cuffing him away. It took Adrian long seconds to see what was happening: They'd stalled out between the fire and two newly-arrived fire engines, and the firefighters were rushing the scene, with Ray and Adrian in the way.

"Get back!" one of them yelled at Ray. "GET THE HELL OUT OF HERE!"

More came, each dressed for the scene in a way that the Porters were not. The responders all wore heat-resistant gear, duly clasped and buttoned: hard hats on, collars high, boots heavy, faces covered with high-temp breathing equipment. After the first wave, Ray and Adrian did as they were told, accepting now that they had no business even being here.

They shunted aside, attention now on the big gray wall. Whatever it was seemed to have come down like a hammer, descending with enough force to blow bits of concrete all the way to the street beyond. Near the thing, a shattered parking lot had ripped in a wavelike pattern: bent inward at the wall-thing's base, but broken upward just beyond as if the force of the thing had made concrete whitecaps. Ten feet or so from the wall's base, a second ring of concrete jutted up like a giant, semicircular donut. The surface had spiderwebbed, revealing iron rebar that poked at the sky like rusted brown teeth.

Looking at the scene, deducing the impossible way it must have happened, Adrian thought he understood how an underground tank that should only have been pounded open had exploded instead: The force of impact must have been enough to rub rocks against rocks, iron against ore. High-pressure fumes had filled the air, and all it'd taken to blow the thing was one little spark.

A group of firefighters rushed to a hydrant near the squad vehicle. It was parked too close, but the inventive crew already had an answer to that: One of the engines rolled forward as the men and women in coats came on foot, struck the squad car's bumper, and pushed it noisily away. Watching, Adrian had a strange thought: *Good job taking the captain's car, Ray. When he sees the damage, Kaur's going to be PISSED.*

The engine backed up. With the way now clear, the firefighters ran in, unscrewed the hydrant, attached a hose that ran to the pumping truck, and opened the valve.

But nothing happened.

Seconds later, Adrian saw why: As pressure diverted, water began to spray from a point farther down the big gray wall. The same thing shattered both the ground and the water main feeding the hydrant.

"Can you put it out without water?" Ray yelled at one of the firefighters.

"It's a gas fire! The water's just for surrounding buildings! "Now get the fuck out of here!"

More trucks came. Adrian could only gape, unable to follow what came next.

Something rushed in to spray the area with foam. Some of the crews went into the mouth of the blaze and seemed to seal the hole around the base of the incomprehensible wall, after which the mostly-contained fire began to burn at lower but still-ferocious intensity. This done, the crews turned most of their attention to the surrounding area, using water from a tank to douse vegetation and structures around the blaze to keep the fire from spreading. Then activity mostly quieted, and in time the cut-off fire burned itself out.

The heat slowly abated. Everything was wet; sounds of

dripping water soon filled the quiet. The fire crews went about the business of cleanup. From where he sat, Adrian could see everyone on the scene trying to focus on their jobs so they could ignore the impossibility that had made them necessary.

The area had been cordoned off since they arrived. Inside the circle of temporary barricades now were only firefighters and other emergency responders. They'd already been asked to leave with all the other civilians, but the one thing Ray and Adrian always had on them were their ID badges.

Riftfighters on a fire scene? If anyone thought that was strange, nobody mentioned it. The cop they'd shown those badges to had simply looked from IDs to faces, registering the two biggest fallen heroes the city had ever known: Ray and Adrian Porter, traitors in the flesh.

Press was starting to gather, but not just for the fire or the wall thing, which authorities on-site had thus far insisted they not approach until "proper departments" were called, whatever that meant. Word had spread about the Porters being present. They could see reporters behind orange-and-black sawhorses pointing at them, yelling their names.

"Time to go, Little Brother."

"We need to figure out what this is," Adrian said, meaning the wall.

"Why us?"

"Because nobody else knows the whole truth."

Ray's brows drew together. *"The truth?"* There was only one thing about which *only* the Porters — plus Dixon and Laurel — knew the truth. "You think this is about what Carl said? About the fiend king's plans?"

"Look where it fell. In both directions."

Ray looked from one end of the big gray wall to the other, as far as their current station allowed — something Adrian had done a while back, and spent all the intervening time trying to interpret.

"It's over the Rampart."

Adrian nodded. The Rampart wall surrounding Fortune had only two exit points: one north and one southwest. At each exit, an extensive military encampment guarded 110 yards of space in which there *was* no Rampart, allowing four lanes in each direction of gated highway plus a paved median area between them designated for parking (mostly military carriers and 18-wheeled transport) and refueling.

What looked from here like a civilian gas station was actually part of the massive northern gate complex, most of which presumably cut off and on the other side of whatever-this-was.

Opposite of the now-extinguished fire was a shattered four-lane highway, duly blocked by the huge gray-stone wall. Beyond that — past the highway — the gray wall had smashed into the top of the Rampart itself.

The wall thing followed the Rampart exactly. Past the gate area where the fire had occurred, it was as if the Rampart had been made taller, its peak now higher than the eye could see.

"Listen to the sirens out there, Ray." Adrian pointed slowly down the wall in one direction and then the other. What looked like a raised horizon looked now, with context, to be the perfectly flat top of a miles-high wall. "Bet you anything it follows the Rampart all the way around the city. Bet you anything we're boxed in."

"You think the fiends did this?"

"I don't think humans did. I don't see how. Who's left?"

Ray looked uneasy. It took a lot to rattle the Unshakable Ray Porter. He was letting himself see the truth, and it scared him. A massive, city-sized wall had dropped from the sky with enough force to ripple concrete and detonate a buried gas tank — and, judging by a far off plume of black smoke in the southwest, might have done exactly the same thing across the city as well. That sort of thing just wasn't possible. But people used to say Hell was only a nightmare.

"Carl said that controlling Fortune is the key to his plan. He said, 'As goes Fortune, so goes the war.' Look around you, Ray." Adrian nodded, feeling his own fear. "If the Rampart's now impassable and we're all trapped inside ... wouldn't you say Fortune's firmly in the king's corner?"

"What do we do?"

Adrian shook his head, as if he had no clue, but his mouth gave a better answer. "We ask Laurel. Laurel will know."

"Did she know this was coming?"

The delivery of a lock-in barrier around Fortune seemed like the kind of thing Laurel would have mentioned before now if she'd known about it. Adrian had been hanging on to a certainty that somehow, in some way, she had an ace in the hole against the king and had never truly been part of his plan, and therefore had never actually been on his side. Did the king know that Laurel would conspire against him?

To his credit, Ray didn't ask again. He knew Laurel hadn't known about the wall. It made everything that came next suspect, but Ray was smarter than he seemed from the outside, and plenty smart enough to know that suspect or not, whatever Laurel came up with would be the best chance they had.

While Ray and Adrian sat there gaping at each other, someone approached from the rear.

A voice — strange, almost chattering — said, *Are you the Porter Brothers?*

While Ray turned, clearly ready for a quarrel, instinct told Adrian to do something very different. Because although it was a clever mimic of human, the voice had not been out loud. They'd heard it, disguised as audible, inside their heads.

A shadow sliced through the air. Adrian dove for the

ground with barely enough time to grab Ray's arm and drag him down with him. They hit the dirt as something whooshed by above.

Adrian looked up from the dirt, expecting to see a fiend wearing human clothes. Instead, he saw a man with black hair and dead, almost black eyes. He looked like anyone else — any anonymous man they might pass on the street — but he could think-speak, and what was inside him bled through his thoughts and into Adrian's.

He felt like someone infected. Someone with the Devil inside him.

The thing he'd swung where they'd been sitting seconds earlier was a Legion's Rollard.

Ray sat up, eyed the Rollard, and started to stand. "You son of a—!"

"NO!"

Adrian shoved his brother aside as the man swung again, this time embedding the bladed end of the Rollard in the wooden bench on which they'd been sitting. Ray again tried to fight; Adrian again pulled him down. The man wore a brigade coat beneath an overcoat, and Adrian thought he even recognized him: a retired Legion from the closed Brigade Six.

The ex-Legion knew how to use the Rollard, but he was too fast for an ordinary Legion. Too strong. Something had *improved* him, like an infusion-improved fiend soldier on the far side of a rift. Something internal. Something that didn't make his skin glow blue. Something that now used him from the inside out, and that was nearly invisible from the outside, making him look like just another man.

Ray hadn't seen and didn't understand. He thought the man was human, and was more offended that some random guy dared to use a Legion's weapon against him than aware of what was actually happening. Unlike Ray, Adrian had spent much more time speaking with his mind and knew how the psychic voice could mimic — how it could hang itself on a person's memory centers and fool him into thinking it was speaking aloud.

But why? Why didn't it speak with the man's own voice — with the larynx it'd had when human?

It hardly mattered. The man worked to wrench the Rollard free while from the corner of Adrian's eye, he saw three more people marching forward to join the party. No more Rollards, but there was a pipe, a machete, and a severed stalk of rebar.

"Let me *GO!*" Ray protested, indignantly shaking away from Adrian's grip. "If this motherfucker thinks he can just—!"

There was no time to explain. Using both hands, Adrian wrenched his brother's head sideways to face the three others approaching. All had fiend-mind inside them, all coming forward to kill Ray and Adrian for daring to be traitors — not to humanity, but to the fiend king this time.

Ray understood.

"RUN!" Adrian yelled.

They ran.

7

COME WITH ME

Adrian wrenched his home's doorknob almost hard enough to break it off.

Ray had always been the strong and impetuous one, more inclined to use too much force because he wasn't thinking straight. Now, though, Adrian seemed more panicked. He wasn't used to being attacked; for Ray it was just another day on the job. Usually it was fiends who came at him. Today, it'd been fiends wearing human bodies like puppets. Same foe, different shape. In a way it was like Ray had already shaken it off, or at least put it on a shelf in the back of his mind for later consideration, when he had more to go on. Adrian wasn't as sanguine. It was hard to believe in a future right now where he'd ever know enough to explain something so strange, so troubling.

Fiends inside Legions. Inside people just like them: men and women whom they used to count as colleagues.

On the rushed drive back (in a borrowed car because they couldn't reach their own; after the earthquake force of the dropping wall, finding stalled-out, driverless vehicles with keys still in the ignition was easy), Adrian's adrenaline had abated. In its wake, he thought he might even know their attacker's name.

Renfield. The man with the Rollard's name was Renfield. I remember because that was the name of Dracula's accomplice: the crazy guy who talked to insects. It even seemed fitting.

He tried to talk to Ray about it, but he couldn't open his mouth. He was afraid to hear what Ray would think. He didn't particularly want Ray's theories until Laurel was there to mediate them. Those theories might be facts that Adrian already knew. A lot of people hated Adrian Porter right now, but it was one thing to spraypaint *Traitor* on FedEx packages filled with shit and quite another to come at him with blacked-out eyes, thinking his speech and trying to kill him.

Was this how the world ended? By comparison, the sundering might almost be a relief. Carl had talked about the king having a kind of mental virus. He'd said this new, sneakier form of sundering had already spread out from the Gore Point. Who still went to the Gore Point? Besides teenagers with macabre minds, courting dark places for kicks or suicidal tendencies, and the retired riftfare workers of Fortune, who'd become glorified janitors when the remaining brigades closed. People tasked with cleaning up the old rift points. Like Renfield.

Don't think about it.

So he didn't. Not until he got home, Laurel's home, and found the door locked even after he'd unlocked it. There was a deadbolt, but it had to be turned from the inside.

Why was it locked now? Laurel had the most level head he'd ever known. She wasn't some housewife from the 1950s, climbing onto a chair and screaming when she found a mouse in her kitchen.

His fist pounded the green-painted wood: side-on like a

cop demanding entry, not knuckles-first like a neighbor paying a visit.

"LAUREL! LAUREL, OPEN UP!"

"Easy." That was Ray beside him. Hearing Ray urge calm was disarming. Troubling. It gave Adrian an idea how frenzied he must look, to have his hothead brother talk him down like that.

"LAUREL!"

"Adrian. Relax."

"Don't tell me to relax. LAUREL! WHY THE FUCK IS THIS DOOR LOCKED? *LAUREL!*"

Neighbors were poking out, craning their heads toward his tantrum like praire dogs checking the surroundings. Seeing them made him angry at their butting-in ... and even more unnerved. At first he didn't understand why, but then it dawned on him: They should be inside cowering with the lights off and the blinds drawn, rubbing crucifixes and crying. Instead, they looked like he'd disturbed their preparations for the bake sale. He'd seen similar things on their drive over here. Pedestrians were out, not in hiding. He'd seen at least three people walking dogs. Had he noticed shops open and doing business ... despite windows broken by the wall's impact, despite all the sirens and black smoke on the horizon? He thought he had. One car on the road had actually honked at him for driving too fast as he screamed away from their zombie attackers and toward Laurel's place. The normality was bothersome.

As if they hadn't just been boxed inside some sort of supernatural container: bugs trapped by kids, kept for observation inside a mason jar made of gray stone. If the miles-high wall that now seemed to surround Fortune even *was* stone.

Now the neighbors on both sides were poking through their doors and staring.

"Get inside! What the hell are you looking at!"

"Adrian."

His attention was on the door again. "Where is she? Why isn't she opening up?"

"Ade."

"LAUREL!" Then his head whipped toward the neighbors again, who hadn't yet gone inside, but this time he didn't yell. "We should break a window. I'm going to break a window."

"Adrian. You need to chill. You're freaking me out."

"Good! *Be* freaked out! Why *are* you so goddamn chill?" Now he projected his voice to the ho-hum faces of Laurel's neighbors again: "Why is everyone so goddamn chill?" Then to Ray again: "What's going on here?"

"Nothing's going on. We got away. Those guys didn't chase us."

"*Guys,*" Adrian echoed. "Those were *things.*"

"Let's not jump to conclusions. Neither of us are favorite sons these days. We don't actually know what happened back there, so let's not assume they were—"

"—Legions? The one with the Rollard was a Brigade Eight Legion. His eyes were black. The shit he said? He didn't say it out loud."

"How else would he say it?"

Adrian tapped the side of his skull. "They were fiends."

"They were people."

"Where the fuck is Laurel?"

"It's okay, Ade. Look around. Nobody's chasing us now. Everything's fine."

It was. It was actually more than fine. It was *superfine. Supernormal.*

A sprinkler cast gentle arcs of water on a lawn two houses down. Sunlight through the mist made a rainbow.

A couple pushed a baby in a carriage down the sidewalk.

Did people actually do that? He supposed they did (otherwise, what were carriages for?), but Adrian couldn't think of the last time he'd seen it. The entire neighborhood, looking around, struck him as a performance. Some fool's vision of what life looked like rather than life's gritty reality — especially these days, since the king of Hell reclaimed his throne and everyone in Fortune started awaiting the End Days.

It was all perfect. If you ignored the straight gray line above where the horizon used to be, reaching high into the sky.

The door unlocked with a click. Laurel opened it, and for just a second she looked at them with pleased surprise, as if perhaps Adrian and Ray had come to her front door selling cookies. Her expression was almost Rockwellian too.

Then it vanished and she was herself again.

"Why did you lock the door?" Adrian demanded. "Do you know what's going on out here? We saw ..."

She didn't wait to hear what they'd seen. She grabbed both men by the arm, pulled them inside, then poked her head back out, seeing the neighbors wave as if they were worried by her anxious, shouting visitors, then closed and re-locked the door.

"Something happened," Ray said, jumping in before Adrian could start to chatter. "I don't know if you heard, but—"

"Oh I heard," Laurel cut him off. "Come with me."

8

RISKY BUSINESS

"Other-plane technology," Laurel explained. "It's biochemical. It reads my unique bioelectrical signature. Like body heat, but ... it's complicated."

"You don't think we'd understand?" Ray asked.

"You wouldn't. But more importantly, you wouldn't care."

"How did you get it?" Ray sounded suspicious.

"I designed it. It's a very different thing to refine Zen over there. Here, it's just a substance. There, it tunes into the hive mind around it. It's one way of making sure only I can open this lock."

Adrian was less interested in the operation of the lock and more interested in why he hadn't known it was here. He lived in this house. Had for over a year, minus the time he'd spent out on his ass, but that was before Laurel was abducted into the employ of the queen. She must have installed it while he was at Dixon's, then never told him about it.

He'd seen the door a thousand times, but never opened it once. Never even thought to try, though if he had, he apparently wouldn't have been able. He'd thought it was a utility closet — the kind of place a house keeps its water heater and circuit breakers. The lock hole was concealed behind a bit of moulding. Her basement door was elsewhere, so it was surprising to see a downward spiral staircase when she opened the door. He could only assume it led to an isolated part of the basement — somewhere not accessible from the main area. Who knew Laurel was so handy?

The room at the bottom was small. Three of the walls were cinderblock but the last looked like sheet metal, not something sensible like drywall. There was no door. The space was lit by a pair of long LED fixtures hanging from the rafters ... which had also been covered with sheet metal.

Adrian was feeling better now. It wasn't that anything had been answered or solved. It was more that he found it hard to be agitated while he was busy being so confused.

He touched the metal wall. It shook a little and made a hollow sound. It seemed to be aluminum, not steel, probably nailed to wooden studs.

"Camouflage," Laurel explained. "Metal or stone will do it, but not wood or sheetrock." She pointed up the spiral staircase, where they saw that the back of the door had also been covered with aluminum.

"What's it camouflaging?" Ray asked.

"Thought."

The brothers looked at each other.

"I'm serious."

"*Thought,*" Adrian repeated. "Like when conspiracy nuts make hats out of tinfoil."

"Don't mock it 'til you try it," Laurel said. "The king and queen — after she overthrew the king on my suggestion — both talked to me using their minds. It's the only way they *can* talk to humans, since even the ones able to think outside the hive mind don't have a larynx. While I was working on their

Zen problem, I conducted a few experiments of my own. I needed to know if thought could be blocked, or if it's just sort of everywhere. Turns out it can. What I wouldn't have given for a tinfoil hat while I was there. Thoughts are tricky. Even if you don't want to think them, they have a way of percolating up ... and I had things in my head I'd rather they didn't know."

"And also you can lock the front door against them." Adrian was being sarcastic, but Laurel actually answered.

"The front door was locked against you."

"Me?"

"I needed time to get out of this room and close it up if you came home unexpectedly. I've gotten pretty good at controlling my own thoughts, at least about this stuff. Turns out meditation has some really practical applications. You, on the other hand, wouldn't be able to keep a secret if you ever found out what I was up to. Or even if you knew I had a secret in the first place."

"I keep can keep a secret."

She tapped her head. "Not from them, you can't. You talked to the king once. More than once, really, since he was at least half of the communication you thought was coming entirely from me while I was in the other plane. You felt how strong his mentality is. Carl's used to the hive mind, even if he has to work hard now to join it, so he really only hears what you want him to hear. The king, though, has always been an individual. For him, individuality is primary and the hive is secondary. And optional. If he wanted to get something out of you, he'd get it. Same for the queen."

"You know," Adrian said. "You know about the king's new plan. For the mental virus."

"'Virus.'" She seemed to weigh the word, then bobbed her head. "I wouldn't have put it that way, but that's about right. How do *you* know?"

"Carl."

"If Carl knows, the plan's moving forward. For a long time, only he and I knew. I thought of it more as a kind of 'mental sundering,' but yes, it spreads like a virus. He needs human accomplices on this side before he can move to the next phase. This is how he gets them."

"You *knew*. You knew this was going to happen all along, and you never told me." Adrian looked around the metal-and-stone-encased room, now seeing it as less like a hidden laboratory and more like a betrayal. Laurel having an affair.

"Don't be offended. I needed a way to work without anyone knowing. The fewer potential leaks in the system, the better. I figured I could control me. I didn't know if I could control you. You could have the best intentions in the world, and still things sometimes just ... slip out."

Again she tapped her head. "You don't even have to open your mouth to blow it. What you called a 'virus' will start making its way around Fortune if it hasn't already, but it's a *thought thing*, not some dumb flu. It's not random. The king's behind every branch. Making it go where he wants. Hearing through its tendrils as it spreads out. So you'd better believe he's paying special attention to the three of us, just waiting to see if we're on the up-and-up or if we're doing ... Well, if we're doing exactly what I *am* doing here. Any one of a million thoughts could give him reason to suspect, and if he started to suspect, he'd dig deeper. You wouldn't even have to think about my work. If you got a picture in your head of the way the basement used to be before I walled this part off, that would be enough."

"I don't remember how the basement used to be. I never come down here."

"Even if you only came down once," Laurel said, "that's enough."

Adrian and Ray looked around. There were benches on the walls, one wet and one dry. The wet bench was full of reagents and glassware like her GEN lab. The dry bench was full of wafer board, soldering irons, and a ring-lit magnifier mounted to the back wall by a double-jointed swing arm. Adrian wouldn't have known what to tell the king about her work even if he'd wanted to.

"Well, we've seen it now," Ray said, picking up a cone-shaped contraption, turning it over, and setting it back down. "Now what?"

"I just finished testing these. I wouldn't have shown you anything if they hadn't worked."

Ray held out his hand and she filled it with a pair of classic, black-frame Ray-Bans, or a good imitation.

"Sunglasses?"

"Obfuscators."

He put them on, then gave a wide and sarcastic smartass's smile. "How do I look?"

"Obfuscated." Laurel picked up a tablet and was checking a series of undulating graph lines, like on an oscilloscope, nodding with approval. "Either your thoughts are being entirely blocked by the chip in the earpieces or you don't *have* any thoughts."

Ray turned to Adrian and preemptively said, "Don't."

"You'll need to wear a pair of these at all times from now on," Laurel told them, setting the tablet aside. "Time was running out to bring you in already, but I heard the crash a few hours ago and saw that the fortification has dropped."

Adrian wanted to throttle her. He'd been thinking not long ago that clearly Laurel hadn't known that was going to happen — and here she was now, casually telling them otherwise.

"That means he's isolated the city."

"The king?" Ray asked.

Laurel nodded. "It'll spread faster now. I was hoping I'd have obfuscators ready in time to bring you in before it fell, but this is close enough. I couldn't tell you until I knew you wouldn't inadvertently give us away."

Adrian had picked up a second pair of sunglasses and was turning them over in his hands. They looked entirely ordinary. "You want us to wear sunglasses. Twenty-four seven. You don't think that'll look suspicious?"

"I have some with clear lenses, too. If you were still on TV, maybe it'd be a problem if suddenly you both developed myopia at the same time, but everyone hates you right now."

"Thanks," said Adrian.

"Nobody's going to notice except maybe Dixon, but I've got a pair for him, too. Wear either the sunglasses or clear glasses all the time and nothing will leak."

"You want us to sleep with them on? And shower?"

"Shower, yes. Sleep, no. You're going to love this."

She reached down the bench and pulled out something they were presumably supposed to wear at night. It looked like a hat with a chin strap. Made of a shiny material like foil.

"You're kidding."

She didn't dignify Ray's question with a response. "Glasses or sunglasses during the day, tinfoil hat at night. When you need to clean the glasses or dry them after showering, put on one of the other obfuscators to do it. Change from one to the other quickly, and hum while you do."

"Hum?"

"Or recite a mantra. Anything to occupy your mind for the few seconds it's unprotected. You strike me more as humming guys than mantra guys, but you do you. Keep them on, and we can talk openly as long as we're alone. The king can't cross over yet, and fiends would attract attention he doesn't want yet.

Even the humans he's digging his fingers into almost surely won't care."

Ray turned to Adrian. "Something tells me she's not going to be too surprised by our news."

"You mean about the fortification now surrounding the city?"

Adrian shook his head. "We were attacked by a group of humans about a half hour ago out by the north gate. Only, I don't think they were human."

"They're human," Laurel said, completely unfazed. "They just have the Devil in 'em. It's influence, though, not control. Tell me. Were you agitated at the time?"

"We'd just watched a gas station explode. And a fucking wall fall from the sky."

"And were you wondering what to do about it? Making some sort of a plan, thinking of some way to stop it, or fight it?"

Adrian thought back, but Ray had already answered in the affirmative.

"It stirred them up," Laurel said. "A lot of it is automatic. Being under the influence of the king's 'virus' is sort of like having a post-hypnotic suggestion. They were nearby and your thoughts were loud. You triggered them, so they reacted. If you went back and met them now with those glasses on, they'd probably smile and shake your hand. The king isn't taking people over, like creating zombie soldiers. It's more like propaganda. Most of the time, his people will tell you all's well, the kids are fine and the weather is nice today … and by the way, the king of Hell has some pretty fantastic ideas, so maybe we should all play along."

"Their eyes were black," Adrian said, though in reality he'd only seen Renfield's. "They spoke to us with their thoughts."

"It's complicated," Laurel said.

"Shit," Ray turned to Adrian. "We mentioned Carl. They heard us talk about Carl."

"I'm sure it's fine. I doubt the king even knows the name 'Carl.' And it was probably your agitation that fired them up, basically making your thoughts like screams."

"Okay," Ray replied. "So. The big wall around the city ..."

"It's just what you said," Laurel explained. "It's just reinforced the Rampart. Made it so you can no longer get in or out. That's why I called it a 'fortification.' It's not a new barrier. Fortune was always designed to be isolated."

She didn't say the rest of the reason the Rampart had been built: In an emergency, the two gates could be quickly closed, isolating Fortune in full. Nothing could get out without being airlifted, and there were drone weapons on the Rampart's top to take down the few known species of demons that could fly.

The nuclear solution, in Fortune's case, was literally a nuclear solution, should the rifts get out of hand. Thinking was, the sheer force of a nuclear blast was akin to striking everything in its radius with a very large Rollard. Brute force had, until they'd discovered blue-skinned, Zen-enhanced fiends, been the only thing capable of killing every kind of demon. Even now that people knew the blue ones could function even after getting cut to pieces, brute force remained effective if enough of it was applied to the pieces.

If Fortune went to Hell, a nuke would obliterate it and every fiend — and, unfortunately, every human — inside the Rampart. An army of enhanced, emergency-trained Stitchers would spring into action from outside the city after it was done to close any remaining rifts before more fiends could emerge.

"Before now, it was our choice to be isolated," Laurel said. "The king made it his choice. There were problems with the Rampart his fortification doesn't have. He hasn't isolated us so much as made our isolation a lot more effective."

"What problems did the Rampart have?" Adrian asked.

"You could climb it with enough gear. You could fly over it."

"You can fly over this," Ray replied. "Go outside. You can see the sky."

"Try to *reach* that sky, though," Laurel said. "Unless something's changed, he's put some sort of a force field over the top. You can't communicate through it. From the outside, you can't even *see* through it. Even the top part was meant to be sort of like a one-way mirror made of stone. Maybe the military outside Fortune is scratching their chins about it right now, or maybe they haven't even noticed. I have no idea what it looks like to the outside world. I just know they won't be able to break through or tunnel under it. We're completely isolated until he decides to end it. Like I said, I saw the plan."

"We're trapped," Adrian said.

"Yes."

"Why?"

"Because Fortune is where the Gore Point is. It's where riftfare happens. Almost all of the Legions and Stitchers are here. The gear and weapons are here, along with the facilities. The larger world likes to pretend that the other plane's incursions are Fortune's problem. Budgets and initiatives reflect that attitude. *We're* the thin spot in the rug where demons come in, so they walled us off and stuck all the demon stuff inside and out of sight from Washington and New York and LA, who'd rather go about their normal business without considering the burning reality: If they can take Fortune, they won't have any trouble taking everything else."

Adrian thought of Carl: *As goes Fortune, so goes the war.*

"And you *knew* about this," Adrian said. "The 'fortification.' How completely and totally it'd lock us in. You *knew* we'd be entirely fucked, but said nothing."

Laurel answered with her usual scientist's pragmatism —

the same way she'd told Adrian that the planes were going to break apart with disastrous results eventually *anyway*, so letting the king do it now, although horrible, was still the best option anyone had.

"So, what — you'd rather I spread the word just to spread it? It wouldn't have made a difference."

"They could have sent Legions and Stitchers outside the Rampart before he locked it down! Sent out weapons, started making *new* weapons, so at least we could—"

"Uh-huh. Okay; keep going. *Then* what would have happened? It's like with the sundering ... resistance just draws things out. It doesn't change the result — just makes a lot more collateral damage as we try to prevent the inevitable. There's only so much energy in a system no matter how much you spread it around. *We're not prepared and weren't going to be. Period.* Don't you get it? I don't care how many 'new weapons' we managed to build in a month; there hasn't been — and was never going to be — enough time to make a meaningful difference. The way things turned out, we *can't* fight. So we won't. Nobody gets hurt this way. This way, we're still whole enough to be able to regroup and try something different — something we wouldn't have tried if we'd thought we had a prayer of winning the usual way, which in this case we absolutely didn't."

Adrian was still angry, but he could only trip over himself trying to explain why. This was the one aspect of Laurel he'd never gotten used to and hated whenever he saw: She never, ever sugar-coated anything. She didn't see the point in symbolic efforts if they were doomed to be fruitless. Like a doctor who would tell the child of an accident victim, *Well, your mom's dead. I could have kept her alive for long enough to say goodbye, but she'd still have died and do you know how much that would have added to the bill?*

"You could have at least told me!" Adrian knew how he sounded.

The tone of Laurel's response was like hands on her hips. "I couldn't stop him, Adrian. I couldn't change it and it's not like I had any way to sabotage him, so what would be the point of risking the king learning I'd ratted him out? I would have lost his trust, and then we wouldn't have any of our advantages. Same thing if I'd told people what was coming. Nothing would change, except I'd be dead, or in a cell … anything but to be right here right now, able to at least try and subvert him."

While Adrian tried to digest what felt like planet-level treason, Ray was looking around the lab. It was hard to stay mad at Laurel in situations like this. Her decisions weren't always popular, but in the end — so far, at least — they'd always been right.

"You have a plan, don't you?" Ray asked.

"I have a few. My plans have backups."

"What are they?"

"Soon." She held up a warding hand. "But understand, I can and should only say so much. To a certain degree, you're going to have to trust me."

Ray nodded, but Adrian was still sulking.

"Okay," Ray said. "So what do we do?"

"We go to the fortification with our shades on." She tapped another pair of Ray-Bans on the workbench. "And find out if anyone else can see it."

9

THE HALLUCINOGEN

Adrian assumed he'd misheard or misunderstood. But Laurel's plan really did start with a trip to see whether the citizenry could see the giant wall that had fallen from the sky.

Adrian looked at his brother, then at Laurel, as they exited the squad car. In their sporty sunglasses, they looked like Men in Black.

"Watch," she said, pointing.

Adrian and Ray followed her finger. Ahead, a sedan was driving directly toward the old military checkpoint at the southwestern gate out of Fortune, now visible behind the wall. It'd taken them a good half hour to reach, but considering they'd already seen the situation at the north gate, it made sense to check out the other one for a fuller picture.

Adrian had expected the roads along the way to be jammed with people rushing exactly nowhere (wall or no wall, bad shit inside the city would make people try to panic-flee), but everyone they passed seemed to be going about their usual business as if nothing was amiss.

Before the big gray wall — the "fortification," in Laurel's words — had embedded itself in the ground, the sedan would have pulled up to a guard and answered some questions before being allowed to leave Fortune. Now, the guard wasn't even present. Along with the checkpoint building, the refueling pumps, and a lot of military hardware, the guard was probably on the fortification's other side. The scene right now was like something Wile E. Coyote might engineer for the Road Runner: a highway that ran smack into a massive obstruction without warning or fanfare.

Adrian waited for the car to stop, for the person driving it to get out, and finally for a lot of quizzical wondering and head-scratching, if not abject terror. Alternatively, the car might run right into the wall — the driver daydreaming his way through this boring and repeating ritual, somehow failing to notice the barrier.

Instead, the car paused twenty feet from the wall, then entered an apron of concrete meant for service vehicles on the left-hand side. After that, it simply re-entered what would normally be inbound traffic on the other side and drove back where it'd come from. They all saw the driver's face through the windshield, singing along to the radio.

"What the hell?" said Ray.

Another car was coming. The same exact thing happened. This driver wasn't singing, but she was checking her lipstick in the rearview.

"I hate when people do that," Laurel said. "Pull over if you want to put on makeup."

"What's going on?" Adrian asked.

"They're deciding to turn around."

"What?"

"They're changing their minds, Adrian. At the last minute, they're deciding they'd rather not leave the city after all."

Adrian watched as three more cars did the exact same thing. The checkpoint had been more or less erased, so the scene before them was a massive highway barricaded with extreme prejudice. Everyone who lived in Fortune knew the ritual of the gates and checkpoints; everyone knew exactly how driving this particular stretch of road was supposed to go. Anyone encountering what they saw now should be a lot more surprised than to simply *leave* — turning from the big, ground-shattering alien wall the way they'd turn from a grocery store if they realized it was closed today. There were no police on-site, no military, no authorities whatsoever. Traffic hadn't been diverted down the road. Nobody had so much as put up a sign.

"They can't see it," Laurel explained.

"Bullshit."

"Not bullshit at all. I figured this was how it'd be. It's the only way the plan works. You can't convert a population that's scared out of it's mind."

"Bullshit," Adrian repeated.

But Ray was a man of action and tired of conjecture.

Without announcing his intention, he left Adrian and Laurel to stand by the roadside while he re-entered the car, turned on the yellow flashers, and pulled it forward to block the middle lanes.

Adrian watched as a new car approached Ray's. He was standing beside his vehicle like a traffic cop, counting on his Legion flashers to hit the same authority cues as police ones would.

The new car slowed; the window rolled down; the driver and Ray traded a few words. At one point, Ray pointed directly at the wall, and they both looked at it. Then the car made a U-turn and went back like all the others. Ray drove back and parked where he'd been, beside Adrian and Laurel.

"What was that?" Adrian asked.

"I wanted to see what would happen if I told someone the road was closed."

"And?"

"She asked me why."

Adrain looked at the fortification again. From the inside of a car driving this close, it would be impossible to see the sky. A motorist's entire windshield would be filled with what looked like gray rock.

"*Why,*" Adrian repeated.

"She asked me why the road was closed," Ray said again, "and asked if I meant that the *lane* was closed. The specific lane she was driving in."

Again Adrian looked at the wall. This had to be a joke that Laurel and Ray were conspiring to play on him.

"She asked if she could just go around my car. Use the inside lane instead. You saw when I pointed at the wall? I was trying to point about where the truck scales are, by the highway patrol building. I told her that the entire road was closed, because there was something wrong with the scales."

"The scales."

"The scales I was pointing at," Ray confirmed.

"The scales that aren't visible because there's a huge fucking wall in the way," Adrian said, wanting to make sure he had this right.

"Correct."

"What did she say?"

"She asked if the north gate was open. I said I didn't know but she could try her luck."

"She must have misunderstood what you were saying."

"I don't know why she would, Ade. I was speaking English."

Laurel seemed to find this all very interesting, as a scientist. She told Ray to try it again, but to do it closer to the wall itself — right at the place where the cars were turning back without interference. So Ray did, this time stationing his squad car a hundred yards or so from the wall's surface — not blocking the road and with his flashers off.

They watched the scene repeat, except that this time Ray only turned on his flashers and stopped the driver after they'd already made their U-turn. He then did the same with two more cars before returning.

"What happened this time?" Laurel asked when Ray's experiment was over.

"The first guy said he remembered he had a conference call. He'd thought it was canceled, but it wasn't, so he couldn't head over to SLC like he'd planned. The second guy said he thought he'd left water boiling on the stove. The third car was the most interesting. She had a cell phone in the cup holder, playing music through her car speakers. But I don't think she thought she was listening to music."

"Why?"

"Because while I was talking to her, she said, 'Hold on, I'm talking to a policeman' like she thought she was on a call instead of listening to music."

"And she wasn't listening to Wilson-Phillips's song 'Hold On'?" Laurel seemed to think this was funny.

"I wanted to be sure, so I asked who she was talking to. She said it was her husband, and she was turning back because he'd just called and told her that their kid fell at school and broke a finger. She asked if she was in trouble for making a U-turn and asked if it was okay if she merged with the traffic entering Fortune so she could get back without having to go all the way out and in again."

"'The traffic entering Fortune,'" Adrian echoed, looking at the empty lanes on the left side of the broken highway.

"I asked her to do me a favor. I told her I was new to town

and wanted to know if she knew the name of the big mountain peak. I pointed at the wall when I asked."

"What did she say?"

"She said she wasn't sure. She said she'd gone hiking in some of the other areas off to the right side, but didn't know the big one. And yeah, she pointed at the 'areas off to the right side' when she said it."

"And she didn't mention a giant wall in the way. A giant, gray-stone wall."

Ray shook his head. "It's like Laurel said. Nobody can see it."

It went on that way for a while. Adrian refused to believe what he was hearing, so after their reentry into the city center, he resorted to asking pedestrians — all of whom had returned to their daily business as if nothing was amiss. Most looked at him strangely and walked away. A few said No, wondering if his was a real question, and a few more seemed to assume he was a rift tourist and told him Yes, it was called the Rampart. When Adrian corrected them and said he actually meant the big wall that now sat *on top of* the Rampart, they gave answers like the others. Two people told him to fuck off, recognizing him as Adrian Porter. One woman slapped him across the face and called him a bastard.

"This is impossible," Adrian said when they were all back in the car.

"The king invades minds," Laurel replied.

"You're saying he's already gotten everyone. And that's why nobody can see the wall. Because he's telling them it's not there."

"No, it's subtler than that. There are degrees to rift opening. You guys know that."

They both knew that. It just didn't usually matter to rift-fighters because even though rifts technically "thinned-out the barrier between planes" before rupturing entirely, the process usually happened too fast for the thinned phase to matter. Paper technically thinned-out and stretched too, before a pencil could poke all the way through it, but poking-through happened almost instantly, so you never noticed the in-between part.

"We used to experiment with pre-openings at GEN," Laurel explained. "They're actually pretty useful — just too energetically expensive to maintain. Pre-openings act like if you stretched thin mesh over a glass before trying to pour water out of it. The water pours more slowly, and all the little solids in it stay behind. My readings suggest that's what's happening out at the Gore Point. There aren't any rifts inside the former dead zone anymore, but right now that's only the case because none of them have ripped all the way through. There are *pre*-rifts out there, though, and all sorts of stuff keeps wafting from their plane to ours without anyone realizing it's even happening."

"What sorts of stuff?" Ray asked.

"It's complicated. For all intents and purposes, we can just call it 'influence.'"

"And that's how the king is reading people's minds. The reason we're wearing these fancy glasses."

"No the thought-receiving is different."

"What's 'thought-receiving'?" Adrian asked.

She sighed. "Go ahead and say 'mind-reading' if you want; it amounts to the same thing. I just don't like that term because it implies intrusiveness, and that's not how it works. Technically, the electrochemical activity of our brains creates tiny signals that can be recorded transcranially, and if they can be recorded transcranially, they can be recorded at a distance if—"

Ray held up a hand. "You can go ahead and assume we're dumb. I don't need to know how it works."

"Then fine. Yes. 'Mind-reading.'" Laurel rolled her eyes as if it was a monumental concession to allow such unscientific idiocy. "The king has sensitive enough systems in place that he can 'read our minds' by 'scooping thoughts out of the air.' It gets easier and easier as more and more citizens are infected with the other phenomenon — the influence thing that Carl called a 'virus' — because it all works like one big mesh network."

"What's a mesh network?" Adrian asked.

Laurel sighed because it was all too much. "You guys really are stupid."

"So he's able to hear the thoughts of Fortune's citizens?" Ray asked.

"Within certain limitations, yes. If they're not wearing blocking devices like ours." She touched her sunglasses.

"And somehow, in the same way, he's able to 'influence' everyone, but not control them."

"Correct. In order to truly *control* minds, as opposed to just sort of swaying them vaguely in a general direction, he'd need to get into their heads. Which spreads slowly, moving outward from the Gore Point. Kind of like a virus, though that's not really accurate, either. You guys *do* know what a virus is, don't you?"

Laurel was impatient whenever Adrian couldn't keep up with her fast-paced, Mensa-level thinking, but she'd always seen Ray as more or less irredeemable. Ray would *never* keep up, she seemed to think. She used to treat him like he didn't know that two plus two made four. No wonder they hadn't lasted long as a couple.

"And lastly," Adrian said, "that 'influence,' which is 'leaking through the thin spot' at the Gore Point, is making everyone inside the city think the 'fortification' isn't there. The king's 'influence' makes them unable to see that enormous wall." He was treading carefully with his words, trying not to get anything wrong lest Laurel call them idiots again.

"That's more or less correct. Maybe a better analogy is like if the air was laced with a hallucinogen."

"So everyone in Fortune is on LSD."

"Sure. Small amounts of LSD. Why not. You can think of it that way."

Adrian let it all settle. Carl had warned them that Hell's king would start to take over the minds of some of Fortune's citizenry, essentially turning them into sleeper agents. That part sounded like brainwashing. What Carl *hadn't* said was that in addition to taking over *some* people and making them do things the king needed done, he could also make *everyone* trip balls.

They already couldn't tell there was an enormous barricade walling them in. What came next — seeing those weird, multicolored Grateful Dead bears marching in lines?

"Everyone but us," Ray said. "We're not seeing shit like we're on LSD because of the sunglasses."

"No. I told you. The glasses prevent the king from 'reading our minds.' That's all they do."

"So why can we see the wall when everyone else can't?"

"I don't know. Maybe we're immune because all three of us have crossed a rift and entered the other plane. More likely it's because all three of us were once mutated by Zen Element so we could *survive* the other plane. When you guys injected that 'Frog' stuff, it was basically the same as what the queen did when they abducted me. It allowed us to live in extreme heat and breathe their air, so maybe it inoculated us against influence. The good news is that if that's what happened, it'll probably inoculate us against the 'mind-controlling virus' too." Laurel tapped her temple. "The king won't be able to get inside our heads like he can with others."

There was silence. Then Ray spoke into the confines of the squad car, summing it all up:

"Okay. Pop quiz, hotshot: You're trapped inside a prison nobody else thinks exists. You don't know if anyone outside the prison has a clue what's going on, and you can't contact them to find out. The king of the underworld is trying to conquer the city and neuter everything that might possibly stop him from taking over the rest of the world — all the rift-fighters, all the weapons, all the researchers, all the facilities. You're the only ones who know what's happening, and the clock is ticking. *What do you do?*"

The air felt like desperation. But then Ray and Adrian seemed to remember at the same time something Laurel had said before they'd left her house: *I have plans, and even my plans have backups.* Both men's heads turned toward her.

"You find a way to pull away the wool that's been pulled over everyone's eyes," she finally said. "And then you escape ... one way or the other."

IO

BAD IDEAS

At the corner of Fifth Street and Spruce, a 42-year-old woman named Jenny Caracas was watering her lawn when the she felt the ground shake just once, very hard. A few car alarms sounded, and inside, her 15-year-old daughter's baby began to cry. The kid was always crying. Probably because his mother was a whore.

Jenny wasn't one to judge her daughter, but the truth was that Grace had always been slutty. It wasn't Jenny's fault. She was a good mother, always let Grace do whatever she wanted. Hell — Jenny wasn't even home most of the time, leaving Grace as free as she wanted to be. Jenny even slept over at the homes of the men she met at Fortune's many bars, giving Grace abundant time to practice Being Her Own Woman. And yet, how had Grace used that gift? How had she used the forward-thinking, liberal-minded, not-at-all-negligent leeway Jenny had given her to Be Her Own Woman? She'd gotten herself pregnant, that's how. Jenny didn't judge her for it. Seriously. But someone had to judge her, and if it wasn't Jenny, who was it going to be?

Jenny thought maybe she'd murder her. Murder Grace and take the baby. She definitely wouldn't drown the baby. She wanted it so she could try again, seeing how poorly Grace had turned out.

Jenny's thoughts on the matter were interrupted when the entire neighborhood shook as if detonated from below. Car alarms, a baby screaming … How was a woman supposed to water her lawn and consider murdering her daughter with all this ruckus?

"Nuts and balls." Nobody was around to hear her. Jenny was just that upset at the state of the world, with all its explosions and ground-shaking.

In the distance, something exploded in a plume of orange-and-black smoke. People ran around for a while, but only for a while. Jenny considered doing the same thing herself, but she was more responsible than that. She'd raised a whore for a daughter, took care of a baby she definitely wouldn't be drowning … was an upstanding gal who'd Been Her Own Woman ever since her mother's addiction sent her off to live with that biker gang. Not that Jenny resented it.

Jenny was wearing her long green dress. Grace said it made her look like an old fashioned housewife, but Grace said a lot of things. The truth was, you had to maintain appearances. Just like you had to get involved in your neighborhood. Jenny was very Involved in her Neighborhood (the Beautification Committee, the Scholarship Committee, Team Mom to the high school soccer team, regular and vocal attendee to Fortune's City Council meetings, and naturally the PTA) and had many opinions about the questionable way the neighborhood had been going recently.

Like this new wall that had just fallen from the sky. It was so unsightly.

There's no wall. Everything is perfect and it's a lovely day, said the man who lived in the corner of her brain.

Was he sure? There'd been all that noise. All that commotion. And right now, she was ninety-nine percent sure the horizon was a whole lot higher than it used to be. As if there was a very tall, very gray and unsightly wall surrounding Fortune, atop the Rampart, that hadn't been there before.

Nope, said the man in her mind. *There's no wall.*

Are you sure? Jenny wondered.

I'M not sure. YOU'RE sure.

Hmm. Interesting. Now that Jenny looked again, it turned out the man was right. She was indeed sure.

Good thing he'd started talking to her. She barely remembered the time before he'd started talking to her. It may have been years ago. Or possibly several days ago. Probably right around the time she'd gone to visit Dr. Gellert, the school superintendent (Grace's grades were abysmal; maybe a handjob for Gellert would fix that) and had entered his office to find his secretary sawing his head off with a limb saw.

She'd been as surprised by that at first as she'd been by the big gray wall that definitely hadn't fallen on Fortune right now, but then she'd looked in the secretary's black eyes and suddenly an epiphany of sorts had leapt into her mind. Literally *leapt into her mind,* like a squirrel jumping from one tree to another.

After that, the head-sawing hadn't bothered or even surprised Jenny. It all made perfect sense. Gellert, she understood without the secretary having to tell her, had been petitioning the state to declare some sort of "school state of emergency" in Fortune. If granted, it would have moved more than half of the school operations into neighboring cities, bussing the kids out as needed. He'd decided Fortune was unsafe for some reason. Ever since that traitor Adrian Porter came back and everyone started talking about the end of the world again.

After his head came off, Gellert stopped asking for his state of emergency and the schools never left Fortune. Jenny helped the secretary bury him in the community gardens. This well-played political maneuver got her into favor with the board, and she then leveraged her position into a second position under the mayor's desk. After servicing the mayor for a while to keep him from asking the Feds for support, that same thing that'd leapt into Jenny leapt from her to the mayor. He became less interested in blowjobs-for-favors and instead became a proper citizen like Jenny herself, doing necessary good like closing dens of free thinking.

They'd sprung up everywhere: groups of Fortune citizens all over the place who said the air was poison now and things had to change. Jenny wasn't sure how exactly they wanted things changed. She didn't care. It stopped mattering when they were all arrested, their rebel groups cut at the knees.

It'd all happened so cleanly. So quietly.

The hose went dry in her hand. Jenny's watering, devoid of water, came to an end. She stood there for a while in her long green dress and matching shoes, then looked to where she used to think a wall had dropped from the sky.

Jenny wanted to laugh. A wall dropping from the sky was a silly idea. Nothing had changed. Fortune was the way it'd always been. Her water hadn't shut off because some sort of cataclysmic event had cut the water mains. It'd gone off because the baby was crying and Grace was probably inside ignoring it, texting on her phone or whatever kids did, with six dicks in her mouth and at least one in her butt because this was Grace she was talking about.

Grace made waves. That was the problem. Making waves Lowered Community Standards. Lowering Community Standards was the opposite of Maintaining Appearances. That sort of thing couldn't be allowed if Fortune was to change in the ways Jenny and the many like-minded people she'd met wanted it to change.

At night, in her dreams, Jenny pictured Fortune burning with righteous fire, finally as pure as it should be.

Goddamn kids today.

Jenny wound her garden hose neatly back onto the reel, picked up the big-bladed hedge shears, and went inside to teach her daughter an overdue lesson.

CRAIG WARBURTON HAD NEVER USED C-4. He hadn't even known "C-4" was another word for plastic explosive. He'd always thought it was an energy drink.

He cradled the bomb with both hands. He wasn't sure, on a conscious level, how to use it. He was a technical supervisor for a company that built and maintained cellular towers, not a demolitions expert. Craig thought demolition was done the way they did it in cartoons: To blow something up, you pushed down on a big T-shaped plunger on a box. Now, however, he knew it didn't have to be that way. "Demolition" was actually a blanket term, applicable in all sorts of informal settings — not just the formal way people used the word to mean something controlled, sanctioned, and permitted by the government. It didn't need to be that way at all. You could demolish anything, and you didn't need a permit to do it.

You could demolish the lock to your boss's office with an axe. You could even demolish your boss with an axe if he had a problem with your idea. And of course, most relevantly, you could climb the big, dedicated cell towers, stick a brick of C-4 right up near the cellular repeaters, and demolish them, too.

Destroy as many as you can, Craig, said the rogue radio operator who'd been broadcasting directly into his brain for weeks. *The fortification should block communication out of the city, but we don't want to take chances of something getting through anyway, do we?*

Of course not. Craig totally agreed with that. His job was all about communication, but recently he'd realized how over-rated it was. He felt the same way about social media — which, by the way, was also communication and which, by the way, he'd been told would be cut off along with the rest of the internet in Fortune very soon.

He looked at his watch. *Very* soon indeed. The man in his head had told him exactly when to blow the bombs, so the noise and commotion they caused would be lost in the noise and commotion of something much noisier.

The man broadcasting into Craig's brain these days didn't want to show his hand just yet. It was important to still keep things on the QT, as the expression went. People weren't supposed to feel like the cell phones had suddenly stopped working because of a catastrophic event like a bombing. Instead, they were supposed to sort of feel like they'd never truly worked in the first place. Craig wasn't sure how that would go down exactly, but it was probably something like the way he felt about his wife.

Had Craig tied her up in the basement when she'd had a problem with him bombing cell towers and taking an axe to work ... or had she just sort of always been down there?

Craig wasn't sure. Soon he stopped thinking about it entirely.

THE VISITING senator didn't think Jason Kelly's idea was a good one. That's why Jason made him drink rat poison.

Jason's official job was that of Fortune's liaison to the

Federal Committee on Riftfare. Because the government was redundant and (in Jason's quiet but oft-stated opinion) more than certainly had its head up its own oblivious ass, his job actually had several different purposes that were more or less contradictory. He was in charge of deciding how Federal funds to the city's riftfighting brigades and ancillary services were distributed, while having been told repeatedly over the past six or seven months to consolidate spending away from most of the brigades and send it to the military installation at the old GEN warehouses instead.

Paperwork was required for this bit of political money laundering (money laundering being okay when the government did it), but as far as Jason could tell, nobody ever looked at it and might, in some cases, never even receive the documents.

Still, it seemed to Jason that diverting Federal riftfighting funds to the military was akin to the government giving money to itself. He didn't think it was intentional; that was the sad part. It cut the brigades out of the loop while insisting that riftfare amp up, starting with the brigades. Yet only Brigade One was still in operation, closest to the Gore Point, and these days spent most of its time sitting around metal tables playing euchre. In the same breath, the Federal Committee would insist that riftfare was more important than ever, then that riftfare was no longer a thing.

Jason's opinion was that after the literal motherfucking Devil went back to Hell, that was a bad sign for interplanar relations. He'd asked the Feds to allow him to double-divert some of his previously diverted funds back from the military installation at the GEN base and into the brigades again. He wanted some of the old brigadehouses re-opened, their Legions and Stitchers restored. He also wanted weapons budgets re-diverted: taken from the testosterone force of grunts at the base and given back to the men and women who actually knew how to use them.

The base was a fist; brigade workers were fine tweezers. You couldn't just punch the shit out of this problem; that's what the Committee didn't seem to understand. Fighting rifts intelligently took precision, strategy, and intelligence. The military preferred to fuel tanks that never went anywhere, developing bombs that, if allowed to detonate, would cause approximately one hundred trillion times as many problems as simply addressing the issues correctly would solve.

More brigades. More Legions and more Stitchers. And more research. Denny Brennan, who used to liaise between Brigade One (tip of the entire effort's spear) and GEN, kept telling Jason that he needed more funds to pay more scientists to do a lot more tests that Jason didn't understand other than that they were important. Brennan thought there was more happening since the Porters returned and the dreadnought went home than the government believed, but the answer whenever Jason raised it was to threaten Brennan's job.

Everyone had it wrong. That's what Jason had felt absolutely sure of for a while. He had been mostly alone in his quest to undo the head-up-ass moves the Feds kept making and do something intelligent instead. For a while, Jason had been telling everyone who'd listen that the science all pointed to catastrophe on the horizon.

Something *big* was about to happen in Fortune, and meanwhile Fortune was the only basket in which all of the riftfare eggs were kept. For a while, Jason had urged diversification. He didn't just want the brigades back, he also wanted brigades formed *outside* of Fortune. He wanted research done *outside* of Fortune. He wanted weapons built and emergency forces trained to fight fiends *outside* of Fortune.

What happens if something happens to Fortune? he'd asked

the Committee. *Last time, the sundering nearly punched Fortune into the pit of Hell like the bottom dropping out of a wet bag of groceries. Shouldn't we have backup plans? And shouldn't our backups have backups?*

For a while, Jason had argued for not just a Federal Committee on Riftfare, but an actual Federal Department of Riftfare. Army, Navy, Air Force, Marines? Add the Rift Force to that list, motherfucker! For a while, the senator who'd come to visit had been his only true ally. The government wouldn't listen? Then okay — Jason and the senator, working together, would have to bust some heads to make things happen ... to keep the whole world safe, rather than keeping the whole world oblivious, with Fortune its one and only safeguard against the end of the world.

That's what Jason had said and done for a while.

For a *while.*

Until he changed his mind. Right after his housekeeper of all people had convinced him he'd been thinking wrong. Jason remembered the exact moment of his change-of-heart. He'd been paying her usual weekly wage, but when she'd smiled at him and said thank you, Jason had noticed that her eyes had gone jet black. They weren't usually that way. He was quite sure.

Svetla was Scandinavian, and Scandinavians usually had blue eyes. Maybe green. Sometimes brown. But never *black.* And it wasn't just her irises, it was her *entire eye,* as if both orbs had been replaced by obsidian stones.

At first, it'd alarmed him. But then he found it interesting. Her eyes didn't *stay* black; soon enough they'd reverted to blue. Her eyes couldn't have *really* been all-black, of course not. Then the thought vanished from his head. He didn't think about her eyes, or their color, anymore.

That was the day Jason changed his mind about the way

ninety percent or more of the world's riftfighting capability was housed within the single city of Fortune, Utah. He used to think it was dangerous, how undiversified things were, but after that day with Svetla, it suddenly felt right that as far as riftfare went, it was Fortune or nothing.

What used to feel *dangerously singleminded* now felt *focused* instead. Svetla didn't even need to say a word to convince Jason; that was the funny part. The voice of a new person inside his head did the actual convincing.

Cancel your initiatives. Withdraw your requests for change. Stop rattling cages. Join the crowd.

When Jason told the senator (who considered Jason his best ally in the fight to spread riftfighting resources outside of Fortune's Rampart) about his change of heart, the senator hadn't reacted well. At first, he'd thought Jason was joking. Then he thought Jason had been paid off. Around that time, he became absolutely furious.

The senator doubled his resolve, insisting that he alone would do the work that Jason now refused to do. He'd speak in front of the Senate. He'd talk to the president. He'd talk to every news outlet that would book him, exposing the ice-thin vulnerability inherent in the current way of doing things.

That's when Jason had suggested they both calm down and have a drink. Jason's was water; the senator's was ginger ale spiked with d-Con. Rat poison changed the taste of ginger ale, though, because instead of simply drinking it all, the senator had been repulsed. That's why Jason had needed to pin the senator down with the help of a chair's leverage, then pour the rest of the spiked cocktail into his mouth and cover his nose until he swallowed it.

When it was over, Jason brushed himself off and got to his feet.

How did a person get rid of a dead body without others

finding out? Jason didn't know, but two of the office custodians had eyes that sometimes flashed black like his housekeeper's, and they promised to handle it for him. So Jason left it to them and went bowling, stopping for coffee on the way.

PRIVATE LAURA CRAIG, along with the rest of her unit, had been given extensive training in riftfighting and riftfare weapons shortly after being transferred onto what she now gathered was a permanent base.

At first, when she'd been assigned to the old GEN warehouses and shown the massive rift there, she'd been led to believe the installation was temporary. Soldiers like herself were on-site to mine the rift for Zen Element, which was apparently being used in some way by her superiors to strengthen her side's ability to fight the scabs. It was military because the operation required fragging tons of scabs, carting their corpses off in little rail cars, and somehow squeezing them for magic juice. Laura was cool with it. In the days before brigades, her aunt had been ripped apart by a scab she'd found in her toolshed. Fuckers got what they deserved.

Now, however, the installation felt less temporary. Security no longer put up tents outside; now the engineers had built a proper foyer as a checkpoint. Their IDs used to be clipped on, now they were chipped beneath the skin. The forcefield-things protecting the larger compound from the rift's heat and toxic expulsions were now backed by walls filled with concrete and steel, the way they protected against radiation. Hoop-tent barracks were now real buildings. New roads had been built. Yes, it seemed the Army meant to stay a while.

What had been troubling Laura for a while now was not her assignment or position, per se, but instead the overal integrity of the effort.

She was a grunt; she knew she was supposed to follow orders and not think too much. The Army wanted strong bodies and loyal minds, not philosophers. Laura agreed with this and had no desire to rock the boat. Still, the way she'd been thinking lately seemed to be a justifiable exception to her usual code of order and ethics. It wasn't that she wondered whether the Army was doing a good thing here. It was that she'd become quite sure her superiors were agents of the enemy.

She first got the idea from PFC James Brody. He'd come up to her, whispering like a rat, and before he even said more than hello she knew she'd have to turn him in. But then something changed: Laura looked into Brody's eyes. They turned black as coal, then it was like a whole new commanding officer had taken up residence inside her head.

Brody didn't even end up explaining. He didn't have to. Laura understood the problem immediately: Some of the well-placed brass were sleeper agents for the enemy. This was later confirmed over and over again by others on the base. *Almost everyone*, really. As soon as Laura started hearing her new superior barking orders inside her mind, she also started seeing flashes of black eyes wherever she looked.

Not that she needed to see their eyes turn temporarily black for Laura to know who was on her side; she'd also found she could hear loyalists like herself without them needing to speak aloud. She could do it with nearly everybody, once she got the hang of it. Almost every buck private and PFC were part of what she increasingly thought of as a "group mind" — a whole lot of joes and janes who'd consolidated as if they shared a single brain. So were the sergeants — even a lot of the non-military personnel, like techs and skilled laborers who ran the big machines. All it took to see the loyalty of most of the base was to send her mind out and hear them call back to her.

The same internal CO spoke to every one of them.

Do not act yet, but stand ready. Sabotage the safeties, so that when the systems fail, they will fail completely. Spread my word to others who don't yet have it.

The last task, Laura enjoyed most. She didn't often find people who weren't already hearing the voice of the new four-star general inside their heads because most of the base had already joined the same hive mind as Laura, but it did happen occasionally. Some wrong-minded person would come across Laura, and when they did, she felt something jump from herself into them like a squirrel jumping from tree to tree. Then their eyes flashed black and she knew they were loyal, too.

The only problem was those at the top: the disloyal, traitorous few. *Those* people, reportedly, could not be made to hear the new four-star general who spoke to the group mind of the loyalists. They were somehow resistant to his influence. Laura was a private, too low on the pole to have any idea why they were so stubborn and how they'd made their resistance so strong. They were, though, and they had.

At some point, those at the top of this operation would need to be dealt with. For now, it was enough that when they gave their orders, nobody would follow them. The equipment would fail when the bad guys needed it most, and the good guys would win.

Until then, Laura and the others made their plans in secret, undermining the traitors' effort right beneath their noses. They had no idea how many had turned against them.

Destroy the Zen Element cache, the mental general told them one day. *Burn it to the ground, so they have no fuel for their betrayal.*

Laura was honored with the task of heading up the operation. They could not work in groups, so she would handle the task alone.

It was noon — an impossible time for this, if she hadn't had allies. She left the chow line, crossed the grounds in plain sight of fellow loyalists who would not rat her out, then entered the main facility and the annex thanks to the work of loyalists who'd sabotaged the locks before her so she'd be able to pass.

This done, Laura found the fuel left by another loyal soldier and the flares left for her by yet another. Her job was simple. It would be done with gas and flame. Flame wouldn't destroy the Element, of course, but exposure to bright sunlight — which would stream through once the roof burned off — would. After, the traitors at the operation's top would not have what they needed to power their weapons or enhance their bodies. After Laura's great work, the traitors would no longer be able to fight.

She opened the first can of petrol and began to pour it where the voice in her head had instructed. Then the second, and then the third. She took the first of the flares, then, and held it in front of her to strike.

She readied herself, but then the muzzle of a standard-issue sidearm touched the back of her head. The man holding it pulled the trigger, and Laura thought no more.

Corporal Brett McMurphy used his sleeve to wipe blood and brain from his face, then re-holstered his M9. He looked down at the woman's body and kicked the flare from her hand, away from the spilled gasoline, just in case she somehow still had life in her. This done, he flicked his coded radio to life. Not many had these radios. They were the second safety in the event the first safety failed.

"General Patel, ma'am," he said into the mouthpiece, "it would seem we have a problem."

II

HOW INTERPLANAR ENERGY WORKS

"What?" said Dixon as Ray and Adrian barged into his office, Laurel behind them with what looked like an old-fashioned doctor's bag: carrying case for her many scientific gadgets. "What the shit?"

"What happened today?" Ray asked, aggressively backing Dixon into a corner.

It was excessive, but Adrian knew why Ray was acting this way. If Dixon had been affected by whatever was swallowing so many of Fortune's citizens, he might actually be a threat.

"Excuse me?" Dixon said.

"Ray." Laurel looked back and saw her holding out another pair of her special thought-blocking sunglasses.

Ray took the glasses and held them out for Dixon, dangling by the temple piece. "Put these on."

"The fuck?"

"*Put these on,*" Ray repeated.

"Why?"

Ray sighed as if mildly inconvenienced. Then he pulled his 9mm service pistol from the back of his jeans and sighted it on

Dixon using his second hand. He'd carried the pistol in his belt the entire way over despite Adrian's remonstrations that his brother would "shoot his dumb ass off."

"Because they make you look cool," Ray answered.

Dixon looked at Adrian, who shrugged, and at Laurel, who was straight faced and grave. He put the sunglasses on. "What the hell's going on? Adrian?"

"What happened today?" Ray repeated, ignoring the question to Adrian. "Be real specific."

Despite the gun, Dixon was barely cowed. He was too blustering and self-important to be truly cowed. "I got up when my alarm went off at six. Hit the snooze alarm twice, then took a long piss. I'm thinking thirty seconds. That specific enough?"

"Keep going."

"Had a bowl of Raisin Bran. For my colon. So I can shit."

"Less specific," said Adrian.

"Maybe you could just tell me what the fuck you want to know. You could even ask nicely."

Adrian nodded toward the pistol. "Ray. Stand down, will you?"

Ray hesitated, then lowered the weapon. He didn't return it to its place. Dixon sat behind his desk again as if this was an interview of middling importance.

"What's going on in Fortune right now, in your own words?" Adrian asked. "*That's* what we want to know."

"Your guess is as good as mine. After that big boom, the streets were full of idiots running around like chickens with their heads cut off. Then they all fell into this weird nothing, as if it's all normal. Probably the same freaky shit that made *you* get guns and come at me like *I'm* the problem."

"I don't want your *assessment* of the situation," Adrian said. "I want *the situation*, point by point, just the way you saw it."

"Those are the same thing."

"Pretend we were under a rock and saw none of it. Pretend we just woke up and you're getting us up to speed."

Dixon looked at all three of his visitors' faces. He seemed to realize something dire was happening here, in addition to whatever might be happening outside. Adrian's request to literally recount the afternoon was strange, but he'd better do it anyway.

"Okay. About an hour ago, I thought an earthquake hit. Whole building shook and stuff fell off all my shelves. I looked outside and saw it was that Thor's Fucking Hammer came down on top of the Rampart."

"What's that mean?" Laurel asked. "Tell us exactly what you saw."

"*A wall*, okay? A wall came down from the sky." His hand went to the sunglasses. "Can I take these off now?"

Ray re-raised his weapon, again pointing it at Dixon's head. "Sure. Let's see how that goes."

"Put it down, Ray," Laurel said. "He just said he can see it. That means he's okay."

Dixon left his sunglasses in place. "See what?"

"The new wall surrounding the city. Boxing us in."

"Kind of hard to miss, isn't it?" Dixon asked.

"Actually, no," Laurel said. "Turns out, most people in the city *can't* see it."

Dixon's face scrunched. *"What?"*

And so, now that she knew Dixon's mind hadn't been infiltrated, Laurel spent fifteen minutes explaining all they'd discussed and learned. He stopped asking to take off the sunglasses once he understood the situation, and their purpose.

When it was over, Dixon looked shocked and fell speechless. Both were firsts for Dixon.

"So the whole city's delusional," he finally said.

"The people out walking around like nothing's changed seem to be," Laurel replied. "It's impossible to tell how widespread it is. It's possible there are a lot of unaffected people, but they're hiding in their homes."

"Do you think that's the case?"

Laurel thought for a moment. "The readings I showed you clearly indicate a dozen or more pre-rifts inside the Gore Point. There's no question that ..."

She stopped, and Adrian knew she was consciously deciding not to lapse into science-talk, finding a way to dumb things down for them instead.

"That a whole lot of *influence* must be leaking out given the number of thin spots between the planes. If it was poison gas, I could guess that just about anyone without a gas mask would be dying without having to see it for myself, because that's how poison gas works. So yeah. Knowing how interplanar energy works, I can safely guess that most of the city is affected. The only silver lining is that influence isn't the same as control. Most of the city probably doesn't think anything strange is going on ... but I don't think the king has turned them all into puppets."

"Yet," said Ray.

"Yet," Laurel reluctantly agreed.

"How long will it take?"

Ray and Adrian's eyes went to Laurel, but Dixon answered. "Six days."

All three heads — Laurel included — whipped in Dixon's direction.

"There are things," he said, "that I probably should have told you a long time ago."

12

THE KERNEL

"Spread and Containment discovered a possible extraplanar contagion three years ago." Dixon settled in with a humbled posture Adrian had never seen in the man, all artifice now gone. He was usually filled with self-importance and bluster, but right now he was guilt and regret exclusively.

"We were experimenting with psychological vectors, working through some old government research on the hunch that some of it might apply."

"Whose research?" There was hardness in Laurel's words. She'd been highly placed at GEN, and S&C and the brigades were supposed to play straight with GEN so they could do their jobs. The realization that the government had been keeping secrets didn't seem to surprise so much as disappoint her.

"The CIA's," Dixon said.

Laurel nodded. She didn't look remotely surprised. "MK Ultra?"

"And things like it," Dixon said, cowed even further. "The things society mocks, the CIA has taken seriously since it was founded. You have no idea how many NDAs I'm breaking by telling you any of this."

Ray still held his pistol. It was in his lap, but he looked down at it now: His answer to how much he cared about Dixon's nondisclosure agreements.

"The real purpose of MK Ultra wasn't to explore LSD and other chemicals as weapons. It was partially about mind control — which, more importantly, was based on a belief that things like ESP and telekinesis were possible. And phenomena like remote viewing, where talented psychics seemed able to 'send their minds out' and spy on enemies without getting anywhere near them."

"Horseshit," said Ray.

"Oh, there were people who seemed able to do it. But that's not even the point. The government has believed in the power of the mind for a long time, and for pretty convincing reasons. They noticed the same things that everyday people noticed about rifts since they first started appearing, like how insects form lines around them if they stay open long enough, radiating outward in concentric circles. The government was curious because the pattern of lines and circles looked just like force lines caused by strong magnets. If you put tiny iron filings around a magnet, they'll make the same shapes as insects around a rift. It suggested that there was a force of some sort coming from the rifts, not just fiends. That force, instead of acting on tiny pieces of iron, was influencing living things. Insects, yes ... but living things just the same."

"We had a theory about it at GEN, but it didn't go anywhere."

Dixon nodded at Laurel. "That's because you didn't have the CIA's research. We did. Well ... *I* didn't, but the government did, and around the time Erika Dale and Matt Baker's little sabotage plan was unfolding, that's when the government got involved with Spread and Containment. It made sense. We're about 'spread,' right? Same as the CDC. Looking back, they probably suspected a sundering was coming. I learned most of what I'm telling you now right before we started working together, Adrian."

Dixon said it companionably, but Adrian didn't have fond feelings about his first weeks under Dixon's command. At the beginning, he had stonewalled every attempt Adrian made to understand his orders. He hadn't wanted to betray his brothers and sisters at Brigade One — or any of the brigades — but Dixon had simply seen Adrian as a scalpel and "the saboteur problem" as a cancer. You don't mess around with cancer, and you don't worry about saving the cells too close to it. Cutting out more is better. In the saboteur matter, Dixon had been just fine ruining the entire brigade if it meant catching his man or woman — or, in Dale and Baker's case, one of each.

"I won't bother to take you through every last bit of it right now (although Laurel, whatever you want to know later, I'll tell you), but combining the CIA's psychic research with the idea of a 'force exerted by open rifts' led us to a theory that still holds today: that of some sort of a mental virus."

"Jesus," Adrian said. "So when I said that Carl mentioned a virus—"

"I wanted to look into it before I said anything about it. It's been a day, Adrian. *One day* since Carl said that. But yes. What we're seeing is consistent with our fears about a psychic contagion — one that spreads through thought instead of bacteria and sneezing. The lines of insects we see around rifts indicate the location of peaks in the 'force wave' of the contagion. They radiate outward, causing the simple nervous systems of insects to gather where the force is strongest."

He looked at the three people facing him with accusing eyes.

"You don't understand," he said, attempting to justify. "Insects don't even have a central nervous system. They have nerve clusters called 'ganglia.' Barely pre-brains. We thought the force was weak — far, *far* too weak to affect more sophisticated lifeforms."

"Bullshit," said Laurel.

"Not bullshit! We thought—!"

"You thought what the CIA always thinks. You thought it could be augmented and weaponized."

"No, we—!"

"Don't lie. Tell me about your 'psychological vectors.'"

Dixon looked like he wanted to swear. Adrian had heard Dixon say those words earlier, but years spent living with Laurel had trained him to gloss over what sounded like intellectual buzzwords: complicated-sounding things Laurel added to explanations that could be simple if she didn't feel the need to up her vocabulary and show off.

But Laurel had heard Dixon say "psychological vectors," and Dixon, who was a suit instead of a scientist, apparently hadn't realized it was enough to give him away.

"Fine," he said.

"What were they? Criminals?"

Dixon hesitated, then nodded.

"What the hell are you guys talking about?"

Laurel turned, explaining to Ray while demanding that Dixon go on with her glare.

"A 'vector' is an organism that transmits a parasite from one lifeform to another. Dogs and bats are vectors for rabies. Fleas that lived on rats were vectors for the bubonic plague. Seeing as humans are the only form of life on Earth that people usually attribute 'psychology' to, I assume that Mr. Dixon is talking about an experiment conducted by Spread and

Containment ... one that used humans as vectors for this 'mental virus' we're talking about."

Dixon said nothing.

"And because you probably wouldn't bother mentioning the psychology of someone whose psychology was normal ..."

"You used psychopaths?" Adrian said.

Laurel looked to Dixon, then answered for him. "They used psychopaths. Didn't you? You found people who were criminally insane, and you exposed them to the contagion, and—"

"*Yes! Fine!* It wasn't my work, but I was there. The people working on it knew from earlier CIA research how to do things like amplify thought. They wanted to see what would happen if it was people, not insects, who were exposed to a stronger version of the force coming from the rifts."

"Why?"

"Because we assumed they could do it already," Dixon said, presumably meaning the fiends. "If *we* could do it, and if *they* operated as a group mind, it stood to reason that they'd be a whole lot better at 'thought warfare' than we were. We only tried to weaponize mental rift energy because if we didn't, they'd beat us to it."

Laurel scoffed with derision. She'd once campaigned against nuclear armament and was all too familiar with the argument Dixon was making. *Why would anyone build a force capable of destroying the world? Why, as self defense, of course.*

"When were you going to say something?" Ray asked, still fingering the pistol.

"Now. I decided to tell you as soon as I heard your analysis, Laurel, and recognized what you were describing as the spread we always feared would come."

"You should have told us earlier. Maybe we could have done something, you son of a bitch."

"Weren't you the one who wanted this?" Dixon said,

suddenly angry, throwing looks at Adrian and Ray — but mostly Adrian and Laurel — to get them all to see his point, and to agree. "Wasn't 'letting the king take over' *your* plan? Wasn't it *you*, Adrian, who opened the door and set him free?"

"Because I thought it was going to happen no matter what we did!" Laurel spat back. "Because I thought this was about physics and entropy! Two planes in fragile balance! Already splintering! How the fuck were they *not* going to fracture eventually?"

"And *that* justifies ushering in armageddon?" Dixon said.

Adrian slid between them: the old bald man and the fiesty young woman dangerously close to blows. "Don't turn this around on her. You were on board."

"After it was done! *After* you came back and told me what she told you!" Now Dixon was shooting daggers at Laurel, trying to make her the bad guy — trying to convince Ray that she, not he, was more at fault. "If either of you had bothered to ask me, I would have told you straight away!"

"We didn't know what you knew! Were we supposed to read your mind?"

"*Why the fuck not?*" Dixon shot back, moving chest-to-chest with Adrian. "*You read HER thoughts so much you led two of your friends straight into a trap!*"

Adrian's felt his face fall. His anger deflated like a balloon. He'd managed to forget the deaths of Ollie and Shannon ... and until right now, he'd never quite blamed his own skewed motivations as the center of the target. But it was true. He'd been so determined to save Laurel, hearing her voice inside his head, that he'd charged ahead without thinking. Two of his fellows had died in battle — and for what? When they finally reached Hell's city, Laurel had been colluding with the enemy and feeling just fine.

Ray moved forward. "Step away. Now."

Dixon stood tall, though clearly outmatched.

"I'm warning you," Ray said.

"What? Are you going to shoot me?"

Ray checked his gun's safety and put it back in his waistband. "You'll *wish* I shot you."

"*The golden Porter Brothers,*" Dixon sneered, meaner than Adrian had ever seen him — and why not? He'd been exposed as a villain, and blaming the others was his only chance at redemption. Consciously or not, Dixon was fighting for his soul. "Always trying to look like heroes. But actually, from the very beginning, *the reason bad things happen.*"

Ray moved closer.

"Starting with your father," Dixon added, still holding his ground.

Ray reared back, about to shove him.

"Stop," Laurel commanded.

Ray paused with one hand on Dixon's shirt, about to grab it. His other hand had cocked back, preparing to strike. Adrian was preparing for something unknown — to protest Ray's intervening, to join his brother in beating Dixon for disparaging their father, maybe to argue for pause as Laurel had just done.

Both brothers hitched only a beat, still contracted and ready to spring. But then they paused more seriously after hearing the tone of Laurel's single word after the fact. And seeing the look on her face.

She wasn't angry. She wasn't indignant. She was merely thoughtful. Forehead tense and eyes far away. She had the appearance of a woman with an elusive word on the tip of her tongue.

Ray let go of Dixon. His fist lowered.

Adrian stepped back, and Dixon didn't so much as straighten the collar Ray had crumpled.

"'Starting with their father,'" she said, repeating Dixon's words, still with that thousand-yard stare.

"It's not that simple," Adrian told her. "Our dad—"

"Shh. Shut up." She was very still, one hand hovering as if afraid to flinch. Then she looked at Dixon and said, "Six days."

"What?"

"You said it would take six days before the contagion infected everyone. Six days before everyone in Fortune was loyal to the other plane's king. Six days before Fortune — the center of the riftfighting world and the only force able to stop the king from taking the world — was gone." She looked at Dixon. "Why six days?"

"It's what our research said. *The CIA's* research."

"But why?"

"I don't know. I never understood. I just know that six days was as long as the most balanced people lasted."

Adrian made himself set a troubling part of Dixon's assertion aside: his mention of *the most balanced people*. He'd already admitted that research began with criminally insane "vectors" for the mental virus. If those subjects were crazy to begin with, they presumably succumbed to Hell's control quickly. Dixon's casual mention of "most balanced" seemed to suggest that the experiments had ramped up after their initial trials, to ultimately see how it fared in healthier minds.

So who were those "most balanced subjects" who'd lasted six days before their minds broke? Student volunteers, trying to earn a few bucks for tuition by participating in an experiment? Luckless workers and agents who'd been exposed, perhaps but not definitely by accident?

Laurel had glossed right past that, thinking on something else. "Did your lab identify a *reason* for the people who 'lasted'? Something to explain their lessened susceptibility?"

"Yes. Same reason it didn't spread to everyone at once

despite the theoretically infinite expansion of the force wave. Same reason the four of us haven't been affected yet. For you, it's probably exposure to Zen, but for me and others, there are things you can do to train for extended resistance if they're not already in you, and they're—"

Laurel held up a hand. The thought she'd been grasping seemed closer now, not quite as apt to flee. "Later. What was the reason?"

"There was something in the 'thought virus' itself that kept trying to shut it down. They used words I didn't understand. 'Anti-entropic.' 'Cancelling wave.' 'Titration.' 'Psychic buffer.' 'Seed kernel.'"

"'Seed kernel.'"

Now Dixon stopped. Everyone watched Laurel.

"But it wouldn't really be a *seed*, would it? They'd be using it colloquially." She was talking to herself, working it out. Adrian knew better than to interrupt. But then she looked pointedly at Dixon. "More like an enzyme and its antagonist."

"What?"

Laurel ignored Dixon and rushed to her little doctor bag. She opened its top and dug around until she found the small tablet with digital copies of her research. They watched as she flipped through scans of handwritten page after handwritten page, waiting with stilled breath.

"Insulin and glucagon. Leptin, ghrelin, somatostatin … Jesus, of course." She turned to face them all. "It's just one more living system! Nature isn't all or nothing. Take hormones for instance. It's not just one hormone per job … it's always a complicated dance! You eat and your body releases insulin, but glucagon is right there, ready and waiting to make sure insulin doesn't work *too* well and go *too* low. Insulin and glucagon push against each other, fine-tuning the actions of the other. A bunch of other hormones fine-tune *that* interaction, making it even more fine-grained. Don't you see? In living systems, it's never just push. It's always push *and pull*. I was so worried about physics, I never considered biochemistry! Of course there's an antagonist! It's the essence of evolution! I mean, it's not really biochemistry, not like insulin and glucagon, but you know what I mean ..."

"No," said Adrian. "We have *absolutely no idea* what you mean."

She took a breath, making a visible effort to control what looked like revelatory excitement ... and to control her scientific explanations and vocabulary.

She found what she'd been looking for in her notes, then poked the page as if her intellectual chicken-scratch might mean a damn thing to the three dummies in the room.

"I was looking at planar collapse from the perspective of entropy." She shook her head as if to clear it, then chose a better word for "entropy" — one the men might actually understand. "*Chaos.* We all understand chaos, right? Everything *always* tends toward chaos. Things don't stay orderly forever; everything always falls apart if you give it enough time. Buildings fall to rubble. Bodies decay. With me so far?"

Adrian nodded.

"That's why I told you that the planes — our plane and the fiend plane — were doomed to collapse at some point. There was no way to avoid it. And if the planes had to collapse *eventually*, it made sense to help them collapse *now*. The longer it took for the inevitable collapse, the more strife there would be when it happened. The longer the war would go on, resulting in needless deaths. The goal, when we brought the king back, was to rip the Band-Aid off so we wouldn't all have to live through a long, slow decay."

"Okay." Ray was new to the idea and sounded less than

convinced, but he'd lived with Laurel once, too. He had learned, the hard way, that she was usually right.

"But I forgot that *life itself* is a force, and I didn't even consider it until now. Did we all see *Jurassic Park*? Remember how Jeff Goldblum's character argued that they couldn't stop the dinosaurs from breeding no matter what they tried to prevent it … because 'life always finds a way'?"

"No," said Dixon.

Laurel barged on. "Biological systems are *always* push and pull. Same with anything life touches. Entire ecosystems: *all* push and pull. Forests overgrow, so fire cuts them down. In the wilds, where humans aren't in the way, predators and prey always establish equilibrium. There is always balance. It's kind of like entropy, really — like chaos. Give it enough time, and everything tends toward average. Nature doesn't like black *or* white. It keeps trying to nudge everything toward fifty percent gray."

"What's that got to do with the 'seed kernel' thing?" Dixon asked.

She shook her head, waving it away. "They probably called it a seed because they didn't know what else to call it. I found the same thing when I was working in the other plane." Laurel tapped her incomprehensible tablet again. "All that matters is that there's *something* in the 'thought virus' that isn't the virus itself. Look! I thought it was an artifact, like a kernel, but do you know what I think it is?"

"Laurel," Ray said, "We don't have a single fucking clue. Why don't you just tell us?"

She moved closer to Adrian, as if meaning to speak to him alone. "I didn't tell the king what I found, Adrian. I didn't tell him that there was some sort of an artifact inside his 'mental contagion' because … well … because it reminded me of you."

That was the last thing Adrian expected to hear. "What?"

"We had that link, remember? I could project some of my thoughts into you, and after a while I stared to feel back some of *your* thoughts. CIA experiments aside, humans can't normally do that on this plane. But because I was on *their* plane, and the king was *also* projecting into you, it was like we had a carrier wave to boost the signal. For a while there, I could feel you and you could feel me."

What she'd just said felt beyond intimate, though clearly she hadn't meant it that way. Adrian wanted to turn away, to not let Ray and Dixon hear.

"Whenever the king projected his thoughts loudly enough, that little remnant inside it? It felt like *you*. It's the reason I never really gave up hope."

"*Hope?* Is that all it was? Laurel ... you said you had a *plan*."

"I did. I somehow knew that my ace in the hole was you. I didn't know what it was, only that it was there. I just sort of had to ... take it on faith."

Ray had always been the pragmatist. There was life and death. Black and white. Fact and fiction. But Adrian? From the start, he'd been his mother's son. He believed in things like trust ... and deep down, so contrary to her usual nature, it now seemed that Laurel did as well.

"That's not very scientific," Ray told her now.

"It doesn't matter." For the third time she tapped her notes on her tablet, and for the third time Adrian wished he could understand what was there. "Science deals with what's known, but that doesn't mean we know everything. I trust *my* science. What *I* know, from experience and research. And I'm telling you—" Another tap on the tablet. "—I *already* found what Dixon's describing: that little kernel inside the noise, working as an antagonist to the virus."

"'Antagonist'?" Adrian repeated.

"All living systems have both push *and* pull. We thought

the 'mental virus' was just some sort of plague, out there doing its thing. But it came from fiend-plane energy, and that means it's fiend-plane thought. So it came from fiends. Living things. *Push and pull*, you guys. Part of the virus is there to *moderate* it. To *slow it down*. There's a tiny fragment inside the virus ... and it's been there all along."

There was a long pause, as if Laurel, smiling now, expected them to guess.

"For fuck's sake, Laurel, what is it?" Ray snapped.

"It's the exact same thing that made the king interested in you guys to begin with. The exact same reason this started with a Porter ... and will end with a Porter."

Adrian was starting to understand, if only a little. "Are you saying ...?"

"That's right. I told you that when your father opened the first intentional rift, his mind imprinted on it. That tiny 'seed' of Eldon Porter has been a part of their group mind for over fifty years now. It's part of them, so long as the planes continue to intermingle. Do you understand? It's in *every* part of them ... *including the virus.*"

"How can you possibly be sure it's—?"

"Because I can feel it, now that I know what it is, and because I reached the same conclusion as Spread and Containment, now with context to understand what it means. My research showed that the decay rate of the antagonist made it effectively *non*-antagonistic after around 150 hours, or six days — meaning that after six days, all of its resistance disappears. At that point, the virus really *does* become all push and no pull, meaning it takes over whatever it touches."

Then she smiled wider. "But if that's not scientific enough for you? Well, then, see for yourself."

She turned the tablet so both Adrian and Ray could see, and both could understand.

It wasn't Laurel's handwriting scanned into this specific electronic page. It was Eldon Porter's original research log from all those years ago, which of course GEN had acquired and studied like the Rosetta Stone.

Adrian read. Ray read. Then for Dixon's benefit, once they were finished, Laurel summarized the passage to ram the point home.

"Eldon thought about whether or not he should open that first rift for a long time before he finally did it. He thought and thought ... and in his own words: 'I know I shouldn't, but I can't resist. *I must know what is on the other side!* I've given it God's time to ponder, but in the end I can only ever resist for as long as He chose to labor.'"

Dixon looked confused, but Ray understood and so did Adrian. Laurel already knew because both brothers had told her this most interesting of their father's quirks.

God made the world in six days, and on the seventh day he rested. Eldon Porter (who a long-ago priest had told Adrian was surely going to Hell) had actually been a closet Christian: more superstition, for him, than belief. So Eldon believed that only hubris could make a person indecisive for longer than it took God to build all that existed. And for that reason, he never, *ever* wrestled with an important decision for more than six days.

After six days, one side of Eldon Porter's dilemmas *always* stopped resisting.

Just as his imprint — living on inside the mind of the virus — would decay like the final ember in a dying fire.

I3

TICKING CLOCK

Six days.

Part of Eldon Porter had imprinted upon the first manmade rift, and the imprint was fighting the king's takeover from inside the virus. It was far from a fix, though. After six days, its resistance would surrender and *nobody* would be safe. Everyone in the city — inside the new, impassable wall — would become slaves to the king of Hell. Fortune would fall, and without Fortune's brainpower, technology, riftfighters, and weapons, the rest of the world would follow.

The planes would collapse. Hell would become Earth and Earth would become Hell.

Laurel had argued for ripping off that particular Band-Aid, yes ... but only because she'd believed there was a caveat in her research: a way out of what used to seem inevitable. Now she had her way out. Now she understood what her gut had been telling her all along: The Porters' minds were entangled with the fiends' and that soiled the hive. Eldon Porter's personality was the grain of sand inside an oyster around which a pearl forms. Exploit it, and they might be able to seal the breach — permanently — after all.

But it was a way out with only a six-day lifespan. After six days, even the strongest-minded people in Fortune would be servants of the king. After *that*, as the saying went, resistance would be futile.

"It's only Day One." Ray nodded as if trying to convince himself of something. "It's okay. We still have time."

"Time for *what?*" Adrian asked.

"I don't know, asshole," Ray spat, irritated by the surrender he heard in his brother's voice. "Find a way out of Fortune? Get through the wall and let the outside world know what's going on so they can prepare? Reinforce Dad's 'resistance' somehow? Find a way to show uninfected people what's going on, maybe? If they could just *see the damn wall* and start thinking like human beings again instead of drugged-out zombies, maybe—"

"I don't think that's how it works, Ray."

"We've got six goddamn days to find a way to *make* it work!"

Dixon's head was bobbing side to side.

"What?" Ray demanded, turning on him.

"Well … it's not actually Day One. It's probably more like Three or Four. We didn't notice any of this until the wall came down, but I doubt it just started. Most people can't *see* the wall, sure. That happened right away. But the king would need to *control* — not just *deceive* — at least a few key people inside the city before making his move. You know: keep people from leaving, from causing trouble once the wall came … shit like that."

"You're guessing," said Ray.

"What did you compare the king to, Laurel? A chess player? Chess players put their strategy in place *before* attacking, Ray."

"You're still guessing."

"I agree with Dixon," said Laurel. "I could take you through the epidemiology, or you could just trust me. This isn't actually a virus, but it spreads like one. Based on what we've seen, even the CDC would call this Day Three or Four. To have spread as much as it already has, it must've been happening since the start of the week or so. We definitely don't have six days. We'll be lucky to have have two or three."

Ray seemed so offended by this, he looked like he wanted to destroy truth by beating it to death. "Well, goddammit, which is it? Two or three?"

Laurel tried to look less defeated than she clearly felt. "I'll look into it."

The room was quiet.

"Carl," said Adrian, standing suddenly.

"What about him?"

Rather than explain that they had a trans-planar window in their broom closet, Adrian simply walked over, then came back feeling faint. The portal, which once dominated the small space with its torso-sized Mirror-Mirror presence, had shrunk to almost nothing. It was practically gone: now more like a blemish on the wall than even a fraction of what it used to be.

Adrian couldn't put his eye to the peephole that remained without burning his cornea, but using his phone camera to peer through it showed him nothing on the other side. The window seemed to have moved on the fiends' plane: no longer in the chamber where Adrian spoke with Carl, but opening more or less under a red boulder instead.

There was only one explanation. Seeing as Dixon and Adrian hadn't closed their side of the rift, someone on the fiend side must have found a way to do it. Meaning their communication had been discovered by the king or one of his soldiers — still split open half an inch only because fiends had never been good at closing manmade rifts.

It was as good as gone. Any advice they'd hoped to get from their halfskull informant Carl was gone with it.

"He knew. The king knew the portal was there," Adrian said, returning to the group.

"Not necessarily," Dixon replied. "Cutting off might just be cutting off. He reset all the entrances and exits at once. It doesn't mean he knows Carl was talking to us."

Adrian hadn't said anything about Carl being caught as an informant. The fact that Dixon had gone right to denying his predicament instead of explaining the portal's absence made Adrian feel worse. Carl's personality had developed more and more the longer he was away from the hive mind. He was, without reservation, a friend.

Carl might be in Hell's prison now. Or dead for trying to help.

Something exploded outside. The room barely reacted. They merely peered over, watching as another building began to burn. Eventually there were sirens. Nobody seemed concerned.

"We have to do something." Ray has said it before, but this time it was less testosterone-fueled and somehow sadder. He had sounded ready to rip the world apart his first time calling for action. Now, he was begging support from a group reluctant to give it. Adrian was reminded of their boyhood: times Ray wanted to play baseball in the vacant lot down the street, but when Adrian wasn't interested and his friends were busy, he'd whine, not at all eager to swing the bat alone.

Laurel stood. Ray watched her with hopeful eyes.

"Okay. Let's boil this down. We have a few days before everyone's infected."

"Does 'everyone' include us?"

Laurel eyed Adrian but left his question unanswered. It was answer enough, and made Adrian feel cold.

"There are still people in the city who aren't affected. Have to be. They'll be stubborn people. Strong-minded people. If they live as far as possible from the Gore Point, that would be best because the effect is strongest nearest the Point."

"So we recruit them." Ray nodded, grasping Laurel's words with both hands. "Get a little army together and see if we can take the wall down."

"Or find a way to get over it. Or dig under it. Or communicate through it."

Ray looked at his brother with gratitude, even though Adrian was trying to manufacture hope more than feeling it for real.

"It's not that simple," Laurel replied. "The air's like a hallucinogen, remember. Even most of the people who aren't yet under the king's control can't see the wall and don't seem to feel like anything in town is wrong. They'll think fires and explosions are perfectly normal. I noticed bodies on the streets on the way here. Shot. Stabbed. People either aren't seeing it, don't mind what they see, or are holed up in their houses hiding from the reality."

"We're not affected," Ray said. "We can see it all."

Dixon nodded. "That's because they gave you Frog. S&C thought something like this might happen, so we were all microdosed."

"What if people are dosed now?" Adrian asked. "Can we *make* people see what's going on who can't see it right now?"

Dixon shrugged. "I don't know."

"Laurel?"

"I don't know, either."

Ray stood. Everyone looked at him.

"Ray?" Adrian said.

"I have an idea."

14

LIMINAL

Fortune had one of the stranger interdepartmental overlaps a city could have. Animal Control worked, at times, quite closely with the riftfare brigades.

It hadn't always been that way. Animal Control was Animal Control once upon a time. There was the proverbial dogcatcher, the proverbial negotiator to overtaxed cat ladies, and the not-at-all-proverbial officers in tan uniforms whose tools included raccoon traps and six-foot catch poles. For a long time, Animal Control did what it does in other cities: removing possums from beneath porches, wrangling rattlesnakes that found their way into the crawlspaces of homes, and citing pet owners for not having licenses.

But then the rifts came. And the rifts proliferated. Eventually, escaped fiends started mauling animals the same as they mauled humans, and once the first animal/fiend fight was caught on a surveillance camera, the riftfare department became very interested.

Fiends fought animals differently than they fought humans. It was one of the first pieces of evidence that fiends might not be mindless animals themselves — that they might, in fact, have some idea what they were doing. That was the start of it. But then the bears came.

The Gore Point formed inside a wild, Western United States national park. That put it in close proximity with all sorts of dangerous game: big cats for one, but bears most notably. Grizzlies in particular were particularly adept at fighting fiends to a draw. It happened with no other species — certainly not humans, who, if they fought fiends hand to hand, always died trying.

Grizzly bears, however, were big enough and resilient enough to fight smaller-caste fiends and win. The fiends seemed to figure it out, and to some degree they adapted. It wasn't always adaptation enough. And so, time and time again, the bear would give up and so would the fiend. After staring each other down they would simply walk away.

The riftfare department wanted to understand why and how. Part of their research was to study the fights, if they could get them on video, but more often they could only study the bears. Hunters (but more often, black-clad, mopey teenagers) ran across wounded bears in the Suicide Flats on a regular basis, usually maimed and confused enough to stumble over the down-swept trunks of teardrop trees. The bears were always put out of their misery, but shooting them with big enough rounds to kill them disfigured the corpses. Riftfare wanted the bears whole, so they could study them.

That's why every brigadehouse came to have an Animal Control agent on staff, resident to the brigade. That's why every brigadehouse, in that agent's office, carried a few enormous, bear-gauge tranquilizer rifles. The Legions fought the fiends, and the Stitchers closed the rifts ... and the lone Animal Control agent, whenever necessary, tracked down fiend-mauled bears for analysis and autopsy.

"Not sure what the point of tranquilizing people is," Dixon told his car's passengers as they pulled into the alley behind Brigade One's stationhouse.

"We don't want to tranquilize them. We want to dart them with Frog."

"Uh-huh," said Dixon.

"Dose them with the mutagen, same as all of us were dosed."

"Uh-huh."

"Because maybe if we give them Frog, they'll snap out of it and be able to see—"

"Oh, I understand what you're thinking," Dixon said. "I just don't see how it's going to make any difference. How many guns are even in that locker?"

Adrian had hopped on board with Ray's plan, partially because he wanted to believe that people could be "snapped out of it," in Ray's words, but partially because he didn't want to feel like he was crazy. He could see the wall around the city plain as day, even from here, but the four of them were the minority. For every other Fortunite they'd seen, everything was A-OK in the world. It was hard to feel sane when you were the only one with a different opinion. Sanity turned out to be a "force of numbers" kind of thing.

"One," Adrian answered.

"One?"

"One. One AC agent only needs one dart gun."

"Fuck's sake," said Dixon. "How much can you do with *one gun?*"

That wasn't even the worst of it. The darts for the rifle were, as Dixon said earlier, *tranquilizer* darts right now. They were filled with a sedative. Somehow the darts would have to be emptied, their reservoirs re-filled with Frog. They didn't have any Frog yet, either. There was only one place to get Frog that Adrian knew of, and it would be a hell of a lot harder to get into than their old brigadehouse.

But. One problem at a time.

"Just stay here," Adrian said. "Ray and I will run in. Be right back."

The brothers exited Dixon's car by slowly lifting the latches and gently closing the doors. The alleyway was too quiet. Same for everything else. The brigadehouse lights were on, but at this time of the day, this close by, they should be able to hear music playing in the common room. They should hear voices and camaraderie and laughter. Someone was definitely home. Adrian could see silhouettes walking past the windows.

Once they were out of sight of the car and not yet in sight of the brigadehouse's rear door, Ray turned to Adrian, nodding toward the corner around which they'd just come.

"Think they'll be all right out here?"

"Dixon and Laurel? Yeah. I think so."

"What if some zombies come?"

"They're not zombies, Ray."

"You know what I mean. People under the spell. Not, like, the black-eyed minion fuckers. I just mean blank-faced zombies."

"Again, not zombies."

"They might fuck with them."

"I think Laurel can handle herself." He paused, then said, "Dixon, I'm not so sure."

For some reason, that struck Ray as incredibly funny. It was nerves. They were both keyed up — and, unsettlingly, were keyed up for no real reason. They both used to live on adrenaline. Ray used to drink it for breakfast: front of the Legion formation, almost begging to get himself killed every time they fought a new fight. But this was different. This was the calm before the storm in a horror movie. This was zero action, all anticipation. Adrian for one found it far worse than a visible threat.

He thought of the Legion that had wanted to kill them because he recognized the Porters — and, presumably, saw them as a threat. The king had stopped seeing Adrian as an ally the second Adrian set him free, same as he'd stopped seeing Laurel as an ally. That made them wanted people in the eyes of the king: a pair of wrenches just waiting to throw themselves into the gears.

Adrian kept wondering: Had that Legion tried to kill them because he'd decided on his own that the Porter boys were trouble? Or had *the king* tried to kill them back at the check-point, using the Legion as a puppet?

He didn't like what that implied. He thought again of Carl's portal: taken away either on purpose or as a side effect. What if both things were intentional? What if the king was pointedly after them, and what if he knew through Carl just how subver-sive they'd become?

There were two types of people in Fortune right now: black-eyed folks who had succumbed to the virus, and those who weren't yet infected but had been blinded to the truth by what Adrian increasingly thought of as "LSD in the air." The second group could maybe be turned around. They'd come for the dart gun, so they could shoot the blind ones with Frog and hope for the best. But the first group? Those people had been weaponized, and any of them might be looking for Ray and Adrian right now.

Maybe not passively. Maybe not just "on lookout in case the Porters came by." The king played chess after all, and that meant sneak attacks were a thing. There might be scores of black-eyes following their every move, tipped off if Carl was tortured for information on them. There might even be one of the bad ones right around the corner ahead, or just inside the brigadehouse door.

It took a while for Ray to stop giggling about Dixon and his complete inability to fight in the real world. Adrian had stopped giggling along right away, his mind turned to much more troubling matters.

"I'm good," Ray said, composing himself. "I don't know why that was so funny."

Nerves. For Ray, too much laughter is a sign of nerves. Adrian decided not to remind Ray how nervous he really was.

They peeked around the corner. The rear door was ahead.

"No big deal. You finally convinced me to quit. I'm here to clean out my locker, nothing more."

Ray nodded. He'd been the one to concoct their cover story: their way to explain why Adrian, the pariah, had returned to the brigade today. At first, Ray had wanted to avoid the need for a cover story by just not bringing Adrian. He'd argued that he could just walk right in, say hello to whoever he passed (it'd be a skeleton crew; nobody was truly "on duty" anymore), then duck into the Animal Control office and hope the locker they wanted wasn't one anyone felt the need to lock.

"That's right," Ray said, nodding at their prepared story.

Even that spun yarn was a last-resort sort of thing. The back-alley entrance would let them into the hallway past Kaur's old office. Ahead would be the garage, and beyond that would be the kitchen. The hope was that with no real rift calls anymore, the garage would be pointless to the occupants now: a place where their old response vehicles were parked. Kaur's office would be empty because he'd been let go a while back, the theory being that because the brigades were now relics, the farce they'd become could more or less captain themselves. The only rift-related action these days was done by the military.

Hopefully everyone would be upstairs, sleeping or chatting or watching TV or playing pool. Keeping quiet should get them in and out. Good thing considering how good Harrison Kim was with a knife.

You have no reason to believe they'll be against you. They used to be your friends.

But a second, more reasonable-sounding voice was right on the heels of the first one: *Used to be, yes. But ask yourself: If you were the king and saw the Porters as a problem, where would you plant your spies?*

Adrian reached the door first. He pulled out his keycard, sure it wouldn't work before he even tried it.

The lock's LED turned red and there was a click as something inside the mechanism reset. Adrian flinched. He'd never heard that click before. It must've been drowned in noise from the neighborhood, noise from his fellows, noise from the street. In all this quiet, though, the sound was deafening.

"It's okay. They'd be pretty dumb not to revoke your access." Ray stepped forward. "Here. I may not go in much, but I'm still official."

Ray inserted his card. Then the LED flashed red again. The clicking somehow sounded even louder.

"What the hell?" Ray did it again. And then a third time.

Couldn't he hear how much noise he was making? It felt to Adrian like ringing a dinner bell. "Maybe we should go directly to Animal Control. The actual department. They'll have more than one rifle."

"Yeah, and we don't have a reason to be there. No way to get at the rifles. No access at all."

"We don't have access *here,*" Adrian said as Ray tried the lock, noisily, for the fourth time.

"It's just my card. It's always finicky." Ray moved to re-insert it, but Adrian grabbed his wrist.

"Stop."

"I just need to wiggle it."

"It's not a key. It's not even magnetic."

"I've been using this same shitty card for two years. Kaur bitched about the cost to replace it. Like ten bucks. Can you believe that? I've always had to wiggle it. It's not the size of the card, Adrian. It's how you use it."

Ray's mouth split into a wolf's grin as he put the card back into the slot. It made a noise that was probably just *click*, but struck Adrian's jangled nerves like *CLICKETY CLANKY CLICK MOTHERFUCKER COME GET US!*

"Stop." He grabbed Ray's wrist again — harder this time.

"We have to get in, Ade. We need that dart gun. What do you want to do — tackle people one at a time and inject them?"

Yes. That was preferable to this. They still had to get the actual Frog to put in the darts if they wanted any hope of pulling the blinders from anyone's eyes — assuming the strategy was sound. Getting Frog from the military base was already going to be impossible. Why not add the task of finding the little dosing guns that'd been used on them? "Impossible" was like "infinity." Once you were at either one of those things, the silver lining was that doubling them made no difference at all.

"I have an idea," Ray said, pocketing his card.

"No," Adrian replied, anticipating his brother's idea and not liking it a bit.

"We'll just go around to the front. It's illegal for the front doors to be locked during business hours. You know that. We can just walk right in."

"Someone will be at the desk."

"Come on," Ray argued. "What are the chances someone's actually sitting there? How many walk-ins did we have after the military basically took over? After the *Brigade* show ended?"

"I don't think there were any."

"There were even less after you came back, when I was still coming around."

"You can't get less than zero in this context, Ray."

"Even when Kaur was still here, the desk was abandoned half the time. Shannon just kind of kept an eye on the lobby cam."

Adrian's gut fell. *Shannon.* Didn't Ray know not to mention Shannon around him? His conscience ached enough already.

"The doors will be unlocked, and nobody's going to spend all damn day at the desk for no reason so it'll be empty, Ade. We can just walk right through."

"I said no."

Ray started walking around the building.

"I said no!" Adrian hissed after him.

But Ray was already to the corner, walking the sidestreet toward the brigadehouse door.

Adrian ran after him, ducking low as if taking fire. The sidestreet was empty except for what seemed to be a kid of about six years old walking alone toward the railroad tracks behind them. Alone. A child, on the city streets by himself. It shivered Adrian's scalp more than the clicking lock had.

He kept glancing back at the kid, wondering if he actually expected some sort of *Children of the Corn* response should the boy turn around and see him. When he reached the parking lot and Mapleside Avenue ahead, he turned his attention forward, feeling naked.

Nobody's after you. The Legion who tried to kill you probably just saw an opportunity.

Yeah. Or was Adrian just telling himself that?

Ray was already at the big glass front doors, cupping his

hands around his face to see inside. He hadn't approached slowly; he'd waited until he was right in the middle to peek in. He probably wasn't visible on the security camera yet (and if they went in, there was a blind spot to one side), but he'd be front and center if someone was at the desk.

"See? Nobody's there."

"Good thing you checked before stepping into plain view."

Ray gave Adrian a look, then didn't dignify him by so much as announcing his intention to enter. He simply went inside. Only the pneumatic closer kept the door from slamming behind him.

"Like I said," Ray whispered, ducking into the security camera's blind spot. "Nobody on duty."

But it was more than that. The stationhouse had the feel of abandonment. The small lobby seemed to host a cavernous echo just waiting to reveal itself. Only a lone flickering fluorescent was on. The umbrella stand to the door's right side had been knocked askew, and the single community umbrella was on the floor like a corpse. Someone must have kicked it recently without picking it up, because a fin-shaped clear spot beside the splayed-out umbrella's faded blue vinyl was sharper in color than the surrounding floor thanks to all the dust.

Ray stepped through the blind spot and around the desk without worry, but to Adrian it seemed that the latent echo was still waiting for the best moment to warble his eardrums. The lobby had become an odd, liminal space: nothing like the lively place he'd spent so many of his years — as an adult, but also before that, when Eldon was Fortune's first hero.

Adrian's feet were rooted. Ray waved impatiently for him to follow. So Adrian did, but he walked on the balls of his feet same as Ray was, now hearing chatter above from the common room.

Instead of feeling threatening (even if everyone up there

was healthy and unaffected, they had still learned to hate Adrian's guts), the sounds from overhead were comforting. The world wasn't abandoned after all. This was simply a place that had ... moved on.

Adrian caught up with his brother. They found the kitchen as empty as the lobby and the garage vacant like the kitchen. When they passed under the fire pole, Adrian chanced a glance upward. The human sounds were louder now, unimpeded as they came through the circular hole around the pole. Who was up there? Were they his old friends, or had the brigade replaced them with stooges and fillers? He received occasional updates on station goings-on from Ray, but he and Ray hadn't been on the best terms since his and Laurel's return. She wasn't welcome here anymore, second only to Adrian. That was one thing Ray had told his brother, when he called once, drunk: *They call her Yoko. You abandoned us and everyone, just for her.*

Into the back corridor. Past Kaur's office, unlocked and open with its contents denuded. It felt like a million years ago that Adrian used to use that office for his own private research, spreading maps on the desk and running through his files. That's where his old life had ended, Adrian realized. The captain had called him in and requested that he stay in Fortune, making him break his promise to Laurel before informing him that there was a saboteur in their midst.

Then suspicion, in both directions.

Alienation.

Reversal. Betrayal. The near-ending of the worlds.

He'd been happy once.

Their luck held. Whoever Animal Control had sent to run the small office at the back clearly didn't come in anymore. The office was as thick with dust as the lobby: abandoned more than formally scuttled. Adrian was sure that the arms locker would be empty or at least impossibly locked, but neither thing was true. The "arms" in this particular locker was a non-lethal sleep agent: a tool more than a weapon. It was where it should be, free to grab. Adrian made sure to pocket a fabric wallet full of darts as well.

Ray slapped Adrian on the back: more a push than a smack to minimize sound. Then quietly he said, "See, little brother? No big deal, just like I told you."

Ray headed toward the back door, preparing to exit.

Adrian said, "Wait."

Ray looked back.

"The alarm will sound if you open that without a keycard."

Ray clapped his shoulder again as he passed with a grin. "There's my bro, finally using that big brain again."

Adrian took an extra few beats to stand beneath the fire pole, listening for voices he recognized. Now that their mission was over and successful, nerves had been replaced by something close to regret, or at least loss. He hadn't thought much about how much had changed. How much he'd once loved but taken for granted was now gone forever.

His father's presence was huge here. This place had been built by Eldon Porter, with deeds if not by his hands.

Adrian's nostalgia snapped. He blinked, a bit bothered by how unconsciously he'd slipped into reverie.

Ray was looking at him: hips forward but torso turned back toward his brother, waiting patiently. He raised his eyebrows: *Coming?*

Adrian nodded: *Yep.*

The shotgun kitchen cut through to the garage on one end and the lobby on the other. There was a third door to the right, leading to a short hallway and the stairs, and in normal times that was the only door in use. The one leading to the lobby (with its ordinary civilians) and the door to the garage (with its gasket against carbon monoxide poisoning) were kept closed. Now they were flung open like a gaping throat.

From the garage, through both open doorways, they could see the lobby and the glass doors to the street beyond. They'd done it: No big deal, just like Ray promised.

"Now we just have to hope it'll work. And *quickly*. If we inject people who aren't happy about it, we'll have a hard time getting our darts back, and we only—"

Ray stopped. It took Adrian a few seconds to realize why.

Jacqui Keogh, once a Legion and still dressed like Tomb Raider, was standing in front of the open refrigerator with a sandwich in her hand.

She'd taken a bite, eyes on them since before they saw her. Adrian watched, frozen, while she swallowed. The faucet dripped in the background.

"So listen, Jacqui ..." Ray began.

"THEY'RE DOWN HERE!" she screamed toward the hole in the garage ceiling.

Ray looked at Adrian, then turned toward the door. Jacqui was prepared for that. She'd always been their best fiend tracer: the brigade's term for someone tasked with chasing down fiends that slipped past the front lines of an open rift. She was also a superior hunter, on the few occasions when hunting was necessary. Fiends didn't slip away for long. Jacqui had the senses of a bloodhound, and always found the loose ends wherever they tried to go.

Ray had spotted the Rollard she'd leaned against the cabinets beside her, but he seemed to be counting on her unwillingness to use it on someone who used to stand beside her in battle. He was wrong, and Adrian had seen it coming. It was hard to spot the whites of Jacqui's eyes from where he stood (he couldn't tell if they'd gone black, and even then the possessed ones were only black temporarily), but her gaze itself told him this was only Jacqui's body they were dealing with.

Laurel's description didn't paint the king's victims as literal puppets. More like people who remained themselves but got bad ideas. Still, Jacqui-in-her-right-mind didn't stand like this woman. She didn't make the micro-gestures this woman had already made: telltale signs of paranoia and waiting that weren't usually there. Jacqui was fierce with her enemies, warm with people she'd known forever. Even if Ray and Adrian were both of those things now, the old Jacqui's body language should have given them the benefit of the doubt.

This Jacqui didn't.

She'd gripped the Rollard within a second and was swinging it at Ray's head the next second. He only kept living because instead of trying to run himself, Adrian dove for his feet in a tackle.

They hit the floor. The rollard's blade end, heroically launched, embedded itself nearly to the hilt in drywall right where Ray's neck had been.

The sounds of tumult came from above. The rush of stomping feet split in two directions: toward the pole as expected, but also toward the building's front. Half of the people in the common room were now headed for the fire escape, on the facade because a change in Fortune's streets had made its front out of what used to be its rear. They were about to be surrounded, in 3 ... 2 ... 1...

The brothers slithered below Jacqui's arms. She pulled one last time on the pinned weapon, got it to move a half inch, then turned and left it so her quarry wouldn't get away. She rushed over to them instead, stomping at the brothers like roaches. Her flare for dramatic costume always had her in high-heeled boots — something Kaur hated because boots like that should make her slow. *Should.* Kaur never actually ordered

Jacqui to find better footwear because somehow, in some way, she stayed fast as hell.

After two misses, Jacqui's second stomp speared Adrian in the calf with one narrow heel. It wasn't a dagger; it didn't impale him. That might have been kinder. This was a thousand-pound blow directed to one tiny spot, smashing in a single point it could not penetrate.

Adrian yelped, feeling like the back of his leg had split open.

He winced and rolled, accidentally taking out one of Jacqui's supports. She staggered but did not fall.

Adrian rolled back to neutral and found himself on his back with one of Jacqui's legs on either side of his torso. She'd grabbed the ancient little cathode television someone had left on the kitchen counter back when the thing still worked and was already in her upswing, prepared within moments to bash his skull.

Ray was right there. He'd found his feet and grabbed a wire-frame chair. He didn't call to Jacqui or hesitate, he just swung the thing hard by its handled top. The arc was long, the chair fully extended to maximally fuck her up with physics.

He hit her hard. The legs collapsed her abdomen and the chrome arm support smashed her full upper lip into her teeth, splitting it like a nightcrawler under his boot.

Jacqui cried out. Staggered back, striking the still-open fridge door and making it rebound. The appliance shook and jars fell to the floor: mayonnaise, relish, something that looked like slaw dressing, all shattered and spewing. Someone's orphaned can of Dr. Pepper rolled up to Ray's foot and stopped there like an obedient dog heeling.

Jacqui, finally dazed, tried and failed to grab the refrigerator shelves to right herself. Her eyes had gone black now, confirming what Adrian already knew.

"Look. She's ..."

"I know. I see it. Come on."

They weren't going to get an actual reprieve. Jacqui wasn't defeated, just knocked down. She was already scrambling up, her mouth foaming blood. Adrian and Ray rushed through the door into the foyer.

Where others were waiting.

Six of them.

Three were people Adrian would once-upon-a-time have named among his closest friends: Lee Barnes, Elaine Price, and Harrison Kim. They now wore hard stares, poised to rumble, some with weapons — though blessedly none as deadly as Jacqui's Rollard. Jacqui was a bit of a dramatist, as displayed in her wardrobe, so while the other Legions were retiring their gear, she seemed to have kept hers as an affect. Knowing Jacqui, she probably used the Rollard like a gentleman's cane.

The weapons the others held were body-worn or improvised. Harrison, of course, held a blade. A woman Adrian didn't know had a baseball bat. Lee's weapon should have been funny, but wasn't. It was a toilet plunger, or once had been. He'd snapped off the rubber end, leaving sheared wood like a spear.

"Um ..." Ray said. They'd stopped, now frozen in a living diorama. Jacqui was back in line behind them, her attack paused now that so many others had arrived. There were arrivals behind her as well — folks who had slid down the fire pole or simply taken the kitchen stairs. They were in shadows or obscured by the intervening wall, so Adrian couldn't tell who they were.

"Oh, hey guys!" Ray said, trying in vain to sound cool and casual.

"Don't," Adrian told him.

It was clear what this was. The brigadehouse should have

been on a skeleton crew. He'd been surprised to hear more than one or two people upstairs to begin with. Despite there being no real need for Legions or Stitchers, almost everyone who had ever been here was *still* here, and that meant trouble.

Half of these people weren't even employed by the riftfare department anymore. Abid Sher had supposedly quit Stitching to become a realtor. They could only be here now for one reason: They were a standing guard, at the station specifically to stop the Porters if they returned.

They could no longer go back to Dixon's office or return to their homes. If the king had seen fit to stake out the brigade-house, it meant Adrian, Ray, and anyone who sided with them was officially *persona non grata* in the other plane.

All pretense was gone; they were clear and present enemies now. God knew what that might mean about the king and his knowledge of the situation ... or maybe it wasn't *God* at all.

Ray, Adrian knew, was considering turning on the charm. These had been his buddies for longer than they'd been Adrian's. Technically — if the Legions and Stitchers around them were in their right mind — they should *still* be Ray's buddies. But they were infected, clear as the bloody gash on Jacqui's face.

"*Harrison. Bud.* Remember when we went through Hell together? Literally?"

Harrison flicked his knife.

The circle marched toward them, closing.

"Okay." Ray raised his hands. "You got us. We surrender. You're on the other side now. I get it. You do you."

Jacqui had finally freed her Rollard from the jamb. She inched toward the head of the rear contingent and said to the others, "Let me do it."

"Hey. Hey. Come on. Your boss almost recruited me last year. He specifically wanted both of us for the other team. I—"

"Stop talking," Jacqui said.

Ray shut his mouth.

She raised the Rollard like a battle axe. It was all show, nothing a self-respecting Legion should do with a precision-trained weapon.

But before she could swing, several piercing alarms started screaming in unison, coming from the lockers in the garage. Adrian recognized them at once — he and Ray had heard those same alarms before.

They were coming from the suits. The rebreathers. Zen Element alarms — the same ones that had screeched like banshees on the day of the sundering, when the air filled to toxic levels with spilled Element.

Zen. Fickle stuff. Unrefined, it was dodgy at best. Refined, it was like plutonium: able to do tremendous things, but deadly when you got too close. Zen treatments had cured their mother's cancer and healed Adrian's last-year's burn, and the whole reason they'd come was for a way to inject people with Frog — a Zen-based mutagen that would, if they were lucky, clear their brains and let them see.

But in close quarters? With doors shut, like all but the front door was right now?

Suits had alarms to warn people when too much was around, in the wrong form, breathable like poison.

There was a SLAMMING sound. Adrian registered it as the shutting of the front door — the only way out, the only vent for all this toxin in the air. Now they would smother in it. He caught a flash of someone outside: their murderer, it seemed: someone small, with hair that belled out at the bottom. A woman, with an above-the-neck silhouette that looked like a triangle.

Almost immediately, Adrian felt himself going faint. The leak in the stitching rigs must be enormous. The sundering's

Zen had been unrefined, but even rig Zen would take a lot to black him out this fast.

Jacqui felt it, too. What had once been a confident pre-swing became hesitation. Then the Rollard fell from her hands — fallen, not intentionally dropped. Her knees buckled along with Adrian's and Ray's. Infected or not, their would-be killers were still human, and every one of them would die right here.

Everything went still. A bluish haze lit the air, like a concert fog machine making light visible. It was the Zen above him. His eyes were half-open, his consciousness barely there. He couldn't move. Nobody could. He could only lay on his back in paralysis, watching as the small woman who'd closed them in reopened the door and began walking through felled bodies like a scavenger among the dead.

She stood above Adrian. His eyes were bleary. He could still only see her as a silhouette, with an up-pointing triangle for a head. Only the upper half of her face was visible. The lower half was covered with the mask of a rebreather.

"Dumb fucking move." Through the mask, her voice came out like Darth Vader's.

Adrian tried to answer the insult, but he felt very tired.

Then he saw only darkness.

15

NOT THE FROG

He woke as a prisoner, tied to a bed.

Except, no, he wasn't tied. So he was a prisoner *laying* on a bed? That didn't make sense.

Someone was standing over him. This one didn't have triangle-head, but instead a head of long, heavy hair like ropes. And this one, this jailer, was coming closer and closer. As if to whisper a taunt before dying.

She kissed him instead.

By the time the woman pulled away, Adrian's foggy mind had come most of the way around. He'd begun confused, kissed by an unknown. He'd ended the kiss as a willing partici-pant: no idea why Laurel was here, but happy she was.

"You saved us. Somehow."

"Yeah," said someone else. "Because *that* makes sense."

The voice was hard: no bullshit. The woman it came from was small and lean. She had the build of an acrobatic warrior. The kind everyone underestimates until it's too late.

"Dee?"

"In the flesh."

"Are you …?" Then, realizing he was asking a biased source, Adrian sat up on his elbows and said it to Laurel instead: "Is she …?"

"Oh, fuck off, Adrian." Dee sighed like it was her purpose in life. "Maybe I should have let them kill you."

"She's not infected," Laurel said.

"You're sure?"

"Are you dead?" Dee asked.

"I'm sure," Laurel answered. "The EEG of infected people shows an interference pattern, as if one set of brain waves is cancelling out another. Dee's waves are normal."

"You did an EEG?"

"I did an EEG." Dee took a large bite from an apple and then continued around her food. "You're welcome."

"How do you know what EEGs look like for infected people?"

Laurel's eyes flicked toward the door of the bedroom he now realized he was in: not a prison after all. "I'll tell you later."

Dee came closer, now right in front of Adrian and still holding her apple. "*I'll* tell you now. When we dragged you two idiots out of the station house, I made the executive decision that we should take an experiment with us, too."

"What?"

"It's not a what. It's a who." Dee eyed the door as well. "Harrison is tied up in the living room. I couldn't see anything in his brain waves, but Laurel did."

She nodded. "It's a data set of one person, but at least it's something. If Harrison is any indication, it's like Dee said. The virus leaves a fingerprint even when Harrison seems to be acting like his old self. The EEG can tell the king is still in there, waiting to give him orders. Until something says otherwise, I guess we'll have to trust that people without the same EEG fingerprint are clean."

"Where are we?"

"Someone's house. Don't worry, they're not coming back. They seem to have shot each other in the back yard."

"We can't go home. *Any* of our homes. Or the office. Or—"

"—or the brigade house? Jesus, Ade, keep up. You don't think I know they've targeted you after embedding with them for the past two days?"

"Embedding?" Adrian repeated. Then something else occurred to him. "You're not wearing the sunglasses." He looked around the room. Nobody was wearing sunglasses, Adrian included.

"Relax," Laurel said. "Yours got knocked off when you were fighting. It made me think we need something more secure, so I pulled the little chip out of the temple arms and put an adhesive on the back. Feel behind your ear. You're wearing a pair right now."

Adrian wondered how long he'd been out. Decisions seemed to have been made. Actions seemed to have been taken while he was away.

"Where's Ray?"

"Right here." The bathroom door opened and Ray emerged, his hair a mess. He looked sleepy and beaten as well. The thought of battle reminded Adrian of the spot where Jacqui had speared him with her heel. It hurt, but not as much as it should. He rolled and saw why: someone had stuck a medical Zen patch over the wound.

Zen. Dee had used Zen against them.

Laurel, seeing the confusion in his eyes, sat on the bed next to Adrian. "Lay back and rest, and I'll catch you up."

· · ·

Dee explained that around 48 hours ago, Captain Kaur had called and told her to take a shift at the brigade house. She asked why, but he would only tell her it was a hush-hush sort of thing and he'd explain later. She asked if he was working with the brigades again, seeing as he'd been laid off, and he promised to explain that later, too. But she found all of her old brigade mates and no Kaur upon arrival.

"They were acting really fucking weird. It was like they didn't even remember who Kaur was. I get a feel for people pretty quick. You guys know that."

Ray and Adrian nodded. Dee's ability to read people was usually annoying because she often refused to work with folks others saw as perfectly fine, but this time her person-sense seemed to have saved her neck in a way she'd yet to explain. She'd gone undercover, basically, living for two days among Legions and Stitchers who acted normal most times but clearly weren't. It took the tingling of Dee Sense to navigate something like that. Since she'd saved their asses, Adrian for one was glad she had it.

Dee had deduced then a lot of what Ray, Adrian, Laurel, and Dixon would realize a day and a half later. The idea of a "mind-control epidemic" seemed outlandish, but it was the only way to explain what she was seeing. Her old friends were just a little … *off*. Sometimes they were *very* off. When she saw the first flash of black eyes, she took it as fact rather than trying to convince herself she hadn't seen it. Someone as vibes-centric as Dee was required to reach a crazy conclusion quickly, simply because it was the only explanation fitting the evidence. Laurel, the scientist, had accepted the same sorts of evidence more slowly.

"I had to pretend to be one of them. I could just tell. I can't even tell you why. It was just in little things they said. The way they chose to phrase things. Even when they were shooting pool, doing all the old-normal Brigade One stuff, it felt like they were Bizarro versions of themselves. So, and this is just a for-instance, I heard Lee describe something as 'unacceptable.'"

"Okay."

"Lee doesn't say 'unacceptable.'"

"Everyone says 'unacceptable.'"

"I'm telling you," Dee insisted, "the way he said it, the sentence and context and tone of voice, that's not what Lee sounds like. Lee would say 'bad' instead. Or he'd say it's 'not right.' 'Unacceptable' is something rich people say when there aren't enough forks at the table setting."

"Dee, that's ..."

She shook her head. "It's not a Lee word. You don't have to agree, but it's true. It was stuff like that that told me something was up, and they weren't what they seemed to be. All sorts of little details. The way Elaine wore her hair the second day. Daniel started doing this thing where he constantly ran his hand over his face, like checking to see if he had stubble. It all added up to *something's-wrong-here*. I can't tell you how I knew they wouldn't let me leave, but after seeing what they tried to do to you, I figure that's what they would have done if they knew I wasn't like them. So I stayed and listened. It became clear after a while that we were there to intercept *you*."

"Me?" said Ray.

"Both of you. I hoped you were smart enough not to come to the brigade house, but—"

"We needed the bear gun."

"Oh, I know. We'll *get* to that," Dee said, stern as if she'd hassled them about this repeatedly in the past. "Laurel told me you knew more for-sure about what's going on in Fortune, and yet your dumb asses came right to one of the places everyone expects you semi-matching set of idiots to be."

"We ..." Adrian started to say, but Ray had already said why they were there, and clearly Dee didn't think the tranquilizer gun was reason enough.

She told them about the preparations she'd made, just in case. Brennan's research was still on Kaur's hard drive, and it included the exact parts-per-million concentration of Zen Element in an environment that was both toxic and deadly. She'd split the difference, knowing that Zen toxicity at high enough doses caused unconsciousness, and pre-opened stitch canisters in preparation for opening them all the way if needed.

Dee didn't want to hurt her brigade mates, since "the old them" seemed to still be inside Hell's programming. She just needed a way to get herself, Ray, and Adrian all out. It'd been a shot in the dark — as likely to kill or merely alarm them as it was to knock everyone out — but she'd nailed it just the same.

"Dee," said Adrian. "Can you see the wall around the city?"

"Of course I can see it."

"I'm not talking about the Rampart."

"Of course you're not talking about the Rampart."

"So you can see it? The new wall?"

"Am I stuttering? Yes. I get why you're asking. Even if Laurel hadn't told me your theory, I knew it already. Mother-fuckers walking around on the streets like nothing happened, or in the common room acting like it was just another day on the job, talking about things they were going to do twenty miles up the road after work. But your theory's wrong. That 'Frog' stuff they gave us isn't the reason your heads stayed normal. It's not why you think things are weird in Fortune while nobody else does. You figure out why I'm saying that yet, or should I draw a map?"

"Shit. Harrison was given Frog," Adrian said, realizing.

"Lee too." Dee nodded. "And me, of course, but I'm okay so

I don't count. So you get it, right? Even if your plan to dart people one by one to 'wake them up' made a goddamn bit of sense—"

"It was the best we could come up with," Ray.

"The best you could come up with," Dee replied, sharp and sarcastic. "Walking around town with a goddamn game gun, tranq'ing people one at a time. *That* was the best you could come up with?"

"Well ..."

"Doesn't matter. It's not Frog keeping you sane. Or me. Harrison and Lee got it, and they're crazy as everyone else. Think all's well. No wall out there. Nothing to see here; move along."

"So what is it?"

Laurel stepped in. Meditation was her happy place. Because Adrian spent so much time with her, he'd picked up the habit. Ray was a far less meditative sort, but he, too, had once been under her spell. Everyone knew Dee was into it. She'd once taken two weeks off for a retreat at an ashram in the Sonoran desert.

"Mindfulness. I think it might be as simple as that. Mindfulness is simply being aware of what's happening while it's happening. But most people aren't remotely mindful. They're on autopilot most of the time — with their heads in the future, worried about the future or their to-do list, or in the past, dwelling on mistakes and regrets. Even if people manage to be in the present, they're usually preoccupied with what other people think of them, not mindfully considering how things actually are."

And it made sense. It really did. Laurel hooked herself up to the EEG and showed them how her brain waves changed when she focused on the present and stayed mindful. It was a flatter brain profile, less a match to the interference caused by the virus.

But common sense, not EEG data, made Laurel and Dee think their theory was right. Propaganda only changes minds if it's not thought about too much, and is instead simply accepted as true. The virus — that voice of the king inside people's heads, telling them what's right and wrong and what's best to do — was just one more form of propaganda.

"Mindful people will get this last," Laurel said. "They might feel it coming at them, but it'll strike them like a bad idea. Kind of like you might see an ad for fast food and want to eat some, but then think twice and decide it's better for your health if you don't. It won't last forever — not as the kernel's internal resistance dies off — but for now it's probably our best defense."

Ray looked unsure.

"What?"

He shrugged. "What about you, Dixon? You don't strike me as a 'meditation and mindfulness' sort of guy."

Dixon sighed before responding, somehow embarrassed by the forthcoming mar to his hard-charging brand. "Some of the same thinking came out of our S&C research, especially after we moved to the base and started working with Patel's people. We all ..." Another sigh. "... trained in it."

Adrian, feeling better, stood. His injured calf twitched, but he found it was well enough to bear his weight. "We can't shoot people with darts to make them be mindful, so there goes that."

"I have some thoughts. They're ... unconventional."

"What thoughts?" he asked Laurel.

"Let me unpack it a bit more before I commit. I just keep thinking the king needs the mind in a certain state in order to change what it sees."

"Are you talking about reversing the mind control? Like ... curing Harrison?"

Laurel shook her head. "I want to try, but my gut says no. Once it has you, it has you. We all know how hard it can be to dissuade someone of an opinion they've decided to stand behind, and this works like that. I'm talking more about removing the blinders. Even if we can't get the king out of Harrison's head, we might be able to make him see the world for what it is. Make him see the wall and the strange things going on. But what we really need is a way to do that *en masse*. That's what I didn't like about shooting people with darts. It was one-at-a-time. We need everyone seeing the truth at once. A way to mass-remove everyone's blinders. Snap them out of it."

"How? Can we put something into the air? Or into the water? Or ... I don't know ... blow up a broadcast tower to shut it all down like in that John Carpenter movie?"

"What movie?"

"Let Laurel do her thing and forget about it for now," Dee said, and right there Adrian understood that she knew the plan that Laurel didn't want to tell anyone else yet — presumably because it was "unconventional," which meant that practical-minded Laurel was embarrassed by her strategy. "We need to focus more on the *other* major objective."

"What other objective?"

"Getting out of this box they've put us in, or at least sending word to the people outside it," Dee said. "But I guess the wall goes down far into the ground and I hear there's a clear cap up there, so it's not like we could ever get over it. I listened closely at the brigade house, but I still can't figure out a way. But we *need* a way, you guys. All the meditation in the world won't help when the rest of Fortune is taken over by this 'virus.'"

They were silent for a while.

Until Dixon spoke. "I know a way out."

"How?"

"We'll have to go through a rift. Our plane doesn't map exactly to theirs. *You* figured that out last year. Poke around long enough inside a rift and you're bound to find something on their end that's outside the city wall."

"I thought of that too," said Laurel. "But the city alarms. The monitoring systems. It's not like the old days, where rifts could open willy-nilly. Even if we *had* the equipment and supplies to open a rift, which we very much don't, any effort would be noticed. Even if humans here don't see it, I'll bet the king will."

"Right," said Dixon. "So we have to go through a rift that's already open."

"Except that there aren't any rifts already ..." Adrian saw the look in Dixon's eyes. "No way."

"The Magnitude 35 rift," Dixon confirmed with a nod. "At Patel's Army base."

<h1 style="text-align:center">16
NIGHT</h1>

Adrian hovered over Dee's shoulder. It was something like three in the morning and he couldn't sleep. She was sitting in front of the former owners' home computer in the home office, watching what looked like a static camera somewhere in stark — almost ghostlike — black and white.

"What's this?" He thought too late that his words might scare her. He'd approached quietly in deference to the late hour, thinking only now that it might amount to sneaking up in the dark. But Dee only turned her head, nodded as if to say, *Yeah, I'm secretly as much a mess as you,* and then turned back.

"You don't recognize it? Pretend the lights are on."

He assumed she meant onscreen. There was a light on back in the small home's kitchen, but turning on house lights wouldn't suddenly give him new information about what she was watching.

"Is that the common room? At the brigade house?"

Dee's curly head bobbed. "There was an IP camera in one

of the cupboards. Found it when I was there the first night and couldn't sleep any better than I can now. The kind of novelty camera people buy to watch their pets while they're away. It looks like a little bubble gum machine with a ring of infrared LEDs around it.

"Infrared," Adrian said. "Wait. So they can't see?"

It changed everything. It made the already-creepy black and white a whole lot creepier. Now that a bit of mental gymnastics had let Adrian recognize the view for what it was, he'd adjusted and begun understanding what he was seeing. The wedge shape to one side, splash-lit with infrared light enough that it looked like metal reflecting the sun, was the close corner of the pool table. The light gray rectangle at the back was the open second-floor window to the street, where there should have been a streetlight but the one there had burned out months ago and nobody had fixed it.

The lay of the land made sense to Adrian. And so had the people in the scene. Dee's plan to flood the station with Zen Element seemed to have worked, because the people were ones he knew, alive and well once they woke back up: Daniel, Elaine, Lee — even Jacqui with infrared-black blood running uncleaned from her mouth and into her accentuated cleavage.

Only now was it dawning on him that the scene was live — all of them awake at 3am just like him and Dee. Only now that she'd explained the infrared did the casual scene give him the shivers.

The milling about casually, the conversation between Lee and Elaine, and the quiet way a Stitcher named Jason Chase was sitting on the couch, his face toward the TV — all those things were happening in near-pitch darkness.

"Nope. The last of the moon went while I was there. When I was awake with them, I couldn't see a thing with that streetlight busted. Only the thing is, I didn't *know* I was awake with them. I could hear someone moving around, but I thought it was someone headed to the bathroom or looking for something." Dee shook her head. "But no. *This* was going on."

She turned in her seat. Adrian lowered himself into a second desk chair, settling in beside her.

"It's gotten strange, Adrian. Since you left, yeah. Since you went to Hell and back and let the dreadnought free, of course. But—"

"Look, Dee, there's more to it than you think. I wasn't trying to—"

Dee held up a silent hand. In the dim, he knew what it meant: *I don't hate you. I don't think you're a traitor.* He assumed Laurel had explained her theories to Dee while he'd been unconscious. Or, just as likely, living for two nights in the undead scene onscreen now had been enough to change her mind — to tell her that Adrian Porter might be the most hated man in Fortune, but that hatred came from the perspective of a crumbling "normal."

"But, you know I'm an intuitive person."

"Intuitive enough to tell when 'unacceptable' is a strange thing to say."

The joke — a callback to earlier — didn't land in all this darkness.

But Dee seemed to understand his intention, and took it in kind. "I'm intuitive enough that I think I can tell you exactly when this began. When the first things started to get strange. When it was a lot more subtle kind of 'strange' than this." At *this*, she tilted her head toward the onscreen screen.

Adrian almost didn't want to ask. He almost didn't want to know how much time they had left. It was quiet. If not for the strange nocturnal behavior the camera was catching and the memory of the day, it would probably be peaceful. Dixon had conked out early. Harrison had spent the afternoon arguing that he wasn't affected at all, that they should just let him go, and had eventually grown agitated enough that Laurel had used some of the dart gun's sedative after all, to shut him up. She was in the master bedroom, snoring loudly enough that Adrian had had a dream about earthmoving equipment. They could hear her from here, sawing away.

"Laurel told me she thinks it'll take six days."

Adrian nodded.

"I don't know shit about this kind of thing, but you know what? I agree. The first time I felt anything weird was Wednesday afternoon. I was shopping. I had a can of green beans, and I was looking at the label to see how much sodium it had. You've gotta keep an eye out. When they can't add sugar to things, they like to jam-pack it with salt."

Adrian smiled.

"Anyway, there's this guy farther down the aisle, and he's doing exactly the same thing with a can of mandarin oranges, only I'm guessing sugar in oranges, not salt. I didn't think anything of it, but then I got to the end of my list and realized I hadn't gotten a bag of dried lentils. I'm doing this thing with soup recently. I walked back past that same aisle, and the guy is still there. It must have been ten minutes later, and he hadn't moved."

"Maybe he's a slow reader."

"Then I got to the checkout, and there was something off about the checker. She looked into my eyes when I got in line and took way too long to look away. When she was scanning my stuff, she did it like this."

Dee pantomimed. Her arm, as she pretended to check out an invisible customer, was slow and metronomic. "When I was all finished, she gave me my receipt. And I can't tell you what was strange about that part, but trust me, it was. She gave me this tiny, barely-there nod. Like she was acknowledging me in a fraternal sort of way. As if there was an understanding between us, almost like a private joke."

"You think that's when it started?"

"It's when I noticed. But then I thought back and remembered stuff that was a lot more subtle the day before. My neighbor Sam painstakingly straightening his garden edging. Dude barely mows his lawn. Clara Whitney walking hand-in-hand with her little boy down the sidewalk, but when the kid turned to look at something, Clara not even noticing, just pulling him on."

"Tuesday was four days ago." He had to say it aloud just to get it out, wanting to disbelieve.

"Four days yesterday," Dee corrected. "It's technically Monday now."

Adrian felt cold. If she was right, they had maybe 36 hours before the mindful stragglers of Fortune succumbed and the king had his prize. 36 hours until the hour when future historians, if there still were any, would say the old world truly ended.

"We still listened to all the police calls while I was at the station just like we used to. Nobody responded to any of them — not even Elaine, who's got EMT training and is supposed to be a first responder. But there's a lot of shit going on out there, Adrian. A lot of shit."

"What kind of shit?"

"Fires. Shootings. Stuff blowing up. I think he's taking out infrastructure. Laurel says cell phones probably can't reach outside our bubble, so the only reason towers would be taken out is so the few normal people left in the city can't call each other. There was something at the dam authority the other day. I think maybe they're putting something in the water. The power grid's changing somehow, too. Lights seem to still be on everywhere, but not everything inside the Rampart is served by Fortune Edison. A lot of the east side still draws power from the Baylorville co-op, so you'd think they'd be cut off by the wall, right? But no. And you wanna hear something weird?"

No. The answer was no. Adrian had heard enough.

Dee held up her cell phone. "My phone uses one of those inductive charging pads. I just set my phone on top of it and it juices wirelessly. I forgot my charging pad at home, though. But look."

She tapped her screen to wake it, then pointed to the upper right corner. An icon showed the phone as charging.

"Been doing that since Saturday. But, okay, the phone's meant to charge that way, so I can imagine some reason it'd be charging now even without the pad. But then look at this."

There was a printer beside the computer. She reached under the desk and unplugged it. Then she pressed its power button, and the thing coughed to life. She look at Adrian with perplexity and shook her head. "Why?"

"I guess that's what we're supposed to find out," Adrian replied.

She kept looking at him. Dee was one of the most hard-charging, unshakable people he'd ever known, but as she kept matching him eye to eye — as they watched each other, weighing out the meaningful silence — he saw fear in her for the first time.

"I'm scared, Adrian. I'm scared because even with Laurel's theory, I still don't know what's happening. I'm scared because I feel like the walls are closing in and I don't know who to trust. Harrison is godfather to my nephew, and yet I'm positive if I untied him, he'd cut my throat with a knife from the butcher block. But what scares me most is that I'm starting not to trust *myself*. I'll pick something up with my right hand and say, 'Wait. I'm left-handed. Would I normally pick something up with my right? Was the right hand just closer to what I wanted, and *that's* why I used it?' Or I'll look in the mirror, and it's like ..."

Dee paused, looking for words. "It's like my own face is a mask. Like I can see someone else behind it, looking back out at me." She faced Adrian with an ill-fitting smile on her face. "But that's crazy, right?"

It wasn't crazy at all. Dee had just described something Adrian had felt a time or two now himself, rationalizing it away as the hangover from a terrible day.

Dee was still watching Adrian. Waiting, with the shamelessness of a child, for someone else to be brave for once, and tell her it was all going to be okay.

"You know ... Ray was always just like our father. They're both 'act first, think later' kinds of guys. That was always their way of being in control: They just always ... *stayed in control.* When they *didn't* have control, they faked it. I'll never forget when our grandmother was sick, near the end of her life. She was only seventy. It seemed unfair. We were all upset, and so at one point Dad stood up at the dinner table and told us all, 'Don't worry. I'll take care of it.'"

Dee laughed, but kindly.

"I wasn't anything like our father. That's probably why Ray and I fight so much, but it's also why, once we get over ourselves, we make such a good team. I was more like Mom. You know, it's funny: I never really thought about this, but she was never worried about the cancer — not even before there was a chance they'd end up curing it. Scared to die, sure, but not as much as you might think. Sad to leave us, to not see our futures? *That* was most of what bothered her."

He pushed on, feeling a well of emotion he didn't want to let overwhelm him.

"But Mom was never worried. Not really. 'Worry' is what

you do when you predict the future, but only a worse future. What the doctors said was going to happen with her was terrible, but Mom didn't fret it. Instead, she kept insisting on staying in the moment, always saying, 'Everything will work out exactly as it's supposed to.' When Ray rolled his eyes, she'd get mad. She had a whole list of things she'd been worried about in the past, but even the ones that turned out bad changed things for the better because they'd put her on a new, better path. So when Ray rolled his eyes, she'd say: 'Don't laugh. Everything's always worked out in the past. So it always will in the future.'"

"And you're like that. Like your mother."

He nodded. "I wish I was as strong as her. But yes, I try to be."

Dee sat more upright, facing him earnestly. "You don't think you're strong?"

"I think Ray has always been stronger."

"And yet you went through literal Hell for Laurel."

"That was different."

"*And* you're a Stitcher. You fight creatures for a living."

"I used to."

"And now you don't. Because you were okay with everyone hating you as long as you did what you felt was right."

He laughed. "Look how well that worked out."

"Yes. Look how well it worked out. Here you are." Dee pointed at her screen, full of brainwashed zombies that were once his coworkers and friends. "And there *they* are. It's almost like everything worked out exactly the way it was supposed to."

Adrian thought about that. He'd felt like a sack of shit since returning, and over the past few days he'd felt like that same sack of shit had been hung from rafters and used by a boxer for punching practice. Still, the truth was that he really *was* like his mother and always had been. His measured and trusting approach — even when Ray thought it was naive — was the reason the first sundering hadn't turned out nearly as apocalyptic as it otherwise might have. Sometimes force was the wrong answer. Sometimes, allowing yourself to be defeated was the brave way out.

Adrian really did believe that all things worked out in the end, or at least tried very hard to. He'd heard his mother's list of unfortunate events that revealed blazing silver linings, and he'd been around for most of them, seeing them just the same as her. In Mom's world, the evidence proved her belief true. So could Adrian look at the same evidence? Could Adrian, through sheer force of will, find a way to make it true even now?

What's gone wrong? he asked himself.

They were trapped, cut off, and had maybe a day and a half before the timer on humanity's last real chance at surviving ran dry. But in addition to the "wrong" of it, did those bad things create any opportunities? Was there anything that might be true now *because* of those terrible events that wouldn't be true otherwise — a truth they could turn to their advantage?

At first there was nothing. But then he had an idea Mom would say proved there were two sides to coin.

"To end this, we have to get outside the city before everyone's infected, but there *is* no way out of the city except for what Dixon said: going through the big rift at the Army base."

Dee nodded.

"But the problem is, we'll never get into the base. It's too well guarded."

She nodded again, seeming to suspect Adrian was building up to something. "Most of the city is under the king's control by now. We'll be caught the second we get close."

Adrian looked toward the door leading into the kitchen,

thinking about not worrying and trusting. He could hear Harrison in the kitchen, snoring lightly through his tranquilized haze.

"I wonder what would happen, if when we got to the base, we'd been *caught already?*"

17

THE PRISONER

"Harrison."

His eyes came open. It was morning now. The last half of Harrison's sleep had been drugless and more or less natural. They'd moved him to the couch, his wrists and legs bound. Dixon had added elaborate rope work to keep him in place.

"Adrian?" Harrison said, fighting through drowsiness.

"Yeah. How are you feeling?"

"Better."

"Better than what?"

His face twisted. He was having a hard time finding the words to describe what he felt. The way Laurel described the virus, it was like having a second person in your head. Funnily enough, the "devil whispering in your ear" metaphor seemed spot-on. But that also meant that it wasn't one hundred percent about control, and was instead more like hearing a very convincing argument that victims ended up agreeing with. It meant that he was really still Harrison ... but thanks to the voice inside, he was something else as well.

"I remember being really mad. I ..."

"But you don't remember why?"

Harrison shook his head. "That's what's weird. I remember *exactly* why. It just doesn't make sense."

"The thing you thought doesn't make sense?"

"It doesn't make sense that I'd get mad about it. Why the hell was I so *mad?* Hell, Adrian — I wanted to knock you out. All of you."

Adrian could have asked more, but Laurel's eyes, as she watched unseen from the kitchen, told him to keep things moving.

"The rest of us need to leave, Harrison. We can't stay in this house. But there's an issue with leaving. You remember how you were last night. You remember how bad it was, right? How *hard* you tried to knock us out?"

He was being kind and Harrison seemed to know it.

"We had to sedate you," Adrian said.

"Probably a good move. Was I ...?" Adrian felt bad for Harrison. He seemed so honestly perplexed, looking for a way to justify the murders he'd almost done. "Was I *drunk?* Did someone serve me a drink spiked with PCP or something?"

"I don't know why it happened," Adrian lied. "But that's why you're tied up. You get that, right? You understand?"

Mortified and confused, Harrison nodded. He was a proud man. It would take an Earth's-weight of remorse to humble him like this.

"We need to leave, and we won't be back. That leaves us with a problem, and maybe you could tell me what you think is the best way to solve it."

Happy to have a chance to repent, Harrison nodded again and sat up as well as his bindings would allow.

"I don't want to leave you tied up here without us. Dixon's great with knots. I don't think you can wiggle free no matter how much time you have, and the people who live in this house …" Adrian hesitated, knowing the city felt normal to Harrison. "Well, let's just say I doubt they're coming back to untie you. I don't want you to starve, but if *we* untie you …"

"I'll be okay. I promise. It's cool. I'm myself again."

"Then who were you yesterday?"

Adrian knew the answer, but it seemed Harrison didn't. The king's ideas supposedly felt to subjects like ideas of their own. Laurel said there should be no sense of invasion, or being under anyone else's control. That meant Adrian was forcing Harrison to confront a tricky dilemma, knowing he had no way to take it literally.

To people in Harrison's position right now, everything in the city of Fortune was A-OK. Everything was as it had always been. There was no crisis, no wall, no cutting-off of communications or ways to leave. To Harrison, there'd been no bombings, fires, or shootings — not even anyone acting strange. Except for Adrian and Ray, of course. The Porters were traitors.

When Harrison didn't respond, Adrian took it as him agreeing that the dilemma was a rough one. "So you see the problem. I can't trust you not to hurt us. Do *you* trust yourself not to hurt us?"

Harrison almost said *Yes, of course,* but then his face relaxed and he fell back in defeat. He remembered what happened, but the king was gone from his mind now. "You could hold a gun on me."

"What if you attack the person right in front of you, though? Not the one with the weapon, but the one setting you free? You weren't in a hostage-taking mood yesterday. It was more frenzied than that."

"Hold the gun *close*," Harrison suggested.

"If we do that, I'd have to shoot you if something goes wrong, I don't want to shoot you."

"If I come at you, *please* shoot me."

Adrian looked at Laurel. From the doorway, she gave him a subtle nod. Her go-ahead to tell Harrison a bit of the fiction they'd already agreed on.

"I didn't want to freak you out, but the truth is I actually *do* have some idea what's wrong with you. There's ... some sort of a disease in Fortune. It makes people rage."

He watched Harrison's face, unsure if he'd buy this line of totally-invented horseshit. Laurel had said he would, and he seemed to be ... but maybe only because his behavior last night was that inexplicable.

"If you were a psycho, maybe I could justify shooting you if I had to. But that's not the case. You're *not* a psycho, Harrison. At least not permanently. Laurel thinks this disease passes, and if that's true, you might be back to normal tomorrow. Or the next day. I can't risk killing you over something temporary. We used to be friends, Harrison. Still are, in my book."

Harrison seemed to think. Adrian, watching, wished he would reach the conclusion they were leading him to reach faster.

Then his eyes lit up. "Give me a knife before you go."

"A knife?"

"Sure! That way I can cut the ropes, but it'll take me a while to get through them. You'll be gone by the time I'm free."

Laurel moved closer, letting herself be seen now that Harrison had "come up with" their target idea. Adrian looked at her, and she nodded her approval.

"Where's his knife?" Adrian asked.

Laurel reached into her pocket. Harrison's blade was one of those butterfly jobs, like ninjas use. She pretended to hesitate, then handed it to Adrian.

He unfolded the blade, but paused before giving it to Harrison. This next part was the riskiest, but he didn't want to end up stabbed to death.

"I'm not a traitor, Harrison," he said, still withholding the knife. "Before we go, I want you to know that."

"Of course. Of course." Adrian could see the change starting to happen deep in Harrison's eyes: an eagerness to hold the blade. They hadn't put thought-blocking chips behind his ears like the rest of them wore, and that meant the king was hearing what Harrison heard. The king was rising inside him again now, telling Harrison exactly what he should do once the blade was in his hand.

Adrian continued, talking less to Harrison and more to the king inside him. "Don't just say 'Of course.' I mean it."

"I know. I believe you."

"The king told me and Ray that he wanted equilibrium. He wanted peace. When he changed his mind, I was as surprised as anyone. I *did* set him free. I *did* know there'd be bad stuff to follow — something like the sundering, even. But I only did it because the alternative was worse."

Harrison was growing impatient. Greedy. The king's will was present in him now, barely concealed. Adrian looked at his face, knowing he was speaking to the Devil.

"But I haven't told anyone why I'm *still* sorry, despite all that. Something about my family's energy is inside the rifts. That energy is like a key to a lock — something the other plane needs in order to do what it wants. The fact that Ray and I were 'keys' meant the dreadnought had to keep us alive. He *needed* us, and he needed Laurel's mind. That meant he was never going to kill us. I went into that bargain knowing I'd be safe, Harrison, and *that's* why I'm sorry. I knew I could be weak, because in the end, he needed us all."

Adrian stopped then, watching the king in Harrison's eager

eyes. He had no way of knowing if his message had been received. What he'd said had been true once: the king *did* need them alive. That might have changed, given the multiple times his new soldiers had tried to kill them ... but hopefully a reminder, now, could keep them alive a little bit longer.

His mother's voice spoke inside Adrian's head: *Don't worry. Have faith. Everything always works out the way it's supposed to.*

It was a sentiment Ray would never agree with, which was why Ray, on this particular gamble, had been placed on a need-to-know basis.

"It's okay. Really. I forgive you, man."

Was that Harrison speaking? Had the king heard him? Had he understood? There was no way to be sure.

Adrian put the knife in Harrison's hand. What came next happened in a flash.

Harrison gripped the handle, flipped it around with one bound hand, then wrenched upward through the outermost wrap of his bindings. The rope was not particularly thick, and everyone knew Harrison kept his knife so sharp that the cutting edge was almost invisible. There was barely a snag as Harrison's practiced hands ripped up and across in unison.

With one hand free, Harrison reached up and grabbed Adrian by the collar. Adrian, who'd known something like this was coming, resisted the impulse to wrench away. Harrison swiped through his right hand's ties, then raised the blade to Adrian's throat once both were free.

Adrian let himself flinch, trying to move away from the couch, but Harrison held fast, pressing the flat edge of the blade against his throat, knowing the sharp edge might flinch and start opening arteries. That was a good sign. If Harrison had meant to kill them, he would have done it already. Adrian's reminder, to the king not to kill them, had been received.

"You," Harrison said to Laurel. "Untie my feet."

With Adrian held hostage, Laurel obeyed. It seemed a further good sign that Harrison didn't slash at her. He must still find value in their lives. The only one he might have killed was Dixon — but as the second part of this plan, Dixon was already gone.

Ray, hearing the commotion, ran into the room. He held a crowbar he'd found somewhere, but when Harrison saw it he hugged Adrian closer, using him as a shield.

Harrison stood carefully, keeping Adrian hostage. Ray's crowbar made little circles like a batter preparing to swing, but he didn't advance.

"We're leaving," Harrison said, backing toward the door and dragging Adrian with him. His eyes had gone black. He wasn't really Harrison anymore.

Adrian made himself walk, keeping up with his abductor. If his feet dragged, the knife might cut. Harrison had him too tightly, though. His windpipe was constricted, lessening his oxygen and making dark spots swim before his eyes. What would happen if he lost consciousness? How would Harrison keep from opening his throat then?

But something was strange, as Harrison backed Adrian toward the door. Instead of keeping eyes on Harrison and Adrian, Laurel and Ray kept glancing at the windows.

Adrian understood: He wasn't seeing black spots because he was about to pass out. He was seeing black spots, outside the windows.

Along with a sound, like heavy leather fluttering. Enormous bats, perhaps, with canvas for wings. A low, undulating hiss warbled beneath it. He heard small ticking noises on the stoop of the door to which they were headed: the sound a dog with untrimmed nails makes crossing a tile floor.

"What the fuck is that?" Ray asked.

Black spots were eclipsing the morning sun.

Harrison, whose unshielded mind had conveyed everything to the king and those he controlled, gave his answer. "Backup."

18

ENERGY TO SPARE

Demons had filled the street, ready after Harrison bound his prisoners and escorted them out.

Hundreds of them.

"Fuck," Ray whispered to Adrian. "Didn't think of *this*, did you?"

Adrian didn't reply, not wanting any of the fiends to wonder just what Adrian had and hadn't been *thinking* about this moment. They still wore Laurel's thought-blocking stickers behind their ears, but the words they said aloud could still be overheard. Ray's irritated question suggested a plan. Adrian didn't want them wondering what that plan might be.

In truth, Ray was both right and wrong. Adrian hadn't known there were so many fiends already inside Fortune — and blue-glowing, Zen-strengthened fiends at that. Seeing it now was a gut check. They had gone into their little ruse assuming that Harrison would recruit mush-brained human helpers once he "captured" them or that (ideally) he'd try to manage tied-up Ray, Laurel, and Adrian by himself. The fact that so many demons were here in the open changed the game.

They didn't have Legion weapons. They didn't even have a Rollard. Any thoughts of using "escape by any possible means" as Plan B were out the window now. They were only alive because Adrian had reminded the king why he hadn't wanted to kill them earlier, but chances were slim that they were one hundred percent necessary to his plan. Break Harrison's ropes and the prisoners would probably become more trouble than they were worth. They'd be dead in seconds.

But Ray was wrong to imply they shouldn't have let themselves be captured — that they shouldn't have gone to such lengths to make Harrison think he'd defeated them. Because if they hadn't played their ruse, what would have happened? The street around them was a cornucopia of horrors: crawlers, half-skulls, panther-rats, chatterers, and three or four different kinds of what they used to call gargoyles.

The fiends had descended so thick, Adrian wondered how they hadn't smelled sulfur inside. It made him shiver, thinking of what might have happened. They weren't attacking because Ray, Adrian, and Laurel were Harrison's prisoners. If he was still the prisoner, how might things be now?

His thoughts turned to Dee and Dixon. Had they gotten away? Adrian had no idea whatsoever where they'd gone — only that they *had* gone, and in separate directions. The case Adrian had made for the king being able to use the minds of himself, his brother, and his girlfriend wouldn't extend to Dixon and Dee. If they hadn't been sent away before dawn, they would have been slaughtered when those who stayed let Harrison take control.

Ray, unanswered, continued to sulk and mutter, but Adrian kept thinking about the talk he'd had with Dee earlier. Eldon and Ray had always felt that working on faith was passive and pointless — something you did because you were a fool or because nothing else was possible. Adrian and his mom had always felt the opposite. Faith was *active*. It took strength to hold firm while everything fell apart. Never mind that he was facing Hell, and that every holy book treated faith like a weapon against darkness.

Surrender. Stop fighting and see what happens. You don't have to know what comes next. What happens next is exactly what it's supposed to be.

His mother's voice. Good thing Ray couldn't hear it. As far as Ray was concerned, they'd had the upper hand until Harrison woke up without thought-blockers behind his ears and an occupied mind showed the king his situation. This was the result: tied up and headed to God-knew-where. In Ray's world, this could and should have been avoided. They had two goals: free minds and escape the city. Even with no idea how to do either, they'd at least been free to act. Ray didn't know all the nuance because he would have fought the plan.

In truth, there *was* no nuance. Even Laurel didn't know the depth of Adrian's total and complete lack of a plan. Dee had understood, but she was gone now. Nobody else would. So he'd let them believe "the mysterious and powerful Porter-family influence on the rifts" was somehow guiding him. If there was a kernel of Eldon in the creatures around him, it was of no help ... and, if his guess at the timing was right, that kernel would be gone tomorrow anyway.

"Where are they taking us?" Ray whispered after Harrison handed the prisoners off to a trio of winged throat-rippers.

Adrian shook his head, eyeing the demons with claws around their shoulders: *Not now. Don't talk. They're listening. Trust me.*

"Trust me" was something Ray might be able to do, so long as Adrian didn't have to explain, even though he'd never be able to trust the plan Adrian didn't have.

Letting Ray believe he had a clue was a harmless deception.

If everything went to shit, they'd be dead by the end of this anyway. No time for one last brotherly quarrel.

Adrian had only known that struggle was getting them nowhere. They had fought through the city and the brigade house to end up with a tranquilizer gun that would do them no good. They had learned that dosing people with Frog wouldn't show them the truth of the world around them. Mindfulness wasn't something you could inject. And he knew that the enemy controlled everything in Fortune now.

With only a day remaining, the spark of Eldon hidden in the virus couldn't be keeping more than ten percent of the city sane. That was especially true of the rift that Dixon said was their only way out. How could they get near the rift? The military controlled it, and the military was the first group the strategic-minded king would infiltrate with his mind virus. They'd never get close without being seen, and stopped, and killed.

If the enemy controlled everything, the only way they'd get close to anything would be if they were with the enemy. Tied or untied hardly mattered. It was either this or hiding until time ran out.

There were humans among the demons. Some were black-eyed but others appeared normal enough. Adrian even recognized a few of them: a woman from the laundry that cleaned the brigade's uniforms, a clerk at the Quik Stop, the husband of the Realtor who had sold his friend Chip's house.

Many, he didn't recognize at all. That meant little; Fortune wasn't a big city or a small town. They struck him as strange. All had black hair — even a few with otherwise Nordic features. Most were dressed in black, wearing black eyeliner and black fingernail polish regardless of gender. Many had tattoos, piercings, and ear gauges the size of a quarter.

Suddenly, he understood. They were the outsiders who

lived in the forest around the Gore Point. In Suicide Flats. Kids and cultists who worshipped Satan before it was cool, living among the teardrop trees and praying to death.

Adrian didn't think the last ones had been taken over by the mental virus. The way they stood and stared and stretched sores up and down their arms — as if their skin was a too-tight suit — told him this was something more. This was *infiltration*. There were classes of demons that GEN said existed but the brigades never saw, because they couldn't survive on the human plane. But they were here now; Adrian felt certain. The way the kids in black breathed wasn't quite human. Because they *weren't*. Not anymore.

They were fiends shoved inside living bodies, co-existing inside them like tumors. They were beneath the skin and between the organs, using their hosts like spacesuits to survive on the Earthly plane.

A pale woman with three rings through her eyebrow approached the group. When she spoke to Laurel, her voice was like gargling glass.

"I told you this was inevitable."

Ray looked like he was about to speak — to ask Laurel how this woman knew her — but Adrian glanced over to silence him. The woman *didn't* know Laurel. She was a demon, another mouthpiece for the king.

Laurel didn't flinch. She either wasn't surprised or scared, or hid it well. "And I told you the same."

"Yet you betrayed me."

"I haven't betrayed you."

The woman looked to Adrian but still spoke to Laurel. "You went to him."

"He hasn't betrayed you either. Look around. It's happening just like you wanted."

"Not exactly like I wanted," said the woman with the king's voice.

"We never talked about cutting off Fortune. We talked about a cataclysm so the planes could heal."

"Yes," said the woman. "Because until it ends, nothing can heal."

Adrian was trying to follow. There were assumptions here that the conversation wasn't re-stating. Laurel had spent months with the king before calling him to save her. What had they spoken about during all that time? He only knew what Laurel chose to tell him.

"It's clear that you've tried to subvert me," said the king. "You found the signature. The signature of Eldon Porter inside the wave."

It was talking about the virus. About the Porter imprint that lived inside all things made by the intermingling of planes — including its kernel that fought back, moderating the virus's measure of control.

"Yes. I found it. The question is why you hid it from me."

"I did not know."

"You didn't know it would fight back. But you knew it existed, all the same."

"It was irrelevant," said the woman's mouth.

"It was *all* that was relevant. You asked me to back-calculate entropy to the day of the first human-made rift, and you didn't tell me the impression of that first event was still around?"

"I owed you nothing. You are human."

"I am human. But before that, I am a scientist. If I'd known there was another factor, my recommendations would have changed."

The woman in front of Laurel did not respond.

Ray was trying to follow, looking to both of the others in the silence that followed.

Adrian kept his eyes on the women, knowing that engaging with Ray could only make things worse. Adrian understood little more than his brother, but he knew this was the reveal of a horrible truth. The king had used Laurel. Given her incomplete information, then caused her to draw faulty conclusions without the whole story.

It was the most offensive thing anyone could do to Laurel. Worse than insulting or imprisoning her. Worse than enslaving her, the king had intentionally given Laurel false data and led her to an incorrect conclusion.

When the woman still didn't answer, a half-defeated, half-furious look crossed Laurel's face. Her head bobbed slowly. "You didn't tell me about the kernel *because* my recommendations would have changed."

The woman — the king in her skin — smirked.

"What's going on?" Adrian asked.

"There's another way," Laurel said. "I should have known. Science is never black and white. Science is chaos."

"I thought science was the one thing that *was* black and white."

"Frail human thinking," Laurel said. "The foundation of everything is indeterminacy if you go down far enough. Nothing is more creative — more 'it depends' — than nature."

"What do you mean, 'There's another way'?"

"I mean that your family's imprint on the rift is a wildcard. I knew it was there, but the king hid it from me. He let me believe collapse was unavoidable, giving me only the information he wanted me to have ... and like a good little worker, I concluded exactly what he wanted me to."

Laurel had told him the planes were doomed to annihilate

each other eventually, so they would do best to get it over with now. Then told him to free the king and hasten the inevitable.

Now it seemed there had been yet another game inside the game — a chess match that started before she even set up her pieces. Collapse wasn't inevitable; he'd just let Laurel conclude for herself it was by holding back a few of the most important chips.

It seemed Adrian and Laurel had doomed the world after all. Now it was almost done, their time nearly up.

As went the city of Fortune, so went the world.

"What 'other way' is there other than letting the planes collapse, Laurel?"

"I don't know. I'm not sure. I told you. It's a wildcard."

"You must have some idea."

"I'd need time. My calculations were correct, but I only had part of the context before now. I know what the thermodynamics say. That there's a whole lot of pent-up energy that has to be dissipated. I thought collapsing the planes was the only way to blow off that energy, but now I see there are factors I didn't consider. There's an excellent chance that collapse is *not* the only way because the scope of things just got a whole lot bigger. Because of Eldon. And good old fashioned human free will — the least predictable thing in all the cosmos."

Adrian didn't know that that meant.

"The king let me believe that letting him take over and collapse the planes was the only option because when everything is in ruin, they'll be able to survive what the world becomes ... but it won't be as easy for us to live in their atmosphere as it is for them to live in ours."

"You said we could survive after the collapse if we survived the collapse itself."

"I said we would find ways to *adapt.*" She looked at the pale woman. "But that assumed peace. That assumed we were in this together. We aren't, are we?"

The woman smirked again. So Laurel hit her. Hard. With a closed fist.

"You waste energy," said a new mouthpiece behind the woman — a teenage boy who now spoke with the king's voice as he stepped over the stricken women.

"No worries," said Laurel, rubbing her hand. "Turns out we've all got energy to spare."

19
HEARTS AND MINDS

You may speak freely, said a voice inside Adrian's head.

It felt like forever since he'd talked to a fiend in their native tongue of telepathy. In reality, it had only been a few very full days. He'd discovered a virus doomed to take over the city. A wall had fallen from the sky, cutting Fortune off from the rest of the world. Citizens had turned into enemies. The Porters fought old friends, nearly died at least twice, then unboxed more science than Adrian had hoped he'd hear in a dozen lifetimes. His brain hurt. What once passed for normality in Fortune (which wasn't even normal, though it was far more normal than this) seemed a very long time ago.

He looked up. A hellbringer walked beside them as the procession made its way down the center of Route 113. There were still cars on the roads. They drove around the huge mass of marching demons, either on their side or oblivious to their presence.

Adrian looked at the thing. Its massive face was staring right at them.

We are isolated. None hear me.

Adrian had to focus to remember the trick of telepathy in these oddest and most disturbing of circumstances. Finally he said the most intelligent of things in reply: *What?*

None hear. We are individual. We are a separate mind.

We are not the hive, added a second voice.

It sounded like a clarification — an elaboration on what the first hellbringer had told him. Adrian looked over to see a second hellbringer.

We are friend, said the first when Adrian still didn't understand. Then it said something even less sensible: *There are worlds between us.*

A hand touched Adrian's shoulder. Their ropes had been traded in for restraints that seemed to have come from a prison. They were a chain gang today, being marched north to places yet unknown.

Adrian jumped. The hand was Laurel's.

"I hear them, too."

Adrian looked around, sure they'd be overheard. But no; he and Laurel and Ray were more or less alone as they walked, protected by the flanking hellbringers that seemed to have been assigned as their guards for this hike.

"They're fifth column, Ade. It's okay."

"'Fifth column'?"

"Sympathizers. Like Carl."

Adrian's head darted around again, sensing a trap. He didn't dare hope. So far, his mother-inspired plan to give up and roll with the punches wasn't going well.

But could what Laurel said be true? He desperately wanted it to be. He remembered Carl telling him that he wasn't alone in having problems with the king's rule. He'd hinted at the existence of resistance groups, though Adrian had never met any fiend members.

After the king's return, it stopped feeling relevant. All

fiends seemed like enemies again after that, though Adrian did remember proposing a change in the term humans used for them because he'd thought otherwise: not *fiends*, but *visitors* instead.

He whispered, "Are you sure?"

"What that one just said. *'There are worlds between us.'* It's a code phrase. It's a thing the fifth column says to identify one another."

"Is there a countersign I'm supposed to say, so they know we're with them?"

Laurel laughed. "You're Adrian and Ray Porter. I don't think they have to wonder."

Your friend has taught us to pinch from the collective, said the first hellbringer. *He has shown us how to think so the others do not hear us.*

Carl? Adrian replied.

Just as you may speak now without others hearing, the second one answered, nodding its enormous head.

"I'll go," said Ray, clearly sick of holding his tongue. "Where the fuck are they taking us? *Ade?*"

"Why do you think I know?"

"This was your plan."

"I assumed they'd take us to the military base."

Ray looked suddenly aghast. *"Assumed?"*

"I couldn't be sure. It was a gamble."

"Fucking great." Ray looked ahead, probably trying to spot Harrison. He had been against letting him go at all after the man tried to kill them the first time. Adrian argued that it was their only option, and Dee and Dixon, before they'd run off in different directions, backed him up.

Captive now, Adrian had no idea why. He didn't even know where they'd gone. Laurel was worried the king could get their locations out of her and the brothers' minds, so it was safest if even they didn't know where Dixon and Dee had run.

If Harrison was in sight, Ray probably would have run up and tried to strangle him with his wrist chains.

"Maybe we should have compared notes," said Laurel. "I guess it's too late now."

"Why compare notes?"

"Because Dee told me something funny seemed to be happening at the base. They heard about it on the scanner while she was at the brigade house."

"Funny how?"

"Funny because they didn't hear anything. Funny because the base wasn't chattering at all after a while. They heard about explosions and fires and masses of people in public places right up until the police dispatchers stopped thinking any of it was worth mentioning. During that phase there'd be regular bulletins from authorities at the base, but then they just stopped."

"Maybe they got infected like the police dispatchers," Ray said. "Just stopped seeing any point in telling people about things nobody had a problem with. Hell — that almost nobody in town could even see, like the wall."

"I don't think so," Laurel argued. "When the others were asleep or distracted, Dee would go to the radio trying to reach them. It was the only line of communication that still worked. For a while, it sounded like a few people there were still unin-fected. They knew what was going on. They were trying to stop it."

"A *few* people," Adrian repeated.

"But then they went dark. Stopped responding."

"Yeah," Ray said. "That tracks, doesn't it? No more fighters. No more free minds."

"Right. I thought the goal was to get us to take them to the reservoir."

"Why the reservoir?"

"Sat maps show a lot of activity up there. It's got all that concrete around the dam, so probably an ideal second head-quarters for them. As far as *our* goals are concerned, it's not far from there to the Boons. You know the Boons?"

Adrian nodded. "Not the best area."

"Right. Lots of drug dealers. Lots of drugs. I figured maybe we could get our hands on some after we managed to get away from them, if we *did* manage to get away. Feed those drugs into the outgoing water supply. Nothing shakes up perception like getting high. Maybe if people got drugs in their water, it'd take off their blinders. Let them see the wall, maybe build up some allies to help us."

"You think that would work?" Ray asked.

"Probably not. Even fed directly into the outgoings instead of the main reservoir would probably dilute it too much, and unless we found a shitload of LSD, most perception-altering drugs can't just be drunk anyway. If it worked, we'd have to find all those people and organize them somehow. In one day."

She shrugged. "That's why Plan B was to jam the upstream gates and swim through the dam. You can see on the Water Authority feed that water's still flowing into Fortune from the lakes to the east."

"*That* was what you and Dee came up with?" Adrian asked. "Swim what might be a quarter of a mile underwater to get outside the Rampart?"

"Sometimes they have to do maintenance in the reservoir," said Laurel. "I figured they'd have SCUBA rigs."

"Dee and I talked about the Army base."

"She remembered after you went to sleep that the base had gone all ghost town. I figured she told you before she left."

Adrian sighed heavily.

"Well, who cares?" Laurel said. "They were always going to take us wherever they took us. It's not like we had any control."

"I wouldn't have green-lit the plan to let Harrison capture us if I'd known the plan was to *spike the water supply.*"

"And SCUBA out of town! Is that really any worse than your plan to run into an enormous fucking rift?"

Adrian said nothing. It was moot. Laurel was right; they really *did* have no control over where the fiends took them. This plan was always a leap, judged as marginally better than staying hidden and affecting nothing. At least being captured meant they'd be taken to somewhere important to the king — somewhere that, if they were lucky, would prove a vulnerable place to exploit.

The road curved ahead.

"Anyway, doesn't matter, 113 loops around. I think we're still headed toward the base."

Adrian wondered if he was supposed to applaud Laurel's announcement. He didn't exactly want to. The wind had left his sails. He'd started this trek with the slim hope that they could be escorted to the base, escape, and run through the rift. Now that hope seemed to have gone from non-zero to zero. Dee said the base had stopped responding — that it'd gone total ghost and was now some sort of a dead zone. Adrian might have made different choices if Dee had remembered to tell him that earlier.

He'd forgotten the hellbringers. They'd been politely silent through his and Laurel's argument, but as the quiet resumed, their huge clawed-and-booming feet recurred to his senses like a metronome made of dragging boulders.

Carl taught you how to be individuals, he projected to one of them now.

How to pinch off from the hive. To be private just to those we choose to hear us. Yes.

How many of you are there? Adrian asked. *How many ... visitors ... are in your "fifth column"?*

Thousands active. An unknown number silent.

What do you mean by—?

"Hearts and minds," Ray said, interrupting his thought-speak. "They're talking about hearts and minds."

"What's that mean?"

"It means they're not one mind anymore. Haven't you been paying attention, Adrian? Our whole march. The entire time we were back. All that studying you do. I thought you were the observant one."

Adrian was going to ask, but he took Ray's point.

Carl was the first fiend he'd heard of who acted like an individual, but even Carl's promise of more sympathizers suggested he was far from the only one with at least some subversive thinking. Since the old ways ended and this new world of uncertainty began, more and more humans had begun to question the way things were. Adrian had to admit he'd seen signs that the fiends *(visitors)* were doing the same.

"In any conflict," Ray continued, "there are soldiers and activists — people who stand up and speak their minds. People who fight. But then there are a whole lot more people who stay quiet. Those people lean one way or the other, but keep it to themselves."

Hearts and minds. Ray was saying that in addition to the thousands of fiends who stood strongly against the king, millions more might be silently against him. War, like Laurel's view of science, was not as black and white as people believed.

Adrian supposed he hadn't thought it through. Despite meeting and liking Carl — despite all the help the visitor had risked his life to give them — he'd never really considered how badly even the other plane would suffer. Laurel talked about "all the pent up rift energy" like it was a bomb that needed to blow: one reason she'd thought at first that collapsing the planes was necessary. Ever since she'd told him that Eldon's kernel suggested there might be another way, Adrian had started to think of that "rift energy grenade" as something they could lob somewhere to save themselves.

So why not find a way to shunt the metaphorical bomb into the fiend plane and blow *them* up instead of obliterating both planes? He had no idea if something like that was possible, but now realized it didn't matter. Not with all the hearts and minds over there who didn't even like the king, who wanted him gone. What Adrian had in mind would be like diverting a nuclear weapon to a suburb. You don't save anyone that way. You just make death from innocents — those who'd never wanted war in the first place.

Have you heard from Carl? Adrian asked the hellbringers.

Not for days, said one.

Not for days, echoed the other.

Adrian thought of the window rift in his broom closet. He thought of the way it had shrunk so far, it was effectively closed. He thought of how it'd been moved and buried. That meant Carl's deception had been discovered. He'd be dead by now, if even his fellow fifth columnists didn't know where he was.

"Fuck." Adrian's swear directed at the cruel world itself.

We go there, said one of the hellbringers, pointing ahead, but not where the hangers stood.

Adrian followed its clawed finger, indicating a building maybe a mile from the base: an old motor depot GEN had used when it'd taken up residence here, if he remembered correctly.

So close to the base.

So close to the ghost town — to the hornet's nest that was both goal and bad tidings.

20

YOU DO YOU

Laurel was silent after that.

Adrian knew that look of dire pondering — of an intellectual splinter that had wiggled beneath the skin of her thoughts. Something troubling had occurred to her, born from her talk with the king, he imagined — something realized after she saw what he had been hiding.

What troubled Laurel seemed to have something to do with Eldon's kernel — that bit of himself and his human will that had impinged itself on the interplanar boundary all those years ago. To Adrian, the kernel was the last bit of an ice cube melting in warm water: something that had mattered a week ago because it resisted the mental virus from the inside, but that soon wouldn't matter at all because its six-day lifespan was almost gone.

Yet the realization that the king had *known* about Eldon's counter-influence all along had shone new light on something for Laurel — some consideration the king had hidden from her while she worked for him in Hell. The discovery of a new ingredient in her grand equation seemed to have changed everything. Adrian just had no idea how, or what it meant.

His mind kept flashing back to the day of the near sundering: the day Matt had opened all those rifts, perforating a hole around the Gore Point before Erika stepped in with her evolutionary ambitions and tried to cozy up like a second queen. Adrian and Ray had entered the warehouse thinking they'd come to battle a rift and had instead ended up facing the king. But he hadn't killed them that day, had he?

No, instead he'd sent wave after wave of fiend soldiers at them to see what they could handle. But even that battle had had a non-lethal feel for the Porters. The fiends weren't really trying to kill them. It had been more … *scientific* than that.

What had the king said that day? That he wanted the Porters to join him? Now with more context, Adrian didn't understand why he'd asked. What could the Porters really do in Hell other than take up space? They were a mental and spiritual match to their father's "imprint" on the boundary between worlds — that bit of Eldon that'd shaped the character of rifts and riftfare from then on — but what actual *use* were Adrian and Ray because of it?

Adrian had wondered that at the time, but not for long. He'd focused first on getting rid of Erika Dale, then on negotiating the end of sundering. Afterward, he hadn't cared about himself or his value in the least; grief over losing Laurel had been all he could think of.

Then they'd taken that trip through Hell. Then his return as a traitor. Since the moment he'd learned he was important, he hadn't had time or inclination to wonder *what* exactly his value was to the king.

He pondered it now.

The grand importance of the Porter brothers, such as it was, seemed to be tied to the ace the king had kept up his lack of a sleeve, hidden from Laurel. Somehow that ace, once revealed, had upended her entire theory. Eldon's kernel had been a revelation to Laurel just days ago, but the king had known it from the beginning. That — not the kernel itself — was the crux of what was bothering her now.

But what did it mean? Why would the discovery of what the king had been hiding (not even what it was, but the fact that he'd hidden it in the first place) irritate Laurel so much?

You didn't tell me about the kernel because my recommendations would have changed.

A chess master indeed. All that remained was checkmate.

Today had started with the goal of trying to leave Fortune through the Magnitude 35 rift. Now Laurel seemed to have given up on that goal because it had been based on bad information.

Adrian watched Laurel as they settled in at their new destination. She'd gone ahead of him and Ray, either to get some space or because she was ashamed. She hurt to look at. There was surrender in the set of her shoulders. In the downcast, head-shaking way she held her eyes to the ground as she walked.

Was she thinking — trying to find another way out? Or had she already given up?

"This is on us now," Ray said in a low voice, standing beside Adrian. They'd cleared the depot's front gate, guarded by infected humans alongside a line of blue-glowing fiend soldiers: mostly halfskulls, some chatterers. The fifth-column hellbringers had been shunted ahead of them. None of the other fiends were close enough to hear.

Ray reached up with his chained hands, then covertly tapped the spot behind his ear. It meant he'd re-donned the tiny blocking chips they'd put in their pockets before letting Harrison take them — a move Adrian now feared had been pointless if Laurel's understanding was wrong and their goal, therefore, incorrect all along.

Taking his brother's lead, Adrian reached into his pockets, letting his own small chips stick to his fingers. Making a show of straightening his hair, he slipped his own thought-blockers into place. The fiends were too far off to hear their words, but without precautions the king might still hear their minds.

"Do you hear what I'm saying, Ade? It's on us. We have to fight. Laurel's finished. Just look at her. We tried this your way. We tried it her way. Now we're going to try it my way."

"You're kidding. Look around, Ray."

They were surrounded. *Boxed in.* The depot's grounds were fenced like the nearby base's grounds. They had no weapons. There were countless guards who didn't need weapons.

"Here's what I know, baby brother. I'm not going to let them put me in a cage, where I'll sit back and watch this happen. I'm *Ray Fucking Porter.* You better than anyone knows I'll only go down swinging."

It had been true of Eldon, too. Ray's bravery had always gone hand-in-hand with a streak of suicidal self-destruction. It was easy to face danger when, deep down, you subconsciously wanted to die.

"You can't make a difference. Your chances of getting away aren't small, Ray. They're zero."

"Did I say I wanted to get away?"

"You said this was on us."

"Exactly. *On us* to choose how it ends. What's that poem? Do you want to go with a bang or a whimper?"

Adrian's head turned toward Laurel.

"She's out of ideas. She was wrong," Ray said, reading his thoughts. "You were wrong, too. Plan A didn't work out. We'd have a hell of a time getting to the rift when it's inside that building way over there."

Adrian had assumed they'd be taken to the base instead of a facility several guard stations away.

"And besides," Ray continued, "I get this feeling the rift's not the place to go anymore. Or am I wrong?"

Again Adrian stayed mute. He still thought leaving the city through the rift was worthwhile (they could tell the world what was happening, at least) but the first issue remained: There was no way to get there.

"Eventually they're going to try to put us in a cell," Ray said, looking across the fenced-in grounds they'd been crossing for the past few minutes, "and when that happens, some motherfuckers are going to get a big surprise."

"Ray ..."

"You do you," Ray said with a stone face, "but dammit, Ade, don't you dare stop *me* from doing me."

He wasn't going to talk Ray out of fighting when their captors moved them to jail cells, but that was mostly because Adrian didn't think they'd be put in cells in the first place — at least not long-term.

His "reminder" to Harrison, he knew now, had been unnecessary. Harrison was never going to kill them when he got free. Just like the king wouldn't kill them now. Just like the king hadn't killed them months and months ago, or any time in between. If all Ray and Adrian were to the king were prisoners, they wouldn't *be* prisoners. They'd been *captured*, but not killed — for a reason. But Adrian couldn't figure out why.

The question remained: *What* were *the Porters to the other plane? Why did they matter?*

Laurel might know the answer, but she wasn't talking and had never been so completely defeated. She was an eternal optimist despite her scientist's skepticism. There was always a way around a problem for Laurel ... until now. She'd finally gone quiet because she didn't see the point in trying.

Ahead was the door to the main building. The fiends ahead were stepping aside without entering as they reached it, making a gauntlet the Porters would cross before entry.

"Some motherfuckers are going to get a surprise," Ray muttered.

But the building wasn't a prison.

It was something much stranger.

21

THE OTHER SIDE OF THE COIN

The scientist in charge was a Dorn-class being called a stiltwalker. Adrian had only seen one of its kind before. Even for a man used to fighting demons, it'd scared the hell out of him. It was all legs with a fat, spider-like body whose belly brushed the ground, its frame sagging between those up-bent legs, again like the abdomen of a spider. Its body was snowy white, billowing with what looked like short hair.

A pair of jim-jams — Classical-class things that looked like large halfskulls with their necks bent backward — had led the procession and approached the stiltwalker as if it had all the business in the world being in charge.

Your subjects, said one of the jim-jams.

I saw them coming, the stiltwalker replied, turning to a dashboard full of unfamiliar instruments. The place was clearly a lab, apparently run by this extraplanar version of Laurel.

And to think, they used to believe fiends were all mindless.

Stiltwalkers were semi-boss caste and therefore often separated from the hive mind. This one seemed almost individual. Eccentricities in the way it moved and gestured deepened Adrian's sense of the creeps. Of all the fiends he'd had for nightmare fodder as a child, this particular species had haunted him the most.

One of the thing's white, fuzzy, spider legs raised to adjust the instruments. It had nine legs still on the ground: plenty to spare.

Electronic sounds began to come from the few controlled human guards who'd entered the building. More came from a bag being carried by a halfskull: Adrian, Ray, and Laurel's belongings, including their cell phones.

A guard nearby took his out. It'd just powered up. An icon on the screen said it was charging. Adrian remembered Dee's demonstration of the printer that ran without being plugged in. Whatever changes the king's helpers had made to the power grid — pushing power through the air instead of requiring batteries or plugs — its center and purpose was inside this room.

Adrian's hair tried to stand on end. Small sparks leaped between his fingers and legs: his body's ill-distributed static charge arcing to even out.

If you have eyes, the stiltwalker said to the group, *shield them.*

The small blue arcs that'd been dancing around the room became enormous as the fiend scientist turned a dial. The air became one big Tesla coil, the sparks connecting everyone inside to every other. It kind of tickled.

Shields, the walker repeated, casting its alien gaze at the Porters.

A halfskull nearby extended what looked like two pairs of welding goggles. Laurel, closer to the scientist, was already wearing a pair. Around the room, humans and fiends alike had donned similar goggles, clearly knowing what was coming more than the Porters.

Adrian put the goggles on. He looked to Ray, wondering if he planned to comply or cause trouble. He donned them without a word.

The static charge increased by a factor of a hundred. Every hair on Adrian's head rose now, as did every hair on his arms and legs. The air was suddenly dry, like the air around a raging fire. Adrian tasted metal. The crisp, blue scent of ozone permeated the room.

Then something strange happened: A rift opened directly in front of them, glowing blue instead of the autumn hues of the usual aurora.

Laurel gasped. Heads turned, but only the scientist's, Ray's, and Adrian's stayed on her.

You understand, said the scientist.

"I *suspect,*" Laurel answered.

"Laurel?" Adrian didn't like the look of the rift. It was alien. It was *cold*. A slow breeze blew into rather than out of it, stealing heat from the room. "What's going on?"

She moved toward the thing before answering, intellectually fascinated more than frightened. Her hand went up; Adrian thought for a moment she was going to try and touch it. She knew what she was looking at. That didn't mean it wasn't dangerous. Intellectuals had a history of courting fascinating phenomena even if they were deadly. See also: Oppenheimer and the atomic bomb.

"It's an anti-rift," she said.

Ray and Adrian looked at one another. Those words, put together, made no sense.

"We considered the possibility of anti-rifts almost from the start," she said, still watching the thing, "but they were only theoretical. For the most part, we invented the idea of them because we needed something to explain the math. It's the same as how astrophysicists came up with the idea of dark matter to explain universal movement. Nobody really knows what dark matter is — only that if you give it mass and factor it in, the way things work makes sense." Her hand hovered closer, now moving through the undulating blue aurora. "Same with anti-rifts. They were a concept to us, not anything I ever expected to see."

She looked to the stiltwalker like an equal, her fascination with the anti-rift sifting away from her earlier dour mood. To Adrian's eyes, she seemed almost excited.

"How did you open it?" she asked. "Where does it go? Have you taken readings from inside?"

Adrian wasn't as excited. What Laurel seemed to be forgetting — or no longer cared about — was that they'd been forcibly abducted and brought here by their enemy. This was the king's doing, and his many goals included taking over Fortune and significantly deprecating human existence by basically ending the world. His researchers hadn't opened a previously-unknown theoretical phenomenon for shits and giggles, or for Laurel's amusement.

The stiltwalker didn't answer.

Laurel moved closer, now standing in front of it the way Adrian so often stood in front of the heat of his closet portal to Carl. Adrian had always kept his sessions at the portal short because if he stayed too long, he got a sunburn. By contrast, the blue rift was stirring a delicate breeze.

She turned more pointedly to the stiltwalker, which still hadn't responded. Some understanding seemed to pass between them, scientist to scientist. Adrian would have heard if it had told her mind that it didn't know or refused share the answers, so whatever came was truly wordless.

The fiend seemed to be saying, *I have no answers for you … but go ahead, fellow traveller, and take a look.*

Laurel did, her questions temporarily set aside. Adrian watched her at three-quarters view, unable to see inside the thing himself. He could only view her face, and the strange rapture making it glow.

"It's empty," she said. "There's nothing at all."

"What do you mean, 'nothing'?" Ray asked.

"I mean *nothing*. It's like three hundred and sixty degrees of cloudless sky. It's …" She searched for the word. "It's *potential.*"

"'Potential'?"

She turned, her worries — abundant as they should have been — temporarily forgotten. This was Laurel in her element, discovering the unknown. "It's astonishing. It's … I don't have the words. Do you know about imaginary numbers?"

Ray and Adrian just looked at each other.

Laurel waved her hands to erase the question. "Never mind. Imaginary numbers are numbers that don't actually exist."

"So far, so good," said Ray.

"Mathematicians use them almost like placeholders. Imaginary numbers sort of get you over the hump of a problem, moving into purely theoretical territory and then back out into the real world again at the end, after you've used the imaginary numbers to get rid of stuff you don't need, then eliminated the numbers themselves."

Laurel pointed at the blue rift. "This? This is something that's basically imaginary." She laughed. "It's imaginary, but there it is right in front of us!"

"Back to Earth, Laurel," Ray said.

She made herself serious. "I said anti-rifts were considered purely theoretical at GEN. We used them like imaginary numbers. They helped the math make sense, but if you actually wanted to draw useful conclusions, you had to cancel them out by the end. The stuff that didn't 'fit' within the confines of our usual planar equations fit just fine if we added the idea of an anti-rift. But it was just an *idea* — get it? We used them as if anything was possible inside an anti-rift, and that was okay because if we later were able to remove the anti-rift from the equation, who *cares* what we said was possible inside them!"

She turned to the rift again. Her face was raptured.

"But one it is, plain as day," she said quietly. "It wasn't cancelled-out of the equation. It's the conclusion itself. Look at it, Ray. Adrian. It's a window into pure possibility. We used them as an intellectual construct: something in which, if they existed in the world we inhabited, anything was possible. Because they weren't supposed to *be* possible. Not by the definition of 'possible' that laypeople use." Her hand again brushed the cool aurora. "And yet, here it is."

Anything's possible. Adrian tried to wrap his head around what Laurel was saying. As usual, he found himself unable. She couldn't possibly mean those words literally. If she did, she'd reach into it right now, because pulling a gun out of thin air would be *possible* inside. Escape, for even people who stayed on the Earth plane, would be *possible* in there.

While Adrian had been thinking, Laurel's face had been changing. He watched it fall from mildly pleased (down from thrilled) to neutral, to concerned, to a terrible species of rock-solid realization. Whatever reason the king had for opening the anti-rift here and now, Laurel had just deduced it ... and wasn't happy at all.

"This is about parity. About equalizing the planes that can't be equalized, isn't it?" Laurel looked at the stiltwalker, whose nonresponse confirmed her theory.

Then without warning she rushed the scientist.

But the guards were ready. They grabbed her as she fought,

thrashed, and began to seethe. They'd known she was smart, that she'd figure whatever-this-was-out, that she'd be furious when it happened.

"Laurel?" Adrian asked.

"The rift is here because it's the only way to solve a paradox," she told him, falling still but not entirely. "Eldon's first rift unbalanced the planes. Ever since, collapse has been the only way to balance them, one way or the other. But there's a problem, and it's the bit of himself he left behind — that tiny piece of 'Porter soul' that keeps the last rifts from ever being able to close. I've been thinking about it since the king admitted he kept it from me, but no matter how I think on it I'm sure that his mind lives on in you — part of the collective consciousness humans still have even though we don't usually know it. Eldon died, but in his sons, a sliver of his consciousness survived."

The brothers waited for their punchline.

"The planes want to collapse because they're out of balance. But they can't, because Eldon's in the way. His kernel expires soon inside the virus, but it's like bubbles of oil in water, making the collapse impure. The only way for the king to collapse is to invoke his version of 'imaginary numbers.' *It's a third plane* inside that rift. There was always *our plane* and *the fiend plane*, but the only way everything makes sense once you factor in Eldon's kernel is for there to be *something else* too. The third plane inside that anti-rift is like dark matter. It's the reason for all the stuff that's never made sense. Do you understand? An anti-rift is the only way the contradictions have 'enough room, inside the math, to be able to coexist."

Ray couldn't possibly understand what she was saying more than Adrian did, but he got enough to become nervous, which made him angry.

"Goddammit, Laurel, nobody but you and that fucking insect understands theoretical math. We're not—!"

"They're going to throw you into it! Do you understand THAT?" Her eyes were wild, her dreadlocks flying as she whipped her head, trying with increasing ferocity to break free. "You're grit in the oyster. The 'Eldon' in the two of you is the only thing keeping the king from collapsing the planes and getting what he wants! Is *that* enough for you, Ray? You're not about to die. *You're about to cease to exist.* Do you understand *that* little bit of two-plus-two-equals-four?"

The answer was no. Obviously, nobody understood. But annihilation was annihilation, and Adrian trusted Laurel enough that what she'd said, however incomprehensible, made his blood go cold.

A small human woman with jet black eyes stepped from among the other guards. She spoke with the voice of the king.

"Do it," she said to the fiends holding Ray and Adrian.

That's when the roof fell in.

22

FIVE BY FIVE

It came down corner-first, away from where Ray and Adrian and Laurel were standing. The lights blew at the same time: every bulb shattered, because inductive power meant they couldn't be turned off.

The commandos had been watching from above using thermal cameras enhanced by Zen Element, their helicopter floating on a cushion of Zen-charged air with the rotors still and silent. There were fiends and converted human soldiers on the grounds, of course, but the helicopter and its occupants were fast and the building's door was barred. They made it, but not remotely in time.

Precision explosives, directional, punching a hole. The intended circle of ingress scored into concrete and rebar for five seconds right before the big boom by a hybrid of det cord and thermite. Like a knife through butter, followed by a punch.

Adrian and Ray, who were used to the tumult and fog of battle, returned to their wits quickly. Laurel, who'd gone from a science fugue to terror in seconds, was not as fast. Adrian saw what was happening by the time the first soldiers were halfway down their drop lines into the room, so he rushed forward to tackle her.

Laurel fought him at first, not knowing it was Adrian who'd taken her low so she wouldn't be hit by crossfire. It seemed like minutes later that she settled, asking to be let up because she could stay down on her own now, but it couldn't have been that long.

The attack was pure precision. Pre-planned, thermally scoped, Zen-swept and electromagnetically vetted. Later they learned that Patel had been watching the depot from the nearby base, noting the curious psychic signatures and deducing their source. The soldiers knew where the Porters were. They'd assumed Laurel would be with them, which was true, but also that J. Dixon might be, which on questioning Adrian hastened to report he was not. Their exchange happened beneath leaning rubble dropped from the room's ceiling, side-lit by the anti-rift's blue aurora.

Meanwhile experimental bludgeon rounds zipped overhead, annihilating the normal fiends and cutting the blue, Zen-filled ones into small enough pieces that they were no longer dangerous.

By the time the room fell mostly quiet and commandos were shouting "CLEAR!" to one another, only forty-five seconds had passed. Volleys of pounding came from the locked and barred doors.

"Come with me, sir," said the camouflaged soldier who'd asked about Dixon. They hustled back to the dangling rappel lines with the silent helicopter above, its moveless rotors beyond eerie. "We're 86ing harnesses to expedite evac. Hold still and try not to wiggle. Ready?"

"N—" Adrian started to say.

The soldier clipped a Batman-type device on a harness around his waist to the rope, then grabbed Adrian in a way he would have found impossible to replicate later. Without pause and before Adrian could finish his single word, the pair zipped upward at speed sufficient to make it feel like they were wearing weighted hats.

A moment of situational vertigo followed, and while it lasted Adrian had a curious feeling, akin to *Hang on; I feel like I forgot my wallet.*

But then it was over and half a dozen camo-clad men and women were grabbing Oh-Shit straps around the transport's edges, their charges — Ray, Adrian, and Laurel — still mostly in their clutches.

The rotors coughed to life, providing increased lift once they were clear of the building now that stealth was no longer needed. The helicopter shuddered as they did.

Adrian grabbed for his own strap. Then Ray did the same and Laurel — who was still shock-eyed, not entirely sure what just happened — eventually followed suit.

Adrian peered at the ground below. The fiends and their human accomplices had massed on the grounds, already through the door of the building they'd just left. Many looked up at the helicopter as its engine started. Some of the humans, holding guns, began to shoot.

The commando who'd escorted Laurel sat in a bay along one wall. He raised his face shield and revealed a visage that seemed too young — just a kid, really. In a stunning display of normalcy, he put on a pair of sunglasses against the harsh morning glare.

They flew on. As they'd assumed, the helicopter had come from the Army base, to which it was now returning.

"You're still human," Laurel said. Its opposite wasn't strictly rational, but the soldier seemed to know what she meant. "We thought the base had been taken like the rest of Fortune."

"No, ma'am. Ain't nothin' but grunts and gruel." He grinned so wide, there should have been a hayseed between his teeth. "Be there in two and you'll see, ma'am: Home sweet home's still five by five."

THEY LANDED on the rooftop instead of the grounds. The grounds were still secure, but a large group of fiends was crossing the land from depot to base, chasing the helicopter and its aggressively-gotten escapees. They'd reach the perimeter fences soon. The Army seemed to be taking the extra precaution of keeping its new arrivals one protected ring closer to the center.

From the air, the rest of the base showed signs of contained destruction. One building looked a little burned and there were corpses unattended on the grass: kills on one side or another that nobody'd gotten to yet.

Patel was there to greet them. Her entire demeanor was different from the last time the Porters had met her. She still projected an air of command, but now it was the aura of a battlefield commander instead of a peacetime one who worked behind a desk — the aura of a leader who still takes orders from ranks above her, but whose discretion allows for bending those orders and improvising because shit was already in the process of hitting the fan.

"Told them it was you," Patel said in greeting. "What was it? Powering some sort of Zen engine? Or charging a weird kind of a battery? You light up like Christmas trees on their equipment. Tell me they brought you in so they could plug you into something."

"It's complicated," Laurel said, butting in.

Patel seemed satisfied enough with this non-answer. She looked out across the grounds, toward the encroaching horde.

It wasn't huge — maybe twenty or thirty fiends. Adrian noticed that the fifth-column hellbringers hadn't rushed over like the others. It seemed Hell's ideological schism was making itself known.

"Let's go inside," she said. "It's about to get shooty out here."

Sure enough, the ping and echo of more blunt-force weapons rang out as they descended from roof into the belly of the building. Nobody seemed perturbed. Like they'd planned for this.

The stairwell they'd entered was concrete and full of echoes.

"Pardon the mess," Patel said, leaving the battle sounds behind. "We had a little power struggle around here. No big deal. It's funny; the worst stuff sometimes has really interesting up-sides. I had no idea what my science corps was working on even though I'm this facility's CO. When the smoke cleared, turned out they'd been working on shit like ET's telephone. You know: the Frankenstein'd Speak-and-Spell thing he made to *phone home?*"

Nobody answered. Adrian knew *ET*, but Laurel was younger and Ray was always too hardcore to stop and appreciate movies.

"We don't know what most of it's for. But rest assured, it told us *exactly* when you showed up over there."

Laurel looked like she might open her mouth and start talking anti-rifts and science, but they'd had enough of the explanations. Did it really matter how and why things were happening at this point? Even Adrian had long ago stopped caring. His last frayed nerve was about to snap. He didn't care how things ended now, as long as they stopped simmering.

Adrian spoke first. "So you're all ..."

"*Human?*" Patel finished. She looked back; the soldier

Laurel had called "still human" was a flight behind them and had apparently thought that amusing enough to pass on. "Yes. Once we knew how to tell the affected people from those who were still in their right minds with sufficient confidence, we pared staff down quite a bit. It was a near thing, though. Almost got our warehouses blown to bits. Fortunately, the black-eyes are sloppy. Going zombie makes them stupid fast."

Adrian thought of what he'd seen on Dee's brigadehouse surveillance cam: his old friends, bumping into each other in the middle of the night.

They cleared the stairwell. Patel led them through a taken-down checkpoint Adrian remembered passing through the last time they'd been here, back when she was their enemy. A clear head in Fortune now put you on the same side.

Nobody manned the checkpoint. There was no intra-facility security. It seemed all guns were pointed outward now, and everyone got Classified clearance by default. Patel was already leading them to a Top-Brass-only section of the ware-house floor, which had been forbidden to them before.

From up high they could see all the machines. They could see how many had been changed by workers who'd been under the king's influence. They'd been made into a new thing: machines, but with a breathing blue pulse that felt almost organic. How near a thing was it, when Patel managed to fight back the king's puppets and keep control of the base? The king's fingerprints were all over the equipment here. He must have been trying to establish this as one of his footholds.

Until someone in Patel's command discovered it, fought back, and won.

Patel reached her destination, then flopped into a huge wheeled chair in front of an array of monitors that mostly showed the grounds. A few showed machine statuses and waveform patterns that Laurel would probably explain in detail if anyone let her. Her flop-down was the least authoritative, least-officer-like thing she could have done. She wasn't putting on airs and barking orders as just another adult like them.

"Let me save us some time," Patel said. "I'll just assure you right now that we're more or less on the same page. I talked to your friend Dee Scott."

"Dee's here?"

"*Was* here. Left. Said there was someone out in Fortune that she needed to find, and I couldn't talk her out of it. Gave her one of the new multi-weapons. I've seen her fight on your TV show. She'll be fine. I liked her. She walked right up to the front gate and rang the buzzer. But yeah, she told me. I know everything you know."

"You don't know about the anti-rift," Laurel said.

Adrian was bracing himself for another deluge of intricate explanation, but Patel didn't even flinch. "Not from Ms. Scott, no. But obviously we have *your* work, Ms. Gantry, courtesy of GEN."

Right. Adrian nearly allowed a laugh. If Dixon had been working with GEN while the CIA looked over its shoulder, obviously an Army base had an even better in with agency types. Patel wouldn't just have seen Laurel's most secret work; she'd also have no-holds-barred analysis of that work courtesy of the most paranoid and devious scientific minds in the country. They'd probably figured out "anti-rifts" before anyone else. Might even have tried to open one of their own. Movies told everyone how much the CIA liked opening Pandora's boxes.

"Like I said. We're on the same page. Now: To catch *you* up on *us*, here are the answers to the questions you're about to ask me: Those of us who are still unaffected have the mindfulness program that Dixon told you about to thank for it. Yes, we know it's not permanent and yes, we know we probably only have a day left. Yes, we have protocols in place to catch new conversions before they become a problem. It's actually pretty simple. Everyone still in the game has to check in with an off-the-shelf mindfulness app that lives on their phone at the top of every hour, or six hours for sleeping. Failed check-ins go to our improvised brig. Two missed check-ins and you're out. No, we're not killing them. Most of them. There were some misunderstandings and learning experiences early on. Yes, that's who you saw dead on the grounds. No, we haven't cleaned them up yet. Until now, when we broke cover, we've been fairly confident the fiends didn't know anyone was here. Not unaffected, anyway. We go outside and start moving bodies, we'll attract attention. Especially now that there's more and more winged species out there. So how did I do? Any more questions?"

Adrian had to admit, she'd done a bang-up job. He'd expected a need to explain themselves, but Patel was way ahead of him. The king *had* tried to take over here just as they thought, but something had allowed the uninfected to see the infiltration in time and prevent it.

If Dee had been here and Dixon had begun here, they'd know everything Laurel had discovered along the way. The only important things Laurel had learned after Dee left the group were things Patel's people seemed to have known in advance, thanks to work with the CIA in Dixon's time.

"No," Adrian said. "That's ... thorough."

Patel's watch beeped. She slipped an Android phone from her pocket and checked the time, seeing it was exactly noon. They all watched as she navigated to a very non-military-seeming app called Serenity, tapped the screen a few times, then stowed the phone back in her pocket: the top-of-the hour check-in, soon enough repeated by every tech in the room and every tech on the machines below.

Patel looked up when she finished. "We survive another hour, it seems. My people predict I can't have more than about another day's worth of sanity left in me, though. Ain't that a bitch?"

"We figured about the same," Laurel said.

"We didn't have to figure. We saw the moderating wave-form from Go and have been watching its effectiveness decline. The downward curve is exponential. For every hour we stay ourselves at this point, the likelihood that we'll *remain* unin-fected until the next check-in gets smaller and smaller. The rate of decay itself is accelerating."

She stood suddenly. "So. No time to waste."

Ray, Adrian, and Laurel looked at one another, then at Patel as she headed for the door. In the silence, they could hear light sounds of battle. There hadn't been an overwhelming number of fiends or human soldiers at the annex building they'd escaped from and the base's perimeter defenses were formidable, but that didn't mean more enemies weren't coming.

The king's many eyes had seen Ray and Adrian stolen, and he'd certainly know what it meant and seen where they'd gone. Two clocks were ticking now: maybe a day left before Fortune was lost, and an unknown time until the armies breached the base's gate.

"Are we going somewhere?" Ray asked.

"*You*," Patel replied, "have a rift to catch."

23
INTO THE EYE

Machines and scaffold had been pulled away from the enormous rift, making it seem even larger.

The last time they'd seen it, an entire mining operation had been built around, in front of, and ultimately entering the magnitude-35 rift in the annex warehouse. Back then, Marines had been on regular duty: platoons of humans entering the rift, killing off as many civilian fiends as they could, then loading their bodies into carts on a heatproof rail crossing the boundary.

Now, all of that was gone. The rails were still in place (they curved into a side room where there'd once been piles of bodies and the facilities necessary to render them for Zen Element), but everything else had been dismantled. In front of the massive thing now was a bare apron of concrete floor the size of a regulation basketball court. Standing at the back of it, even re-dosed with Frog, Adrian felt blown-back by the heat.

It was beyond intimidating. He'd seen the rift before, but hadn't entered the other plane through it last time. Just standing before it now felt like a dare. Nobody would actually step into something that size, would they?

It felt like sliding down the throat of a monster.

"Obviously you've done this before, so I won't over explain," Patel said. "Just like last time, the Zen mutagen eliminates the need for excessive heat protection and rebreathers. We've reduced the load you'll need to carry pretty far over the past few months, so hopefully you can travel fast. Please do. For now, we're not having much trouble holding the base, but that could change fast if the fiends decide they want to get in badly enough to deploy bigger numbers and bigger big-boys."

One of Patel's specialists put something into Adrian's hand. It was the size of a javelin, covered in cooling tubes and heat-proofed wiring. At the same time, Ray was being handed what looked like an improved version of a Rollard and Laurel was being shown the ropes at one of the mission-monitoring machines to one side. They already both wore multi-weapons on their backs.

"We call that device a 'lance,'" Patel said of the thing in Adrian's hand. "You know how to stitch, so its use should come easy to you. It's really just stitching in reverse. See that button?"

Adrian looked. "Yeah."

"Press and hold, then swipe. Start small because it's a hell of a lot more powerful than you think. The current generation of lance opens rifts with about as much physical effort as, say, dragging a sharp knife through a paper grocery bag."

The device was suddenly much scarier. It used to take a room full of equipment to open rifts. Even the micro-rifts Laurel worked with at GEN required teams of people.

"We don't have a map of the plane beyond the rift, so I can't tell you where you should cut to find an opening that'll lead you outside the city. The relationship between our plane and theirs isn't linear. Anywhere could put you anywhere."

"I know." Specifically, Adrian had learned it from Erika Dale.

"We know that Fortune is favored close by, probably because of the proximity of the Gore Point. You may have to hike out a bit. I suggest using the lance to open very small rifts — just enough to see through. If they open inside Fortune, just re-seal them. The other end of the lance is a stitching tool."

"You're kidding." He looked at it. "There's no Zen reservoir."

"I could take the time to explain how military innovation is always a few generations ahead of everyone else," Patel replied, "or you could just take me at my word and get moving before I stop recognizing myself in the mirror and start chanting 'Hail Satan.' Minus the cartridge bay, it works the same as the big rigs you're used to. Do we need to try one now, like a lesson?"

Adrian could tell he was supposed to answer with a *No*. Patel was lively and pretending at self-assuredness, but beneath her facade she was obviously scared. All of them were, Adrian included. His own grace — as well as Ray's — was on thinner ice than he liked to acknowledge.

Mindfulness apparently kept them sane, but neither Ray nor Adrian was doing it on purpose. Maybe their "Porter energy" was giving them a boost, but it was also possible that a general "Laurel-adjacent habit of paying attention" was all that kept them afloat.

Adrian hadn't meditated in years. Ray may *never* have meditated. If they were mindful by osmosis, it seemed to Adrian that his brain might fail at any second, at which point the king could take him over. If that happened, what might he do? Turn on Ray with the lance, and cut him open instead?

"No," Adrian said with all the confidence he could put into his voice — not just for Patel's benefit, but also for his own. "I won't have any problems."

"Okay. This is the fun part. I call it 'the Hansel and Gretel.'" Patel projected her voice to a group of soldiers and techs. "NICK?"

A soldier approached, rolling something that looked like a reel used to store a garden hose. He had a lot of stripes and bars and metals on his uniform. Adrian wasn't military-adept enough to know what rank he held, but it was clearly higher than buck private. The fact that he was dragging equipment around and being addressed informally spoke volumes about what had happened here. It wasn't really military anymore. Now it was a bunch of smart, brave people who needed to get the damn job done.

"I need you to wheel this behind you." Patel handed Ray the handle of the hose-wheel thing, already trailing a braided line that seemed attached to equipment farther back. "I know. Pain in the ass. It rolls easy, though, and it won't bind or snag."

"What is it?" Ray asked.

"Insulated fiber line. There's a receiver in the compartment at the center." She opened a small door and showed him. "We learned from the last mission not to trust wireless anything inside. Pockets in there get so hot, electrical signals don't work because medium gasses ionize. You get in trouble and need us, we'll be on the other end."

"We'll be fine," Ray said, preparing to hand the bulky thing back.

"It's not really for you, cowboy. We've got no idea what Fortune looks like to people from the outside, but the nature of the contagion suggests it must be local-only. Now: Once Fortune's toast and the king opens the wall to let what's currently *inside* Fortune *out*, that might change. For now, though, the wall he put in place seems to be blocking all signals, so we have no reason to think the outside world hasn't noticed — at least — that they can no longer enter the city. They should still be sane out there for now. And *because* they're sane, they'll know something's fucked up."

She pointed at the reel of fiber cable.

"You find one authority figure once you exit the city — a CO at one of the military checkpoints out there would be best, but even a cop will do — and you give them that phone. Tell them the short version of what's going on, and they should believe you right away because of what they must already be seeing. The cable you've laid will let me talk to whoever you put on the phone. I won't bore you with the intricacies of national defense prep, but let's just say there are protocols in place that allow someone in my situation to take remote command of state and local authorities. They'll listen to me, in other words."

Again she pointed at the fiber reel. *"That's* your number one priority, you understand? Getting me on the horn with someone out there. That's how we pop the bubble. That's how we make sure that when the king has Fortune in the bag and opens up again, he can't storm through the country. We know how to keep people from getting infected. We put enough defenses in place and remove enough civilians from the area, and maybe we'll have a chance of stopping him there. Got it?"

Ray nodded. Adrian nodded. It would be at least a day before the king opened anything, and a day — for the government and military, when sufficiently motivated — struck Adrian as more than enough time to mount a defense. They just needed to learn what Patel already knew.

Yeah, but will that actually fix anything? Adrian wondered. *The planes are still due to collapse, surely made weaker by all the king's work so far. Fighting the king back by weapons and force doesn't change the fragile physics of the situation.*

Laurel had told them a lot about this mysterious "Porter imprint," including the reason the king wanted to throw them into a whole new universe so that troubling imprint would be gone. What he hadn't figured out was whether any of this could really be stopped. Laurel had implied that something in the Porters could — or could have once, in the past — negate the need for a collapse, but she'd never said what it was or how it might work.

Time was short. Now was no time to request an explanation.

Adrian nodded his readiness. Then he heard popping behind him, like arcing static electricity. He tasted copper on the air and smelled ozone.

Light flashed on the equipment from a light source behind. A *blue* light source. Adrian turned, somehow sure he already knew what he'd see.

It was the anti-rift, or at least the beginnings as it tried to re-form, sparking into existence above the warehouse floor, opposite the mammoth rift made of fire.

It was here. They'd left it behind at the depot ... but it had followed them here.

The brothers gaped. Some of the techs gaped. But Patel didn't seem surprised at all, and neither did Laurel.

"I told you," Laurel said. "It's potential. The ability for something to happen."

"So why's it following us, Laurel? Why the fuck did it just open spontaneously right behind us?"

"Because it wants to equalize the pressure. That's what the king wanted: to throw you into it so you'd cease to exist. The Porter kernel unbalances an equation."

Ray, who'd seen enough strange things that the arrival of a

blue rift stopped fazing him once Laurel explained it, seemed satisfied. Adrian wasn't.

It'll keep following you, trying to balance it again.

Laurel might call Ray, Adrian, and their father's memory "an unbalanced equation," but to Adrian that sounded more like debt. Maybe even fate. She kept calling the blue rift *potential*. She said *anything could happen*.

Surely *fate* wasn't a crazy concept in that kind of company.

The rift seemed to be calling to him. Stalking him. Following him around like a dog. And why? Because it was owed something, and he feared that "something" was him and his brother.

Maybe it wasn't out-of-line for their captors at the depot to throw them into the anti-rift. Maybe, instead, it was their *fate* to enter it. If so, keeping it at bay was tantamount to cheating fate.

Adrian pushed the thought from his mind. He couldn't cease to exist just yet. First he had a quest.

24
THE HARD WAY

At first, things seemed to go smoothly.

Adrian had no luck opening rifts outside the Rampart in his first few tries, but it quickly began to feel like it was only a matter of time.

The plane was empty. Feeling no heat thanks to the mutagen they'd been injected with, the hellscape might as well have been the red and rocky surface of Mars.

The city of fire they'd entered last time was not visible. What looked like smaller settlements were, but that was by design: The big rift had been opened near fiend towns on purpose, so the government could roll its rail cars in to cart out the harvested dead. Now, those caves and nooks were empty. No fiends in sight. They'd abandoned this place of doom, leaving Ray and Adrian unmolested as they went about their work.

Using the lance was simple. As Patel warned, the danger was actually to overuse it — something Adrian did once, opening a six-foot rift into a school gymnasium. There were six people and around a dozen assorted fiends inside, and while the people ran from the rift (three lingered at the door, their eyes black), the fiends charged it.

Ray sliced one down the middle with his Rollard and it fell dead. Two others made it into the plane: a Dorn-class and a Classical, and they had to rush to deploy the right settings on their multi-weapons.

There were only so many brute-force rounds, so the brothers were reluctant to use them unless absolutely necessary. So they fought in a parody of the old way, finding their prey dead enough as soon as they found their way.

Ray looked at the corpses.

"Dead."

"Like always," Adrian said.

"No. I mean, I'm surprised. That one took a single Rollard blow." He pointed, then pointed again. "Those just took a few energy rounds. It was like brigade fighting all over again."

Adrian waited for the punchline. Ray didn't give it. "And?"

"I thought they'd gotten stronger. Remember?"

Oh. Right. That *was* strange. Riftfare in the good old days had been part sham, part battles the other side didn't care enough to try and win. Eldon had been right about Primordial Form, and that meant any unformed fiend could become any class when it came through a rift. Fiends who'd already chosen a form, though, were slower to change if it was even possible — something Adrian couldn't recall.

The bigger question was that of their recent evolution. Once the fiend plane stopped sandbagging and started fighting for real, they'd unveiled the blue-skinned Zen infusion that made even halfskulls impossible to kill unless you ground them to powder. These weren't like that. They'd died easily: One Legion and two minutes, and it was done.

Adrian nodded to himself. "Carl said something about how much Zen Element it took to improve them — to make them into upgraded weapons. Learning how to refine allowed the Element they have to stretch a whole lot further, but there's still only so much of it. Maybe they only do the blue-skin thing to the royal guard or something."

It made sense. It also reframed the kill for Ray — something he mentioned after Adrian took a full ten minutes to get the big rip closed.

"So I just killed a bunch of civilians." He was looking down at the corpses, thinking probably of fifth column. Or of innocents. Or of others like Carl.

"If they come at you and try to kill you, I think you can fight back," Adrian said. "Let's keep moving."

So they did. Weilding the lance with far more care, Adrian opened and then closed nine more rifts — a nice, round total of ten — before sitting on a rock to rest.

He could feel it burning his ass, but with Frog in him it was merely warm like a luxury car's heated seats.

"This is taking too long."

"It's taken an hour. I'm still me. You're still you. I think Patel can hold the base unless the king really uncorks and sends the masses after her. Not sure why he'd bother, though. It's us he wants, and we're on his turf, not ours. We've got a full day, Ade. The fate of humanity's on the line."

Yes. In theory, that was true. But something was wrong, and Adrian couldn't get it out of his mind. Their original thinking said that the king had isolated and then began trying to take over Fortune because most of the world's riftfare fighters, riftfighting weapons, and riftfare researchers were in Fortune. There'd never been rifts outside the city, so centralizing riftfare made sense. Now it was the way Ray said: Fortune was almost (but not entirely) taken over, and that meant they had until the kernel's clock ran out to reach someone outside the Rampart so that Patel could tell them how to prepare for the wall's falling. The goal was simple: *Escape the city, save the world.*

But something was wrong. If escaping was really the way to end this, they should be facing more opposition. *Any* opposition. The king was smart, so he should know that the Porters could unravel his entire plan by finding the right rift and waltzing through it. Yet they weren't even being chased.

Was this yet another ruse?

"Where are the fiends?" Adrian asked.

"I don't know. Maybe he's massing them somewhere."

"Where's more important than here? *We're* here, and we're the problem. We're the ones standing in his way because we've got this speck of Dad in us. We're the ones threatening to punch a hole into the outside, maybe in time to prepare a defense the king won't be able to defeat."

"So what are you saying?" Ray asked.

"I'm wondering if he's got another ace up his sleeve. I'm wondering if we're doing what he wants us to do, or if what we're doing doesn't matter."

"You think this is all just another con? How many cons and gotchas are there going to be, Ade? This isn't a heist movie. Nothing works that much like clockwork."

It all felt true. But it also felt like something was askew.

THE FIRST TIME they spotted the blue anti-rift on the fiend plane, Adrian startled. He didn't understand how it kept following him, and he didn't get how it could be on the fiend plane at all.

"Why couldn't it be?" Ray asked.

Adrian watched as the thing grew. This was the third time he was seeing it, and was getting used to its patterns. Its final state was always a tall blue eye, about six feet in height —

enough that anyone going through it into the nothingness (the "pure possibility," Laurel called it) would have to duck. It didn't start that way, though. First there was crackling. Then the air — even Hell's air — took on the odor of ozone. Sparks leapt from surface to surface, and then the rift began like a singularity floating at bellybutton level. It grew up and down from there, swelling over the course of thirty or forty seconds.

Ray watched it finish growing and stabilize before he had an answer. Which wasn't really an answer.

"It's a rift. Can there be a rift *inside* a rift?"

"We're not really inside a rift right now," Ray said. "We're on their plane. To them, we're the ones 'inside the rifts.'"

That made sense, but again: something didn't feel right. He wished Laurel was here, though he'd tire from the intricacies of her answer.

He supposed he'd been thinking of the anti-rift as an Earth-side thing. Eldon's spirit — an ill-defined thing Laurel kept calling his *intention* — was the reason for the imbalance the rift was trying to equalize, right? Eldon had opened that first rift on Earth. It seemed right to Adrian that if it was an Earthman's issue, Earth was where it should be.

Adrian stepped closer. The blue rift didn't exhale like normal rifts did, inhaling instead. The subtle in-breath of the thing reminded Adrian of the popcorn rifts they'd seen before he'd been sent through the rift to make contact with the queen ... and to find Laurel. Those rifts — which were normal in every other way besides their size — had only inhaled because the queen's work had been sucking energy and Zen back from the human plane. It was how they knew the queen was stockpiling: filling her guards with Zen fire, preparing for battle.

This in-breath seemed to be thermodynamic, not anything to do with the Element. It was hot here and cold in there, so hot air moved in. But again: That didn't feel right. For reasons unknown, Adrian found comparisons to the popcorn rifts more apt. It was inhaling because it wanted something, and that "something" wasn't necessarily heat.

"It wants us to go into it," Adrian said.

"Good for it." .

"Part of me wonders if that's why we're not finding any resistance. Why there are no fiends here to fight us."

"Because of that blue rift?"

"Because what happens next is inevitable." Adrian kept thinking of the rift as a promise owed. As a debt. And yes, as fate. Their father was responsible for the things that eventually made the anti-rift necessary: Eldon unbalanced something, and that meant it would inevitably re-balance in time.

"So now it's fate?"

"I didn't say fate." But part of him meant it, just the same.

Ray rolled his eyes. "You and Mom. You and your 'everything happens for a reason.' I swear. The two of you would walk off a bridge if you thought it was fate."

"Never mind."

So Ray didn't. They left the rift behind and moved on.

BUT IT OPENED AGAIN behind them again and again. Adrian finally picked up the phone inside the fiber reel, spoke with Patel, and learned nothing at all. Two hours had passed since they'd entered the big rift. One — but only one — member of Patel's crew had failed to check in on his app and been sequestered, on track to become infected like the rest. The gates were holding because no new fiend soldiers had come.

Adrian asked why. Patel told hm she wasn't the king, so she had no idea. Then he asked to talk to Laurel, and he asked Laurel why, too — this time, why the rift was still following them. They'd seen it seven times since crossing over, and the intervals between times seemed to be shortening. Laurel would only say that it was there now because it wasn't open before the depot, but now it was. That didn't answer his question. That only told him why it existed. He wanted to know why it was on his heels. Increasingly directly behind him, like an omen. Or a tail he couldn't shake.

Laurel only repeated that she didn't know.

But Adrian could tell she knew — or suspected — more than she was telling him.

Soon it began to follow them. Literally. It dragged behind them at their walking pace, about fifty feet behind. They could only decrease its distance by walking toward it, not increase it by walking faster or running.

It stayed with them, staring like a big blue eye.

Increasingly, Adrian began to understand what was going on. "This is about us."

Ray was eating rations. They seemed to be boiling. "Bullshit."

"No. It is. The king needs to take over Fortune, and he's going to. That's in the bag. We're not going to stop him even if we find a place to cross outside the city. Even if we connect Patel with someone outside the Rampart, all she can do is help them prepare. Fortune goes either way. Everyone but us."

"We'll go too, baby brother."

But Adrian was sure: No, the virus would never infect Ray and Adrian because they alone were special. He was sure down to his bones by now. Between the two of them, Adrian was the sensitive, intuitive one. Eldon had whispered his mind into the boundaries between worlds, and now it seemed that the blue rift was whispering right back to him. It kept calling him forward. And Adrian, more and more often, kept walking to its edge and looking deep inside. The draw wasn't curiosity so much as the pull of a filing and a magnet.

"No. We'll stay. Because our intentions sound to it like Dad's intentions."

"To what?"

"To the anti-rift," Adrian said. "It ... recognizes us."

Ray laughed, but it was an uncomfortable laugh. "Fuck off."

"Not like it has a mind. It's more like a magnet. I can feel it."

"You're imagining things."

"Ray, what if nothing's happening because it already knows what's going to happen?"

"*It,* meaning that rift."

"Yes."

"*The rift* knows what's going to happen."

"Yes."

"Are you okay, Adrian? You look like shit."

He looked like shit because he felt like shit. It all made sense. Everything worked out the way it was supposed to work out. Until the stiltwalker at the depot created the anti-rift, there was nowhere for the imbalance the Porters represented to go.

Now that the imbalance had a receptacle, it was only a matter of time before it opened under their feet and sucked them in. It was following them around because of a gravity-like force. Flotsam in a bathtub can't avoid the whirlpool above the emptying drain forever. "I think ... I think the king isn't bothering to come after us because he knows the rift will take us eventually. He wants to keep his distance so it doesn't take him, too. But mostly, it just doesn't matter. Maybe once it did if he took Fortune and then took the world, but you heard Laurel; 'the Porter imprint' was always like grit in the oyster. Until we were flushed out, the king couldn't do a thing. We were the only thing stopping him. So he stepped up. Opened that anti-rift."

Adrian pointed, as if it was necessary. "Now it's like a heat-seeking missile. It's locked on to us. Once it takes us, he'll take Fortune and it just won't matter."

"Even if that was true, we just have to outrun it. Cut a hole outside Fortune, hook someone up with Patel, *then* fall into all the rifts we want."

Ray laughed, but it wasn't funny.

Adrian shook his head. "It's going to get us no matter what we do."

"You don't know that."

"I do. I can feel it."

Now Ray looked angry. "You don't feel *shit!* I put up with this in the past because it didn't matter what of Mom's horseshit you believed, but this is different. Adrian? Look at me."

Ray waited until he did. *"We have a chance to save the world."*

But they couldn't, could they? That's what the whisper of the rift — the inverse of Eldon's intention — kept whispering in his ear. Eldon had put something wrong. Now, by the rules of the universe (fate, karma, and all the stuff Ray didn't believe but Adrian and their mother always did), it would be put right ... one way or another.

FIVE LONG AND argument-filled hours later, they hit pay dirt. Adrian cut a small rift that opened on something they knew by sight: a vista of the mountains, seen from just off a scenic lookout up the road ... and outside the Rampart.

The rift was behind them as it'd been constantly for over six hours. When they finished the slice and stepped into cool foothills air, the sun was down and the small blue anti-rift, which popped across the boundary like just one more walker, lit their fronts like a methane fire.

The rig Ray had been pulling was still unwinding fiber. It was astonishingly long, possibly because it was also very thin. They'd made fewer miles in their full day of travel than they would have walking fast and straight, but it was still miles of line. The spool was small now — Ray thought he'd have to go out, find police, and bring them back to the phone instead of taking the phone to them.

As luck would have it, though, a state trooper was parked at the overlook, eating a fast-food dinner.

Adrian anticipated a rough explanation and a lot of laughing, but the cop reacted the way Patel predicted — especially after he mentioned her name. After that the cop sprang into action, took the phone, had a new conversation, and thereafter handed Ray his own phone and drove like hell. He'd promised to call Ray with updates from someone else's phone. Cavalry, he promised, was on the way.

Another few hours passed — by now, Adrian had stopped counting how many. New cops and new government agents came to talk with them, to talk with Patel. Others, they were told, had already been dispatched to the wall with weapons in hand, defenses in place, mindfulness training under their belts, and civilians evacuated outside a perimeter. They'd be ready for the king when the wall fell, they promised.

It seemed to be finished. Their job had been a success. It was too easy, but it had been a triumph nonetheless.

Patel said more of her people were succumbing. By morning, even her and Laurel — and Dixon and Dee, wherever they'd gone, and everyone else — would have succumbed. Prevailing.thought said that if they could kill the king, his puppets would return to normal. The theory felt right to Adrian.

They sat on the roadside, not cold in the same way the Frog kept them from being hot. A crescent moon lit the view from the overlook. All was as well in the world as it could be right now, Adrian knew. But he still couldn't shake the feeling that something was wrong.

Closer enough now to be a third person in their party, the blue rift hovered and waited. Adrain could hear it in his head, though Ray still said he was crazy. He felt like every moment it sat beside them, the more it seemed to be watching.

Anticipating.

Knowing it was only a matter of time before the unbalanced equation balanced itself.

Without a word, Adrian stood. He crossed to the place where the fiber line entered the minimized rift they'd used to enter this place and opened it wide again. Reds and oranges of the new rift's aurora mingled with the blue, making undulating curtains of rainbow hues.

"Ade?" Ray said.

Adrian crossed the rift. The anti-rift followed him rather than Ray, because Adrian had the stronger intention. Adrian, unlike Ray, had made up his mind.

Once in the fiend plane — where instinct had told Adrian to take this — the rift paused.

It allowed Adrian to come closer again, right to its lip.

"Adrian? *Ade?*" Fear in Ray's voice now. Panic. He spilled into the fiend plane, watching his brother.

"Adrian. Don't do it."

Adrian looked at the rift. At his brother. "Don't come closer or I'll go right now."

"You're wrong about this."

"No," Adrian said. "I'm not. I can *feel* Dad in there. Can't you feel it?"

"No. I can't feel a thing."

"They've always talked to me, Ray. They talked to me but never talked to you. That's how Laurel's mind found me. It's why the king found me."

"Found you and *tricked* you."

"This isn't a trick. Something needs to satisfy this rift. We're remainders. If we don't go into it, it'll never be satisfied."

"Then let it be unsatisfied." Ray's voice was almost pleading. "It'll just always be there. Think of it like a pet. It might never come at you. It might always stay where it is."

"It will," Adrian said.

"It ... It will?"

Adrian nodded. "It won't take us by force. That's not how intention works."

"You're talking crazy."

"It's only right, Ray. We did our jobs. The king's going to take Fortune and then he'll come through the wall, and the army on the other side will either find a way to stop him or not. The world will either be able to resist the mental virus, or it won't, and what happened in Fortune will happen everywhere else. We've done all we can do. Now it's up to fate."

"Fate *and people,*" Ray said. "Those are fighters lining up outside Fortune. The outcome isn't decided. It's their choice, how hard they fight."

But Ray didn't understand. Adrian had been thinking. So he understood.

"But what's it change, Ray? Let's say they win. Let's say they even somehow kill the king. Close the last rifts, including the big one. Then what? There's still all this unbalance."

"They'll find a way to balance it."

"Not if it's about deeds." Adrian was staring into the anti-rift, feeling hypnotized by its beauty. "Dad knew what might happen, but he chose to exploit their resources anyway. We're saddled with the sins of the father. This?" He pointed at the blue rift. "It sees Dad and us as one and the same. Blood is blood. Mind is mind."

"That's not true, Ade."

"It is. Everything turns out the way it's supposed to; that's what I always believed. How about another? You reap what you sow. Both things Mom always said. Both things I always lived by."

"Not me. A person makes their own future. You act like there's no free will."

"Maybe there isn't."

Ray stepped forward.

So Adrian stepped toward the rift.

Then Ray stopped and held up his hands. "Goddammit, Adrian."

"Maybe you don't have to go, Ray. Maybe the way you are and the way I am ... maybe that means I'm enough. You were always more like Dad in the obvious ways, but I keep thinking: I'm like him in the way that I think matters most right now. I'm selfish, like he was."

"You're not selfish."

"I hear what I want to hear. I believe what I want to believe. I was the one who had to understand why Dad died. I was the one who never let it go."

"Because you *cared!*"

"My ideas gave GEN ideas. Laurel told me. They never gave up on primordial form because I never gave up on it. I always kept my foot in the door, same as Laurel says we're the 'foot in the door' that won't let the king get what he wants. But now that this rift is here, that doesn't matter. It knows what we're going to do. He's off the hook. He's passed the buck."

Adrian shook his head, brittle emotions finally breaking.

"I didn't give up understanding because I had to know. It stopped being about Dad a long time ago. You were the favorite son, Ray. You got all his attention. All his praise. What was I, but some bookworm who was always thinking, never doing the world any good? That's how Dad saw it. So I kept telling myself, 'Brains can make more of a difference than fists. I just have to study, and study, and think, and think, and eventually I'll prove it.' And that's exactly what happened."

"So what?" Ray said.

"My persistence is the reason groups like GEN and S&C and even the goddamn CIA saw potential after everyone else had given up. Rifts exhaled Zen. Great! That's all that mattered. They harvested the Zen, made things work better, and moved on. Dad made that possible, because he cared more about our side than theirs. He made a selfish decision. But after he died, my need to understand — to prove myself to him, even though he was gone? Well, that was selfish, too. It came out of a need for importance. To be recognized, the way the world recognized you."

Ray came closer, but this time Adrian didn't approach the rift. "They recognized you."

"As Ray Porter's brother. As second best. Runner up. The son of Eldon Porter who never quite lived up to the name."

"You're feeling sorry for yourself. Stop it."

"I'm trying to atone."

"For being curious?"

"For putting myself first. *I* kept the investigation open, and that led to Matt Bakers. To Erika Dales. To the government thinking there might be more to this rift business than monsters and free energy. If I'd let it go, the sundering wouldn't have almost happened. It wouldn't be about to happen again. We went into the rift because I felt guilty about Laurel, who I also sacrificed to save myself. Then I stopped listening to everyone else and charged ahead after losing her signal. What happened then? Ollie and Shannon died."

"We were all taking risks. They were fighters. They knew what they were getting into."

"Exactly. They listened to me, because I told them I knew what was best. But it wasn't what was best. It was *what I wanted*. To reach Laurel no matter what else happened. To prove I wasn't a piece of shit for sending her over in the first place. I was the one who let the king free. I got Carl in trouble, maybe dead, to cover my own ass."

"You've always done what you thought was best!" Ray's begging voice was weaker than Adrian had ever heard it.

Adrian's response was calm. Resigned. He stepped toward he rift. "Maybe not. But maybe it's time I start."

He took another step. Ray threw reticence to the wind and leapt for him, tackling him to the ground. They tussled. They fought. It ended with Ray over his brother, pinning him and furious.

"DON'T YOU GODDAMN LEAVE ME, ADRIAN! DO YOU HEAR ME, YOU SELFISH PIECE OF SHIT?" Then more quietly, he added, "I've never related to Mom like you. You're ..." A sniff. A determined, clench-jawed pursing of the chin. "You're all I have left."

Something shifted. The very air changed. The anti-rift shuddered like a seizure, then retreated slightly. It happened because new possibility had entered Adrian's mind: that maybe trying to erase his guilt through nonexistence was, in this moment, the most selfish thing he could possibly do.

His head rolled. He looked at the anti-rift, sure now that it would never take him, that its nature was to wait for Adrian to walk on through.

But it wants me. If I let it have me, I balance the equation and save the world.

Then a very small voice — his mother's — countered his

own: *Is that true? Or is everything working out exactly as it's supposed to be?*

Maybe this — this here — was the way things were supposed to be.

Ray was right; their possibilities weren't exhausted. He'd been tired, seeking the easy escape. The braver thing — the less selfish, best-for-the-most option — might still be out there, away from this place.

The rift shrunk. It retreated. And there, no longer pulling at Adrian's heart and calling his name, it waited.

Both brothers — the faithful and the skeptic — felt the world change.

Then there was a sudden and complete sense of what Adrian could only call *anger* in the air. It was not their own emotion, but something of this place, of this plane, shivering through its every molecule.

Behind them, the rift to the scenic overlook slammed shut like a door, cutting the fiber line and dropping it to the red dust below. Then a sort of force field, made of shimmering, energetic camouflage, fell away, and behind it the brothers saw what had really been watching them all along, disguised to look like a vast plain of nothingness.

The king of Hell was right there, surrounded by row upon row of blue-skinned lessers. The thoughts streaming from him were something Adrian had never felt from this frequency before: Total fury.

The kind of anger that sends one out of control.

Fine, said the enormous, red-horned dreadnought. *We'll do this the hard way.*

25
ENTROPY

There were tens of thousands of them. Hundreds of thousands. Millions.

There was no way to be sure. The red-rocked hellscape rose and fell, its surface dented at random like steel art from a blind metalsmith. The topology hid much of the land and the soldiers on it. They weren't organized like an army. They were scattered like minglers at a party. One last dance, at the end of the world.

All glowing blue, infused with Zen Element in the way of the New Ones: things that nearly could not die, that had powers they'd never been meant to have. It wasn't only the Earthly plane that knew how to pervert nature for its benefit.

Adrian thought of Laurel, wherever she was right now. If she were here, the word she'd use would be *entropy*.

Even staring at the enormous king and all his legions, even knowing this time no punches would be pulled because the final game had been played — even then, Adrian had to laugh. There was nothing else he could do; the moment was too bizarre, and if he didn't laugh, he'd lose his mind.

Minutes ago he'd been ready to enter oblivion. He'd meant it as contrition and sacrifice, but after Ray tackled him and insisted he'd never do it — not if Ray had a damn thing to say about it — Adrian started to wonder if the idea had been more about self pity. There was no obvious side-up to that coin.

Was it noble to sacrifice, or was sacrifice just making things all about you?

Ray said, *Leaving now would leave him alone.*

And Laurel would talk about entropy. She would see it all as artifice. As the inventions that conscious beings use to explain their unexplainable world.

There *was* no good and bad. There *was* no right and wrong. There *was* no Heaven and certainly no Hell. All of those things were just names given to facets of apathetic existence, which had no preference other than to destroy the things that consciousness attempted to create to explain its existence. There was only the way things were, and the arrow of time, and order and disorder.

Order and chaos: the cosmic push and pull of intelligence versus instinct.

There was only the forward march of entropy.

In the massing of fiends and the way the king had changed them, Adrian saw an excess of order.

From her scientist's vantage, Laurel would tell him that the way things were now was not the way nature wanted them to be.

And he understood.

The moment Eldon Porter decided rifts could be exploited for the Zen the other plane contained, that was the first act of bringing order to what used to be disorderly. Element was distributed evenly over there, but after the first rift, that Zen was suddenly being separated from the bodies that contained it and siphoned from the thickly swirling air. It was stockpiled.

Put into reservoirs and tubes. Refined — made less chaotic in service of magnificent wonders like power engines and healing wounds.

The other plane responded to all that order, and riftfare began. The *war* began. Cause and effect handled the rest, events falling like inevitable dominoes.

Maybe fate was a thing and maybe it wasn't, but choice had had little to do with what happened yesterday.

That's why the planes were supposed to collapse. That's why Laurel had thought it was inevitable: because humans and fiends had both built so much that wasn't supposed to be there. Each side consolidated its offenses and defenses. Structures were built. Zen was put into larger and more orderly — less chaotic — piles. Weapons were made. Armies were formed. And now the king had refined and sequestered even *more* Zen and filled his soldiers with it. No wonder things had gotten out of balance.

But there was a way out. The anti-rift was like neutralizing an acid, an antidote to all the troublesome and unnatural order that now existed between the planes, all inevitable after Eldon's greed cast that first stone. The blue rift was like anti-matter to normal matter: combine them, and afterward neither exists. The anti-rift was a master reset button.

Adrian — and possibly Ray as well — going through would have reset the Porter part of the equation. Eldon's will had stuck around long after the man himself was dead: a ghost on the boundary between worlds. Adrian, sent through a rift that was opposite of the first rift, would annihilate it.

The Porters would be gone. The "foot barring the door the king wanted to open" would be gone. Adrian saw now that it would have been the wrong thing to do. Eldon Porter's memory was all that stood between the king and his domination of both planes.

But the anti-rift was still there. Pulsing as if alive and trying to speak. It still demanded satisfaction. A bubble waiting to burst.

If Porters weren't the right way to satisfy it, what was?

What it wants is to restore entropy. A memory of Laurel's voice was clear inside his mind. *What the anti-rift needs is to undo the out-of-control and unnatural order this war has imposed on the world.*

The king didn't want that. He liked the unnatural sequestering of Zen Element inside his troops, which made them more powerful. He liked how much the planes had come to hate each other. He liked the massing of weapons on the human side, so long as those weapons never defeated them. He liked the hard rule on both sides, whereas before the war, Hell barely had a ruler. And most of all he liked the way that polarity between planes made the balance impossible to maintain.

Laurel had been right about that one: If things stayed the way they were, soon enough the whole system would fall apart. That is what the king wanted, because once it was over, he and his blue-skinned minions would rule the rubble, and rebuild it in his image.

That's why the king wanted the Porters to satisfy the anti-rift. If Adrian and Ray went through, enough of the imbalance would be gone to allow his own, much larger breed of imbalance to remain.

If the Porters failed to go through, then the anti-rift would continue existing, waiting for *something* to collapse.

The world wasn't big enough for all of them — not with the amount of power-consolidation the king wanted to do.

The fiends came at the brothers.

The soldiers did not run. The soldiers did not rush. The

only exit to the human plane had closed behind Ray and Adrian, giving them nowhere to go.

Defeat was inevitable.

They had all the time in the world.

26

BROTHERS

There was a brief battle, barely more than a skirmish. As the soldiers came on, Adrian lost sight of the cool blue anti-rift. At first, because he was fighting, he didn't even notice it was gone. Later, shortly before their doom was sealed and it became clear that continuing was futile, he spied it a hundred yards away or more, undulating atop a small rise. It almost seemed to be watching the fight. Wondering — but only in a disinterested, academic way — who would win. Or rather: Knowing, surely, that the Porters would lose, but curious how it would happen.

There were only the brothers with two guns and one Rollard among them. The lance was the first thing taken and broken: Wouldn't want anyone cutting through and escaping. How would Ray and Adrian be defeated? Killed outright: slashed to pieces like their father? Captured?

Adrian, though he had little mind for such things while fighting demons, wasn't sure how it worked. It was their father's *mind* the king wanted the anti-rift to equalize-out, correct? If so, wouldn't Adrian and Ray need to be alive when the king tossed them through it ... so they'd still have *minds* of their own?

Or did they have to go through the rift voluntarily? That idea was in Ray's head, too. It would explain why the king hid behind a screen and waited for Adrian to sacrifice himself rather than springing forth and grabbing him again.

The scene at the depot must have been for show. Otherwise something would have reminded Adrian of his misdeeds and led him to the conclusion that sacrificing himself was the only way to put things right.

The king had spent time with Laurel; he'd know that Adrian believed that everything happened for a reason. Belief in fate and destiny was a handy lever to pull, if the goal is to make a man kill himself to save others.

But Adrian had no clue. It didn't matter. He knew only that the king's goal was — and had always been — to erase the Porters from the world. Everything before now was just another chess move designed to lead the brothers into this exact checkmate. If he could eliminate Ray and Adrian, he'd be rid of Eldon. The anti-rift could make that happen. And if Eldon was gone, the pressure would diminish and the king would have his collapse, followed by the reign of Hell on Earth.

In order to win this, all Adrian and Ray needed to do was keep on existing. And not go through the rift. Since the king seemed to need Adrian *deciding* to go through rather than be *forced* to do so, their task was probably even easier than that. They simply had to refuse to go through of their own accord.

But *would* it be easy? Surely the king had something in mind to force them: pull Ray's limbs off one at a time until Adrian agreed to do what the king wanted, perhaps.

Or do the same to Laurel.

Or to every citizen of Fortune, until Adrian finally (inevitably) agreed.

So die, said a voice inside Adrian's head. *If you die, he can't make you do anything.*

There was no way to do it himself. The multi-weapon was energetic rather than projectile-based; it harmed human flesh but wouldn't kill quickly enough to do the job. There was a blunt-force attachment, of course, but the rounds that one fired were next-level military: designed for the blue-skinned fiends, which couldn't be shot just once, and as such homed in on fiends instead of humans. A Rollard would do it, but Ray held the Rollard and suicide by Rollard would be tricky — hard to do it yourself in one swoop with an implement so big.

Meanwhile, the fiends clearly weren't even trying to kill them. As happened the first time, before the GEN warehouse became the Army base, the fiends coming at them tried to drive and grab, not impale or decapitate. The king still wanted to keep the prizes he'd made for himself and for the planes to collapse, because doing so meant giving the anti-rift something else to chew-on to stave off the entropy debt. Something Porter-based.

Ray and Adrian backed up a hill to gain high ground, but that only got them surrounded. The way to defeat a Rollard was to storm its holder so they wouldn't have room to swing, but somehow Ray kept the fiends at bay even as they came in number. Adrian was to his side, flaring with the multi-weapon on his back, thanking its makers silently for its newest improvement: an auto-select feature, which chose the right offense for each fiend class automatically rather than him having to toggle attachments on the fly after determining each attacker's class from memory.

They all came. There were Dorns. Classicals. Dolors, Soluzes, Max Jukes. The weapon toggled attachment to attachment as Adrian aimed and fired, but they weren't making a dent. The fiends they struck (Adrian with his multi, Ray mostly with the Rollard) didn't even stay down; they were the Zen-infused kind and stood right back up like zombies.

They came without heads, assuming they'd had heads to begin with.

They came without limbs. Without torsos, even, as disembodied claws and legs crawled forward, taking them by the ankles.

The frenzy, even in its futility, was impressive. Fiend blood spray atomized in the heat, filling the air with the blue gas of boiled-off Zen. The fiends deeper back in the quarter-mile-thick circle around them were showered with gore from the slash of Ray's weapon and the blast of Adrian's.

For longer than should have been possible, Adrian and Ray kept their attackers at bay. They were temporarily seized several times — grabbed and pulled, with the goal of tossing them into the anti-rift or forcing them to go — but each time Ray cut or Adrian shot and somehow they were able to gain a few more inches. Meanwhile the blue eye remained where it was on a rise not far off, waiting to see what happened.

After a while, Adrian swore he felt the pull of it. He swore he saw eddies in the air, as the atomized clouds of element drifted into the anti-rift's maw. There was a breeze in that direction, it seemed: hot air moving toward the cold of the dead-blank third plane: the sky blue nothingness that Laurel called infinite possibility.

Then a stream.

Then a river.

Soon, Adrian could only keep one eye on battle. His other eye was on the rift. It was swelling. Sucking the eddies of Zen forward now as if liking what it tasted and eager for more. And why wouldn't it? The king had defied chaos by filling his soldiers with so much refined Element. The rift wanted chaos back, and was taking its due.

The king sat back. Watching. Waiting for his troops to finally subdue the prisoners.

Finally, it happened. It was always going to happen, unless they found a way to die first. All at once the fiends surged forward from all directions: too many to repel. And after that the fight simply ended: the press of a dozen fiend bodies on the brothers with thousands of fiends behind them. There was nowhere to go.

Very carefully, a macerator pushed its tree-trunk legs through the army until it was close enough to grab the brothers from above. It took them one at a time, binding their arms to their sides using something that looked and felt like wet tree root. The battlefield had gone quiet, the anti-rift's pull swirling the blue clouds above it into a small, transparent tornado as it inhaled the plane's abhorrent order.

To Adrian, watching as his bonds were cinched, it looked hungry.

The macerator returned Ray and Adrian to the center of the crowd of enemy fiends. Then the crowd pushed them as one large, inescapable unit toward the anti-rift at the king's command. The group parted as it approached: now a funnel behind the Porters, pushing them from the rear with the blue eye ahead.

You must enter of your own accord, the king said, moving toward them and settling. *This began with your father's will. It must end with yours.*

"Fuck off," said Ray.

Enter the rift, or Fortune will pay the price.

What came from the king was more than images and sound. It was a full-sense experience, vivid as a waking dream. Adrian watched a horrorshow clip reel unfold: the citizens of Fortune tortured, slaughtered, made to suffer because of him.

Fortune no longer mattered to the king. If it hadn't already been completely taken over by the virus — right down to Laurel and the others — then it would be soon. The king had planned to neuter the city so it could not fight ... but destroying it in the most horrid way possible would do the same thing.

Enter the rift, said the king. *First one brother, and then the other.*

There was a commotion. New energy shuddered through the air. As it did, all heads turned, including the king's.

A huge new army was approaching. All fiends, but almost none were blue. They were not soldiers. They were malcontents of all ranks. They were fifth column. And most of all they were civilians: the farmers and merchants and everyday citizens of Hell. The unsilenced majority, quiet enemies of the king who'd finally stood up to fight.

And at their head was Carl the halfskull, who seemed to have gotten the message Dixon promised to send through the tiny circle of portal that remained.

Your majesty, Carl said to the king. *You have forgotten their million brothers who remain.*

27

THE BALANCE

The brothers could only watch. They were bound arms-to-sides, then to boulders so they couldn't escape. Adrian tried to wiggle from his bonds, but nothing budged as they were trapped in front of the carnage.

It was like Roman times. Like the frenzy of medieval war. Fiends fought hand to hand with the weapons nature had given them. Small fiends compensated for their stature with numbers, overcoming macerators and hellbringers like swarms that climbed and bit and cut. The larger beings, when not overcome, fought much more simply: they stomped, they raked with big, long arms. One class Adrian had never seen before even breathed fire.

It was impossible to say who would win. The blue ones — servants of the king, most of them — did not die easily, but the browns and greens had superior numbers. Adrian had no idea what Carl had done to get so many ordinary fiends (*Friends. They're friends, not fiends*) to rise against the king, but they seemed to outnumber the king's forces by a ratio of four or five to one.

It raged. Adrian couldn't take his eyes off of it. He was surprised, then, when a mental voice spoke from behind him.

Hold still.

Adrian looked and saw a halfskull behind him, using an implement to cut his bonds.

"Carl?"

Carl is below. He sent us to set you free. Keep your mind quiet. Your protection has slipped, and we can hear you now.

Adrian's hand went behind his ear. The blocking chip had fallen off somehow, probably during their fight.

His hands came free. Then Ray's.

"Thank you."

You do not need to thank us. This is our war. We are only doing what should have been done long ago. Look.

Adrian looked. Ray looked, too. The king, who'd been sitting complacently at the head of his blue army, was now covered with brown-skinned demons. He kept swatting them away like ants, but the sheer number was wearing down his defenses. Black blood dribbled down his neck and sides, its flow growing by the minute.

Now run, said the halfskull. *Escape this place.*

Adrian grabbed his lance without thinking, then stared at it, forgetting that it had been broken.

The world was shaking. Adrian noticed it now, as he felt the halfskull's disappointment. He looked at Ray and saw that Ray felt it, too.

Something enormous — an ordinance of some sort, or perhaps just a boulder thrown by a macerator — crashed between them. Several in the new halfskull's party were crushed. Adrian and Ray dove away and then the the battle extended a finger to the hilltop they'd evacuated, leaving them alone and their new friend gone.

"It's collapsing, isn't it?" Adrian said.

"Jesus. I think maybe it is."

Because it wasn't just the ground. It was the air. It was the very energy of the place.

Was the same thing happening inside Fortune right now? Most of the hellscape they'd crossed mapped to places inside the Rampart, around the Gore Point. So yes. It very well might be.

"Too much imbalance. Too much load." Adrian looked to the battle, now partially obscured. Blue clouds overhead had more than tripled in size and density. That's how much killing was happening out there: blue-skinned fiends ripped and ripped again in an attempt to put them down permanently, the corpses never left whole because they refused to be corpses. The result was air full of Zen Element. If Ray and Adrian hadn't dosed with Frog, their human systems would be poisoned by now.

Their eyes went to the anti-rift. The sky above it was a vortex: a whirlpool with a stem, cycling into the mouth of the ice-cold beast. All that Zen was leaking into nothingness as the anti-rift tried to find balance with the imbalance so many normal rifts — so many cross-plane incursions over the years — had caused.

The ground began to settle, dulling from earthquake to harmonic vibration.

"It's slowing," Ray said. "Why is it slowing?"

But Adrian understood. He could almost picture it. This world was a pressure vessel that'd been slowly building steam, but the anti-rift was a leak in the carapace. The pressure could only build so far, because very slowly, the imbalance was quenching itself.

All that refined Zen — the opposite of the universe's desire for chaos — was leaving the plane through the rift. Becoming nothing instead of something, lessening the difference between the planes, making things a bit more equal, more full of entropy and randomness, to oppose the order of conscious beings.

"The anti-rift is eating the king's order. Look."

Ray did. The vortex was even larger now, gaining its own momentum as it grew. Before, the anti-rift had been like the drain at the bottom of a tub: a way through which Zen Element could passively exit the plane. Now it was more like a vacuum. Instead of merely allowing Zen to drain away due to pressure, it seemed to be actively sucking. The vortex's throat deepened, and tendrils of it — new, tiny whirlpools — reached toward the field of battle like sharp little fingers.

One thread of vortex touched a group of the king's army. The blue in their skin faded. First slightly, then entirely. Soon they were brown and green again: their colors in a balanced world.

The civilian fiends fighting them saw it happen. Fervor rose in them, and they surged. This time when they slashed, their enemies stayed dead.

"It's taking their power away," Ray whispered with awe. "It's making them mortal."

The same was happening to the king. His body was too massive to turn blue, so he'd remained red. Tiny vortexes touching his body through the fiends upon him now, though, bled with blue. He'd improved himself upon improving his legions; of course he had. Now that improvement was draining away.

Soon he stopped struggling. He fell to his massive knees, then crumpled sideways. More civilian fiends rushed him, cutting and slashing. Black blood spread in a pool. If he wasn't dead, he would be soon.

Quickly, the entire battlefield grew homogenous in color.

All the fiends looked the same now; it was impossible to tell the king's soldiers from those who opposed them.

The warring groups grew confused. Who to fight? Who to hate and who to kill?

As the ways to tell faded, so too did the will to fight seem to fade. The king was gone and every neighbor looked the same. Groups loosened. Some gave up entirely, and began to disband.

This was their chance. They had a vague sense of the way home, and now was the time to go there, while the warring fiends were distracted. With the lance broken, the only way back to the Earth plane was to find the big rift again. If the king was truly dead, things in Fortune might be okay now.

They might not emerge to find Patel and her people waiting to catch and kill them.

They might even emerge to find that the king's wall had fallen, that the outside world could enter again and that the spell over the city was already fading away.

The hope of it would have to be good enough, because to their knowledge, only one rift between worlds still remained. If they wanted to go home, through the Magnitude 35 was the only route.

"Come on," Ray said, not waiting for agreement before rushing off.

Adrian scrambled to follow. He tripped, fell, and then again found his feet. Ray was way ahead now, soon to pass the still-eating anti-rift. By the time Adrian passed it, his brother was in full sprint.

"RAY!"

He turned and was about to say something cutting about how Adrian was soft, how ever since the day they saw their father die, he had never been able to keep up.

But Ray didn't have a chance to say anything cutting.

Before he could, a snow-white stiltwalker came around a rock and cut Adrian instead.

28

A LEAP OF FAITH

Ray dispatched the thing with extreme prejudice, cutting the stiltwalker into pieces so small, even a blue-skinned version wouldn't have moved again. He finished with his chest heaving, then went to his brother.

Adrian looked down at his chest as Ray came over. The thing's cut was very deep, through his abdominal wall. His guts weren't precisely spilling out, but he definitely had one hell of a hernia.

"Fuck," Adrian said, looking at his bloody hands. "Tell me I'll see Kansas again."

Ray was in no mood for jokes. His big shoulders were still rising and falling with fighting breath. He took one look at Adrian, then began slapping his sides, his pockets, his belt.

"Adrenalix," he said.

"In my pack," Adrian answered. It hurt to talk.

Ray did his best to reach behind Adrian without forcing him to roll over, wiggling his arms out of a pair of straps, then holding up the pack in question. His face fell as they both looked at it. The pack was shredded. Covered in dry-packed red dirt mixed with fiend blood. It hadn't just been ripped open; it'd been ripped open a long time ago — probably when the battle started. They'd crossed the entire field since then, and it still had many pockets of fighting fiends.

They'd never find a single pen-sized Adrenalix injector out there — certainly not in time.

"Zen Element," said Ray. "Remember when you got that burn, and they treated it with Zen?"

"You can't just rub refined Zen on a cut. They do something to it for medical use. You know how toxic that shit is, even ..."

He stopped and moaned, something shifting and shooting astonishing pain up his middle. Something inside gushed blood. A bit more intestine protruded. Horrified and amused in equal measure, Adrian did the only thing he could think of and pushed it back in.

The ground shook again. It was different now, somehow. They eyed the blue rift. It had shrunk — as if partially quenched — but it was far from gone. The shaking wasn't coming from the rift, but Adrian's slit-open gut told him it was related. Spirals of Zen Element flowing into the rift were even larger and farther-reaching now, as if the one tiny rift was determined to equalize the entire plane's worth of work the king had done.

Did that mean it would try to undo Fortune as well? The king wasn't the only one who'd built an army and stockpiled Element. Humans had started it ... and there was the Porter issue left, too.

"We have to get you out of here," Ray said. "I think it still might collapse."

"The planes won't collapse." Adrian eyed the rift. "It's ... letting off enough steam."

"Then it's doing something *else* I don't think we want to be around for."

Adrian nodded. That, he couldn't argue with.

"I doubt you can walk. Right?"

Adrian gave a mirthless laugh.

"Then I'll carry you."

Ray tried, but Adrian screamed.

Something shifted inside and a new gout of blood came through his fingers. He now felt like he was actively holding himself together. If he moved his hands, he was afraid everything would come spilling out.

"I don't think you'd better carry me, Ray."

"Then I'll … I'll …" He looked around and saw the remains of a domicile in the distance: raw materials, apparently, for what he said next. "We can build one of those things to drag you!"

"A travois."

"No, one of those things you lay on and—"

"*A travois,* Ray."

"Fuck you. Is this really the right time for you to word-punch me?"

"I'm just trying to help you out. You're …" He groaned. "So damn stupid."

Ray looked at the ruins.

Then Adrian spoke. "Ray."

"What?"

"I don't think I can ride on a travois."

"Sure you can."

"One bump will kill me. Besides, you don't have time to build one."

A moment.

"You have to go, Ray. You need to leave me."

"Fuck you, *leave you*. I'm not—"

"I die or we both die. Listen to me, will you?"

He searched for something to ram the point home for Ray — any excuse to get him moving.

They couldn't just stay here; something like a collapse (but not a collapse) was afoot. Something that wouldn't be kind to humans who stood in its epicenter.

Ray staying wouldn't help Adrian, and it damn sure wouldn't help Ray.

He just needed an excuse. Something to latch onto as a justification for leaving. If it were Adrian, needing to leave Ray behind, all Ray would need to do was to remind Adrian of what their mother said: that all things worked out the way they were supposed to.

Ray didn't buy that hippie-dippy bullshit, though. Ray needed concrete action. Ray needed a mission if he was to leave: a futile, brother-saving goal — even though that goal would ultimately be impossible.

"Run fast," Adrian said. "We wandered all around, but if you go in a straight line, it won't take you long to find the big rift." That was a lie; they'd wandered some, but the run back was an hour if it was a day. "There's lots of Adrenalix at the Army base. Laurel can help you find somewhere near this place. Somewhere that's not far on our plane. You can cut through. Come right to me. Hurry, Ray! Maybe you can make it on time."

But Ray, for all his practicality and disavowing of things he couldn't see and his frustrating, charming dumbness in Adrian's opinion, didn't believe a word of what his brother was saying. He knew the dilemma. He knew there was no way out. He only had two options: stay and they both die, or leave Adrian to die alone.

But after doing the latter, how could he live with himself?

Ray stood. He looked at the anti-rift. After a beat, he took two steps toward it.

"Ray? What are you doing, Ray?"

"I'm trying to be you."

"W-what's that mean? *Ray!*"

Ray was still walking. He paused, clearly terrified, then turned his head to face his brother.

"Aren't you proud of me, Ade?" He gave a sad smile. "I'm having faith."

"Ray? *Ray.* What the hell are you doing, Ray? You can't … What the fuck do you think *that's* going to do, Ray?"

"It's a rift."

"It's an *anti*-rift."

"Anti. *RIFT.*"

"Ray? Don't! The worst thing you could do to me right now is make me watch you die."

"Laurel said anything's possible in there." He looked into it. There was nothing but cool blue sky.

"That's not what she said. Listen to me!"

"No, Ade. Listen to *me,*" Ray said, some of the usual balls re-entering his voice. "This started with Dad. But not just with Dad, was it? His *intention.* Isn't that what everyone says?"

"Yeah, of course. But—"

"We all know what Dad intended. And a while ago, we both know what *you* intended. You wanted to end it all. The imbalance, the king, the collapse … but more than anything, *yourself.* What's the fancy way you said it that one time, talking about self-destructiveness? When you were going to walk into the anti-rift, you wanted *annihilation.* Well." Ray was looking ahead again, determined. "Let me tell you what *I* think. Let me tell you what *I* want."

"Who cares what anyone wants? It's not a *goddamn wishing well,* Ray!" Adrian's voice choked with tears. He knew his brother; he knew he'd made up his mind and was doing this whether Adrian liked it or not.

"I think you've rammed your bullshit down my throat for almost thirty years," Ray said, ignoring him. "I think that *every fucking time* I've had logical ideas based in the real world, you've bulldozed me with some shit about trusting and having a little bit of faith."

"*I've* bulldozed *you?*"

"And I think you've always pulled the superiority card. Always acted like you're smarter than me. I never *miscalculated*, when you thought I was wrong, did I? I never simply *picked the wrong choice*. No. Every goddamn time, the problem was that I *just didn't understand*. If I'd known what *your* big mother-fucking brain knew — if I was as *smart* and *exalted* and *goddamn spiritually enlightened* as my baby brother ... Well, if *that* was the case, maybe my dumb ass would be able to accept the truth. *Your* truth."

"Ray ..."

He pointed at the blue eye. "*That's* a rift. A doorway between planes." Then Ray slapped his chest, finally starting to tear up. "And *my intention* isn't to do a goddamn thing but to save you."

"THIS ISN'T SAVING ME!"

"I'm sorry, Ade." A wan smile dusted his lips as he stepped to the anti-rift's threshold. "If you were as smart and exalted and goddamn spiritually enlightened as your big brother, maybe your dumb ass would be able to accept the truth."

Adrian tried to crawl forward, but the pain was too much. He stretched out a hand. "Okay. Okay. But if you're going, don't leave me here. We both have to go. Ray? Take me through the rift with you."

Ray's smile persisted. Backlit by blue aurora, he shook his head. "That's not how this works."

"How the fuck do you have any idea how it works?" Adrian shouted. *"You're going to kill yourself!"*

"That's your opinion. But I say everything always works out exactly the way it's supposed to."

Ray stepped through the rift.

And was gone.

29
NEENER NEENER

Adrian's eyes came open slowly. It was like an effect from a movie, where twin lids part to reveal an unknown place, friends and family watching from above.

Laurel was his family. "Don't ask where you are. It's such a cliché."

Adrian blinked. Rolled his head. He felt well, so he came up on his elbows. Laurel didn't try to stop him.

"I'm in a hospital."

"Also a cliché. But better."

"How did I get here?"

"Ray."

"Ray's gone."

And Laurel said, "I wish."

Something occurred to Adrian. He lifted his shirt and saw his usual abdomen. There was only a tiny white scar.

"He saved you, Adrian. He walked right through the big rift at the base like it was no big deal. It was the first thing I remember, after the blackout."

"The blackout?"

"Fortune fell. All the way. We had less time than we thought. Patel tried to kill me. She only stopped once the virus got me, too. You remember how Harrison was, when he snapped out of it in that house's kitchen?"

Adrian nodded. Nothing hurt. At all. "He remembered what he'd done, but not why he'd reacted the way he had."

"Same for me," Laurel said. "I didn't really black out, I guess, but it was like I was watching myself through a TV. I was never present, you know? Never *mindful.* Just ... a spectator. I think it lasted only an hour or so, but then ... Well, I guess that's probably when the king died, according to Ray. And when *that* happened, I blinked like you just did, and Patel blinked, and I just wanted to apologize to everyone. For everything I'd thought, while the king had me."

"Ray's dead. I watched him die."

"Maybe you watched him *disincorporate.* If he's *dead,* then he's got a twin you guys didn't tell me about."

"Ray ... *survived?* He survived the anti-rift?"

Laurel nodded.

"How?"

"He says it had to do with intention. With purpose."

"And you buy that?"

"As a scientist? No. I don't buy it at all. It's completely absurd and flies in the face of everything I know except for one bit of evidence I can't explain away."

"What's that?"

"The fact that Ray walked right up to me and said, 'I need Adrenalix and some Zen balm, right fucking now.'"

"What did you do?"

"I gave it to him. There was a medkit on the office wall. I wasn't really in the mood to ask for a full report. I don't mean to belittle this, Adrian, but at the time I sort of had my own crisis going on, y'know? I'd had the devil in my head. Do you have any idea what it's like to have the devil in your head?"

"Yes, actually." His had been a direct connection rather than control, but it still hadn't been fun.

"Then what happened?"

"He took a new lance from the equipment locker and walked back through."

"Through the big rift?"

"Yes."

"And I suppose it let him right back out of the anti-rift?"

"I don't know *what* happened, Adrian. You were there. I wasn't. I know he used that lance on the other side to cut back and forth and back and forth, going from plane to plane until he finally found you again. I don't have the details. I haven't really wanted to take the time to get a full report from Ray just yet."

"*You* didn't want to collect evidence?"

"Not from Ray. Not now."

"Why?"

"Why do you think? He was right. Righter than you. Righter than *me*. Ever since, he's been *insufferable* about it."

Adrian looked around the room. "How long have I been out?"

"Two days."

"Is the city ...?"

"Whole. And about as normal as it can be, given the circumstances. That new wall vanished, but it made a hell of a lot of destruction. Plowed right through the ground even where it hit the Rampart. But people seem to be okay. Physically. Mentally too, in terms of ..."

"What?"

"The king left their heads," Laurel told him. "Let's just say that much."

Adrian read her face, then read between the lines. A lot of ordinary people had done a lot of terrible things while under the king's influence. There'd been murder and destruction. Not their fault, but tell that to a man who killed his neighbor.

Therapists were going to be in demand in Fortune for a while now. Adrian, who'd gone through Hell in a more literal sense, almost felt lucky by comparison.

A FEW HOURS of bad TV later (it was all over-air broadcast in the hospital, and Adrian quickly lost his taste for the news), there was a knock on the door. Ray entered without waiting for a response.

"Ray. Oh my god, it's so good to—!"

"I was right."

"What?"

"I was right. I had faith. I win. I'm your spiritual superior. Mom's gonna like me better now."

"Buddhists don't rub shit in people's faces, Ray."

"Yeah, I don't really care about that. For once, I'm the smart one. You're the dying brute."

"They tell me I'm not dying."

"Uh-huh." Ray grabbed the apple Adrian hadn't eaten from the hospital meal tray and took a bite. "And who do you have to thank for that?"

More seriously, Adrian said, "That shouldn't have worked. You *should* be dead."

Ray sat in the chair beside the bed. He took a moment, seeming to think. He finished his bite of apple and turned serious.

"I've thought a lot about it. When I did it, I did it from the sack. I did it because my brother's guts were falling out. I talked like I had some idea what was going to happen, but it's not like I *knew*. You know that, Ade. Nobody could *know* about something like that."

Adrian waited. Ray's eyes met his brother's, and then he went on.

"But here's what I did know: I wouldn't *die*. *Dying* is what you were going to do. If anything, I'd just 'stop existing.'"

"That's the same thing."

"No. It's not. Right up until the last moment, I didn't actually know if I was going to do it. But then I looked into the blue inside that rift and I saw how peaceful it was. Everyone dies, but what's beyond it? I thought that maybe it was like that place. Laurel called it a 'third plane.' She also said it was 'potential,' or something, like it might be anything. That got me thinking about how we *assume* that being dead is a bad thing. I'm not talking about *dying*; I'm talking about *being dead*. But it wouldn't be *bad*, would it? At most, it's nothing at all. In the moment, that sounded great to me. It wasn't like when you almost went in. You were all tangled up in guilt and, if I'm being honest, a lot of self-pity."

"Well ..."

"But it wasn't like that for me. It was really rational. I looked in there and I just sort of realized, 'This is a mind place. This is where minds might come from, and where they might go. We're just meat, you know. Bodies are just meat. But minds? It's like there's someone behind your eyes and hooked into your ears, and that's *you*, yeah kinda, but it's not the *you* you think of as '*you*.'"

"Are you saying it's ... what ... Heaven?"

"I'm saying that everything is just a word. Good. Bad. Heaven. Hell. We've done one. Maybe I did the other. Who knows? Maybe what some people call Heaven is just one more zip code."

"I don't understand how you crossed it, Ray. How you came out of the Magnitude 35."

"I don't know either, Ade. I guess that's why it's called a leap of faith. I just knew I didn't like either one of my available options. You ask me, I think the planes listen to the things we think and feel and want — especially *that* plane. And why not? It was something Dad thought or wanted that got us in so much trouble in the first place."

"And protected us," Adrian added. "The kernel inside the virus gave us six days. Six days we needed."

Ray was still speaking. "I ... Fuck. You're my brother. I guess I love you, and all I can think is that my love for you mattered. Don't make me explain too much or I'll have to beat the shit out of you again."

Adrian was touched. Baffled, but touched. They sat silently for a moment.

"So what do they say? Will the planes still collapse?"

"Laurel doesn't think so." Ray said. "She has instruments and readings and shit. You could ask her for details if you want."

"Or not."

"Or not," he agreed, taking a second bit of the apple.

"But the big rift, at the base ..."

"It closed."

"It closed?"

Ray nodded. "On its own. Took a few hours. There's a time-lapse video Patel will probably show you if you ask. It's pretty insane to see."

"So it's over?'

"Who knows?" And the unspoken codicil, which he agreed with this time despite such sentiments usually being Ray's domain: *Who cares?* Now was now. He was tired of worrying about the future.

"Oh," Ray said. "You'll like this. People don't hate you anymore."

"They don't?"

Ray shook his head. "All those people we contacted outside the wall? By the time they came in, it was like FEMA, not just authority-types. They knew all along that weird shit was going on. They could see the wall and everything. Once Patel's information gave them context, it's like the public-relations gloves came off. Half the people who rushed in when it fell were reporters. For once, the truth came out. The *real* truth. Wanna guess who you have to thank for telling the most honest, most formerly-Top-Secret shit he absolutely shouldn't have told the press?"

"Not Dixon."

"Dixon."

Adrian laughed. That fast-talking bastard. Adrian had alternately hated and loved the man, but for all his faults he'd always been on the right side when it counted.

"I don't suppose you know what happened to Carl." Adrian hadn't wanted to ask. Thousands of fiends had died in battle. Thousands of *friends*.

"No," Ray said. "Not exactly. But ..."

"What's that mean, 'Not exactly'?"

"Remember how the portal in your office closet didn't close all the way? Just closed down to about the size of ... What? A softball?"

"Sure. That's how Dixon got his message to Carl."

"Well, I think that's how Carl got a message to *us*, too."

Adrian was about to ask, but it seemed Ray had anticipated this line of questioning. He'd set a backpack down when he came in. He reached into it now and removed something wrapped in a cloth.

"You remember the bobblehead you had in your locker at the brigadehouse?"

"Yeah. The Satan one. 'Know your enemy' and all that."

"What happened to it? I never saw it at the office you shared with Dixon. I'd think that's the kind of thing you'd put on your desk."

"Carl saw it and liked it. I gave it to him."

Ray removed the cloth. He was holding a bobblehead of Satan ... except that someone had cut off the top half of Satan's head, making him look like a halfskull.

Adrian took it and watched it bobble. A smile came to his lips.

They sat a while. It was strange, feeling so normal.

"What the hell are we supposed to do now, Ade?" Ray finally said. "A retired Legion. A retired Stitcher. Hell, Laurel won't have much to do anymore either. We're out of jobs — all three of us. What do you think: get a job bagging groceries? Go back to school, maybe?"

Adrian laughed. "I have no idea, but I do know what Mom would say right now."

Neither of them said it aloud.

They'd taken enough on faith to last a lifetime.

Author's Note

I almost didn't get to publish this series. That would have sucked.

Years ago, the *Gore Point* trilogy was a project that Sean and I ghostwrote for someone else. When that relationship changed, Sean was able to get the rights back so it could be published as a Truant & Platt title. And now here we are, with our demon books back home where they really should have been all along.

It's hilarious to me that anyone thought this series could have worked as a ghost project. When you ghostwrite, you're supposed to write neutrally. You're just supposed to tell the story in a relatively middle-of-the-road way, making it universal enough that any competent writer could have written it. The specific author, in a project like that, is supposed to be invisible. The *story* is everything. The uniqueness of *one writer's voice,* in a project like that, should be almost nonexistent.

Yeah. Seems I'm not able to do that.

These books fail the "ghostwriting neutral voice" test like a motherfucker. The *Gore Point* trilogy is easily one of the most voice-heavy, *firmly-Johnny-and-Sean* series in our catalogs. I take the blame. I'm literally unable to hide my way of writing. I've tried before ... and no matter what, I always sound like me.

This series has *all* the science that hallmarks Truant & Platt.

All the twists and reversals, and plans within plans.

This series has layers. And layers. *And layers.* It's one of those projects where, when I re-read it, I kept hoping I wouldn't hang myself by giving the reader a neverending series of obtuse Russian Dolls. I didn't remember what happened, see. I was a virgin reader just like you when you first read it, and because of that, I was just as nervous as you about whether I'd pull it off.

I didn't know if Ray and Adrian would live or die.

I didn't know whether a sundering-of-sorts would happen or not.

I had no idea how Eldon's actions all those years ago would factor in, why the king wanted the Porter boys, or how it would all work out in the end.

But in my mind, that's exactly what makes a good book good. A good twist, said someone I don't recall, should feel both surprising and inevitable. I wanted to keep you guessing, but in the end I wanted you to nod and think, *Okay, that makes sense given what I've read so far.* That's a tall task, for as twisted a plan as the king and the Porters weaved.

Let's talk about science for a second. There's an assload of science in these books.

I have a theory about fiction. If a story is about unreal things (demons, for instance), it means that at some point, I'm going to ask you to suspend disbelief and come along for a ride. I'm going to ask you to accept that those unreal things are "real enough" for the story to be told.

But in my mind, suspension of disbelief is a limited resource. No reader has an infinite supply. At some point, even the most indulgent reader is going to throw up their hands and say, "Okay, this is too unbelievable. You've asked me to accept too much without any grounding or substantiation, so I'm outta here."

In a truly fantastical story world, the grounding a reader needs eventually starts to come from the story world itself. The universe in an epic fantasy, for instance, may be nothing like the real world, but that's okay as long as that universe's internal logic is consistent. But the thing is, *every* world — including the epicest of epic fantasies — still contains real things. The way people interact has a "realistic or not realistic" feel to it even if they're disguised as elves or wizards. And in my case, even though there are no Hell-rifts out there that I know of, they can't fly in the face of Earth science if Earth is part of the story.

This series does a very tricky thing: it tries to make logical scientific and psychological sense of a lot of stuff that's not otherwise remotely logical. But remember what I said about suspension of disbelief being a limited resource? This is where that matters. Because your willingness to suspend disbelief is limited, I want you to save it for demons, not waste it when I get things wrong that would be easy enough, if I'm smart, to get right.

Hell rifts aren't real ... but if they were, they'd exhale heat instead of sucking in because hot things radiate heat.

Maybe demon telepathy isn't a real thing, but if it was, it wouldn't be terribly unbelievable once you understand that brain activity really does generate detectable current, and that current can be measured across the thickness of a skull.

Entropy really is the driving force of the universe. Entropy is such a big deal, in fact, that it's often entangled with the concept of time. "The arrow of time" is sometimes defined as the direction in which order maximally trends toward disorder — the direction of the most entropy.

I write scientifically because I was almost a scientist. I began a PhD in molecular genetics before I said FUCK THAT WITH A FORK and became a writer instead. But more globally, I write scientifically because it lets me get as close as I can to making unbelievable things believable. I do it because if I can give real, logical reasons for as much of the story as I can, I can save my readers' limited suspension of disbelief for when I truly need it.

Or, put more simply: You're more willing to accept demons and zombies and vampires and aliens because I haven't asked you to take me on faith about about what two plus two adds up to.

When Sean and I wrote *Dead City,* we said to ourselves, "Okay, zombies are absurd and stupid and can't possibly exist. But if they *could* exist, how might it work?" So when we made our way to *Gore Point* years later, we asked the same thing of demons. I don't approach even the supernatural on faith. Instead, I say, "Is there some real thing that I can twist to justify it, using truth as camouflage for untruth? What would be the consequences, if this actually happened?"

The layered story that finally came to an end in the pages you've just read unfolded as a sequence of natural conclusions, framed by real science. I had to bend the rules a little, but that was always on my mind: *What would happen if this was true?* The con, the double-cross, and the inevitability of both sides' actions came from those thoughts. The anti-rift and the Porter imprint, then, came not as real things, but through scientific thinking applied to something that's not normally scientific at all.

It's a weird way of working. I'm sure other writers do it, but

I don't know any personally who insist as fervently as I do that fiction be almost as believable as fact — and are willing to bullshit their way through some otherwise-honest logic and science to do it.

It's hilarious to me that once upon a time, Sean and I thought we could hide our storytelling voices enough for this series to be a ghost series. Who were we kidding? This could only ever have been a Truant & Platt title, and if any of our readers had read these books under someone else's name, they'd've seen right through it.

I'm delighted that these books found their way back home. *Truly* delighted. I'd forgotten how they grew and ended until just yesterday, when I finished re-reading the book you're holding right now.

I love this series, and would have been sad not to claim it.

I hope you loved it too.

Johnny B. Truant
Austin, Texas
February 21, 2005

THANKS TO MY SUPPORTERS!

111 amazing readers helped bring *Plague of Demons* to life as a beautiful limited edition through a 2025 Kickstarter campaign. **My extra-special thanks go to the following backers:**

HELL'S ROYALTY:

Jason Kelly

HELL'S ARMY:

John M North, Scott Casey, Andrew Nicolle, Susan Grubb, Ken Checinski, Neva S, Kimberly Majernik, Will, Joseph Golden, Jennifer McBride, A. Mami, John Barone, Joe Gillis, Nathalie Olofsson, Cynthia, Mark Leslie, Andrew Wainwright, Michele Huber, Katherine W McKamey, Geoff Emberlyn, Amanda Brenninkmeyer, Scott McArthur, Karen, Sarah Brabazon, Nate, Shalene Rod, David Holzborn, Asuberu, Leigh Allen, Fred M Wheeler, Kurt Lucero, Jonathan Bailey, Mike Dailey, John Reynolds, Ashley Bettencourt, Amy, Lucas, Arthur Ni, Florentina Nitschke, David Nix, Chase McGlinchey, Kasey Sargent, David Bock, Kendra Fleck, Nathan Hopkins, Marino Barcos

Thank you from the bottom of my heart for supporting my work. You're the best!

ENTER THE TRUANTVERSE

When it comes to stories and the worlds they live in, books are only the beginning.

Visit JohnnyBTruant.com/join to get my best books sooner and cheaper than the other stores.

My list doesn't suck like so many author email lists. Seriously. It has unicorns.

ALSO BY JOHNNY B. TRUANT

Winter Break

Pattern Black

Pretty Killer

Cursed

The Bialy Pimps

Namaste

The Target

La Fleur de Blanc

Axis of Aaron

Devil May Care

Screenplay

The Island

Burnout

Sick and Wired

UNICORN WESTERN:

Unicorn Western

The Wanderers

A Fistful of Magic

Shimmer to Yuma

The Man Who Shot Alan Whitney

The Spectacular Seven

Open Meadows

The Unforgotten

The Magic Bunch

Unicorn Genesis

FAT VAMPIRE:

Fat Vampire

Fat Vampire 2: Tastes Like Chicken

Fat Vampire 3: All You Can Eat

Fat Vampire 4: Harder Better Fatter Stronger

Fat Vampire 5: Fatpocalypse

Fat Vampire 6: Survival of the Fattest

The Vampire Maurice

Anarchy and Blood

Vampires in the White City

Fangs and Fame

Game of Fangs

INVASION:

Invasion

Contact

Colonization

Annihilation

Judgment

Extinction

Resurrection

Save the City

Save the Girl

Save the World

Longshot

THE INEVITABLE:

Robot Proletariat

The Infinite Loop

The Hard Reset

Cascade Failure

Reboot

En3my

DEAD CITY:

Dead City

Dead Nation

Dead Planet

Dead Zero

Empty Nest

THE DREAM ENGINE:

The Dream Engine

The Nightmare Factory

The Ruby Room

The Pandora Core

COMEDIES:

Everyone Gets Divorced

Greens

Fiends

Decoy Wallet

NONFICTION:

The Fiction Formula

Fiction Unboxed

Iterate & Optimize

The Story Solution

Write. Publish. Repeat.

The One With All the Writing Advice